ALL FOR LOVE

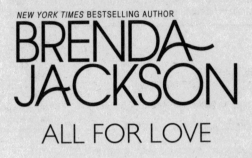

NEW YORK TIMES BESTSELLING AUTHOR

BRENDA JACKSON

ALL FOR LOVE

A Westmoreland Novel

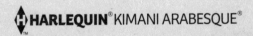

HARLEQUIN® KIMANI ARABESQUE®

ALL FOR LOVE
ISBN-13: 978-0-373-09153-9

Copyright © 2014 by Harlequin Books S.A.

This edition published May 2014

PLEASE RECYCLE
THIS PRODUCT IS RECYCLABLE

Recycling programs
for this product may
not exist in your area.

The publisher acknowledges the copyright
holders of the individual works as follows:

WHAT A WESTMORELAND WANTS
Copyright © 2010 by Brenda Streater Jackson

A WIFE FOR A WESTMORELAND
Copyright © 2011 by Brenda Streater Jackson

Printed in U.S.A.

CONTENTS

THE WESTMORELAND FAMILY

Scott and Delane Westmoreland

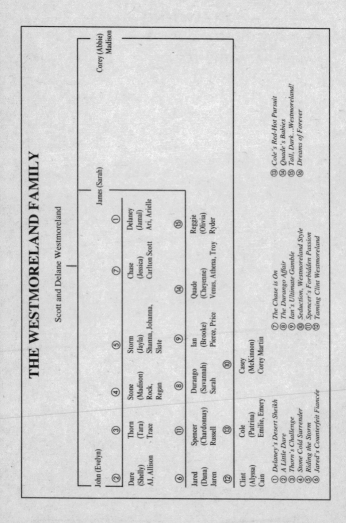

John (Evelyn)

② Dare (Shelly) AJ, Allison
③ Thorn (Tara) Trace
④ Stone (Madison) Rock, Regan
⑤ Storm (Jayla) Shanna, Johanna, Slate
⑦ Chase (Jessica) Carlton Scott
① Delaney (Jamal) Ari, Arielle

⑥ Jared (Dana) Jaren
⑪ Spencer (Chardonnay) Russell
⑧ Durango (Savannah) Sarah
⑨ Ian (Brooke) Pierce, Price
⑭ Quade (Cheyenne) Venus, Athena, Troy
⑮ Reggie (Olivia) Ryder

⑩ Casey (McKinnon) Corey Martin

⑫ Clint (Alyssa) Cain
⑬ Cole (Patrina) Emilie, Emery

James (Sarah)

Corey (Abbie) Madison

① Delaney's Desert Sheikh
② A Little Dare
③ Thorn's Challenge
④ Stone Cold Surrender
⑤ Riding the Storm
⑥ Jared's Counterfeit Fiancée
⑦ The Chase is On
⑧ The Durango Affair
⑨ Ian's Ultimate Gamble
⑩ Seduction, Westmoreland Style
⑪ Spencer's Forbidden Passion
⑫ Taming Clint Westmoreland
⑬ Cole's Red-Hot Pursuit
⑭ Quade's Babies
⑮ Tall, Dark...Westmoreland!
⑯ Dreams of Forever

THE DENVER WESTMORELAND FAMILY TREE

Raphel and Gemma Westmoreland

Stern Westmoreland (Paula Bailey)

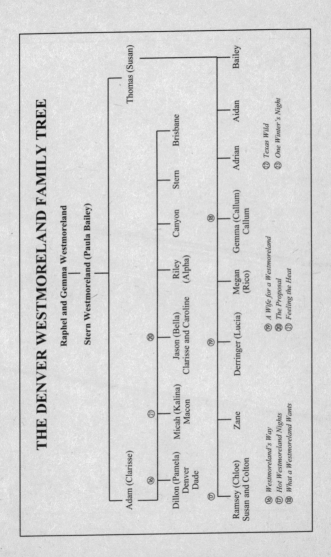

Adam (Clarisse) ⑯

Thomas (Susan)

Dillon (Pamela)
Denver
Dade ⑰

Micah (Kalina)
Macon ⑰

Jason (Bella)
Clarisse and Caroline ⑳

Riley
(Alpha)

Canyon

Stern

Brisbane

Bailey

Ramsey (Chloe)
Susan and Colton ⑰

Zane

Derringer (Lucia) ⑲

Megan
(Rico)

Gemma (Callum)
Callum ⑱

Adrian

Aidan

⑯ *Westmoreland's Way*
⑰ *Hot Westmoreland Nights*
⑱ *What a Westmoreland Wants*

⑲ *A Wife for a Westmoreland*
⑳ *The Proposal*
㉑ *Feeling the Heat*

㉒ *Texas Wild*
㉓ *One Winter's Night*

Dear Reader,

When I first introduced the Westmoreland family, little did I know they would become hugely popular with readers. Originally, the Westmoreland family series was intended to be just six books, Delaney and her five brothers—Dare, Thorn, Stone, Storm and Chase. Later, I wanted my readers to meet their cousins—Jared, Spencer, Durango, Ian, Quade and Reggie. Finally, there were Uncle Corey's triplets—Clint, Cole and Casey.

What began as a six-book series blossomed into a thirty-book series when I included the Denver Westmorelands. I was very happy when Harlequin Kimani Arabesque responded to my readers' requests that the earlier books be reprinted. And I'm even happier that the reissues are in a great two-books-in-one format.

All for Love contains *What a Westmoreland Wants* and *A Wife for a Westmoreland*. These are two Westmoreland classics and are books number eighteen and nineteen in the Westmoreland series. In *What a Westmoreland Wants* I leave no doubt in anyone's mind that Callum wants Gemma Westmoreland, and in this very special story he plans to get what he wants. And in *A Wife for a Westmoreland* Derringer is just as determined to get what he wants…and he's decided that's Lucia Conyers. So just what does this Westmoreland man have to do to win her heart? I think you're going to enjoy the results.

I hope you enjoy reading these special stories as much as I enjoyed writing them.

Happy reading!

Brenda Jackson

To the love of my life, Gerald Jackson, Sr.

To everyone who enjoys reading about the
Westmorelands. This one is for you.

Who can find a virtuous woman? For her price is
far above rubies.
—*Proverbs* 31:10

WHAT A
WESTMORELAND WANTS

Prologue

Callum Austell sat in the chair with his legs stretched out in front of him as he stared at the man sitting behind the huge oak desk. He and Ramsey Westmoreland had become friends from the first, and now he had convinced Ramsey that he was the man who would give his sister Gemma the happiness she deserved.

But Callum knew there was one minor flaw in his plans. One that would come back to haunt him if Gemma Westmoreland ever discovered that the trip to Australia he would offer her would be orchestrated for the sole purpose of getting her off familiar turf so that she would finally come to realize just how much he cared for her.

"I hope you know what you're doing," Ramsey said, interrupting Callum's thoughts. "Gemma will give you hell when she finds out the truth."

"I'll tell her before then, but not before she falls in love with me," Callum replied.

Ramsey lifted a brow. "And if she doesn't?"

To any other woman Callum's intense pursuit might seem like a romantic move, but Ramsey was convinced his sister, who didn't have a romantic bone in her body, wouldn't see things that way.

Callum's expression was determined. "She will fall in

love with me." And then the look in his eyes almost became one of desperation. "Damn, Ram, she has to. I knew the first moment I saw her that she was the one and only woman for me."

Ramsey took a deep breath. He wished he'd had the same thoughts the first time he set eyes on his wife, Chloe. Then he would not have encountered the problems he had. However, his first thoughts when he'd seen Chloe weren't the least bit honorable.

"You're my friend, Callum, but if you hurt my sister in any way, then you'll have one hell of an angry Westmoreland to deal with. Your intentions toward Gemma better be nothing but honorable."

Callum leaned forward in his chair. "I'm going to marry her."

"She has to agree to that first."

Callum stood. "She will. You just concentrate on becoming a father to the baby you and Chloe are expecting in a couple of months, and let me worry about Gemma."

Chapter 1

Gem, I am sorry and I hope you can forgive me one day.

—Niecee

Gemma Westmoreland lifted a brow after reading the note that appeared on her computer after she'd booted it up. Immediately, two questions sailed through her mind. Where was Niecee when she should have been at work over an hour ago and what was Niecee apologizing for?

The hairs on the back of Gemma's neck began standing up and she didn't like the feeling. She had hired Niecee Carter six months ago when Designs by Gem began picking up business, thanks to the huge contract she'd gotten with the city of Denver to redecorate several of its libraries. Then Gayla Mason had wanted her mansion redone. And, last but not least, her sister-in-law, Chloe, hired Gemma for a makeover of the Denver branch of her successful magazine, *Simply Irresistible.*

Gemma had been badly in need of help and Niecee had possessed more clerical skills than the other candidates she'd interviewed. She had given the woman the job without fully checking out her references—something her oldest brother, Ramsey, had warned her against doing. But she hadn't listened. She'd figured that she and the bubbly Niecee would gel well. They had, but now, as Gemma quickly logged into her bank account, she couldn't help wondering if perhaps she should have taken Ramsey's advice.

Gemma had been eleven when Ramsey and her cousin Dillon had taken over the responsibility of raising their thirteen siblings after both sets of parents had been killed in a plane crash. During that time Ramsey had been her rock, the brother who'd been her protector. And now, it seemed, the brother she should have listened to when he'd handed out advice on how to run her business.

She pulled in a sharp breath when she glanced at the balance in her checking account. It was down by $20,000. Nervously, she clicked on the transaction button and saw that a $20,000 check had cleared her bank—a check that she hadn't written. Now she knew what Niecee's apology was all about.

Gemma dropped her face in her hands and felt the need to weep. But she refused to go there. She had to come up with a plan to replace that money. She was expecting invoices to come rolling in any day now from the fabric shops, arts and craft stores and her light fixtures suppliers, just to name a few. Clearly, she wouldn't have enough funds to pay all her debts. She needed to replace those funds.

She stood and began pacing the floor as anger consumed her. How could Niecee have done this to her? If she needed the money, all she had to do was ask. Although Gemma might not have been able to part with that much from her personal account, she could have borrowed the money from one of her brothers or cousins.

Gemma pulled in a deep frustrated breath. She had to file a police report. Her friendship and loyalty to Niecee ended the minute her former worker had stolen from her. She should have suspected something. Niecee hadn't been her usual bubbly self the last few days. Gemma figured it had to do with her trifling live-in boyfriend who barely worked. Had he put Niecee up to this? It didn't matter because Niecee should know right from wrong, and embezzling from your employer was wrong.

Sitting back down at her desk, Gemma reached for the phone and then pulled her hand back. Dang! If she called Sheriff Bart Harper—who had gone to school with both Ramsey and Dillon—and filed a report, there was no doubt in her mind that both Ram and Dillon would hear about it. Those were the last two people she wanted in her business. Especially since they'd tried talking her out of opening her interior design shop in the first place.

For the past year, things had worked out fairly well with her being just a one-woman show with her sisters, Megan and Bailey, helping out if needed. She had even pulled in her brothers, Zane and Derringer, on occasion, when heavy lifting had been involved. But when the big jobs began coming in, she had advertised in the newspapers and online for an administrative assistant.

She stood and began pacing again. Bailey was still taking classes at the university and wouldn't have that much money readily available, and Megan had mentioned just the other week that she was saving for a much-needed vacation. Megan was contemplating visiting their cousin, Delaney, who lived in the Middle East with her husband and two children, so there was no way she could hit her up for a loan.

Zane and Derringer were generous and because they were bachelors they might have that kind of ready dough. But they had recently pooled all their funds to buy into a horse-breeding and -training franchise, together with their cousin, Jason. She couldn't look in their direction now, due to that business venture. And all her other siblings and cousins were either in school or into their own businesses and investments.

So where was she going to get $20,000?

Gemma stood staring at the phone for a moment before it hit her that the thing was ringing. She quickly picked it up, hoping it was Niecee letting her know she was returning the money to her or, better yet, that the whole thing was a joke.

"Hello?"

"Hello, Gemma, this is Callum."

She wondered why the man who managed Ramsey's sheep farm would be calling her. "Yes, Callum?"

"I was wondering if I could meet with you sometime today to discuss a business proposition."

She lifted a brow. "A business proposition?"

"Yes."

The first thought that crossed her mind was that engaging in a business meeting was the last thing she was in the mood for today. But then she quickly realized that she couldn't let what Niecee did keep her from handling things with her company. She still had a business to run.

"When would you like to meet, Callum?"

"How about today for lunch."

"Lunch?"

"Yes, at McKay's."

She wondered if he knew that McKay's was her favorite lunch spot. "Okay, that'll work. I'll see you there at noon," she said.

"Great. See you then."

Gemma held the phone in her hand, thinking how much she enjoyed listening to Callum's deep Australian accent. He always sounded so ultrasexy. But then he was definitely a sexy man. That was something she tried not to notice too much, mainly because he was a close friend of Ramsey's. Also, according to Jackie Barnes, a nurse who worked at the hospital with Megan and who'd had a bad case of the hots for Callum when he first arrived in Denver, Callum had a girl waiting for him back in Australia and it was a very serious relationship.

But what if he no longer had that girl waiting for him back in Australia? What if he was as available as he was hot? What if she could forget that he was her oldest brother's close friend? What if…

Dismissing all such thoughts with a wave of her hand, she sat back down at her computer to figure out a way to rob Peter to pay Paul.

Callum Austell leaned back in his chair as he glanced around the restaurant. The first time he'd eaten here had been with Ramsey when he first came to Denver. He liked it then and now this would be the place where he would put into motion a plan some would think was way past due being executed. He would have to admit they were probably right.

He wasn't sure exactly when he decided that Gemma Westmoreland was destined to be *his* woman. Probably the day he had helped Ramsey build that barn and Gemma had arrived from college right after graduation. The moment she got out of her car and raced over to her older brother's arms for a huge hug. Callum had felt like he'd gotten hit over the head with a two-by-four, not once but twice. And when Ramsey had introduced them and she'd turned that wondergirl smile on him, he hadn't been the same since. His father and his two older brothers had warned him that it would be that way when he found the woman destined to be his, but he hadn't believed them.

That had been almost three years ago and she'd been just twenty-two years old. So he'd waited patiently for her to get older and had watched over her from afar. And each passing day she'd staked a deeper claim to his heart. Knowing how protective Ramsey was of his siblings, especially his three sisters, Callum had finally gotten up the nerve to confront Ramsey and tell him how he felt about Gemma.

At first Ramsey hadn't liked the idea of his best friend lusting after one of his sisters. But then Callum had convinced Ramsey it was more than lust and that he knew in his heart that Gemma was "the one" for him.

For six months, Ramsey had lived with Callum's family back in Australia on the Austell sheep ranch to learn everything he could so he could start his own operations in Denver. He had hung around Callum's parents and brothers enough to know how dedicated the Austell men were once they fell in love.

His father had given up on falling in love and was on his way back to Australia from a business meeting in the United States to marry an Australian woman when he'd met Callum's mother. She was one of the flight attendants on the plane.

Somehow the already engaged Todd Austell had convinced the Detroit-born Le'Claire Richards that breaking off with his fiancée and marrying her instead was the right thing to do. Evidently it was. Thirty-seven years later the two were still married, remained very much in love and had three sons and a daughter to show for it. Callum was the youngest of the four and the only one who was still single.

His thoughts shifted back to Gemma. Ramsey claimed that of his three sisters, Gemma was the one with the fiery temper. The one a man would least be able to handle. He'd suggested that Callum pray long and hard about making the right decision.

In the end, Callum had convinced Ramsey that he had made the right decision and that a hard-to-handle woman with a fiery temper was the kind he liked. He was more than certain that Gemma was the woman for him.

Now he had to convince Gemma… He'd have to be stealthy about his pursuit. He knew Gemma had no intention of engaging in a serious relationship after she had witnessed how two of her brothers, and several of her womanizing cousins, had operated with women over the years, breaking hearts in their wake. According to Ramsey, Gemma Westmoreland was determined never to let a man break her heart.

Callum straightened up in his seat when he saw Gemma enter the restaurant. Immediately, the same feeling suffused his heart that always settled there whenever he saw her. He loved the woman. He no longer tried to rationalize why. It really didn't matter at this point.

As she walked toward him, he stood. She was probably 5'8", but just the right height for his 6'3" frame. And he'd always thought she had a rather nice figure. Her dark brown, shoulder-length hair was pulled back in a ponytail. He thought she had dazzling tawny-brown eyes, which were almost covered by her bangs.

Callum had worked hard not to give his feelings away. Because he'd always been on his best behavior around her, he knew she didn't have a clue. It hadn't been easy keeping her in the dark. She saw him as nothing more than her brother's best friend from Australia. The Aussie who didn't have a lot to say and was basically a loner.

He studied her expression as she got closer. She seemed anxious, as if she had a lot on her mind.

"Callum," she said and smiled.

"Gemma. Thanks for agreeing to see me," he said as he took her oustretched hand.

"No problem," she said, sitting down once he released her hand. "You said something about meeting to discuss a business proposition."

"Yes, but first how about us grabbing something to eat. I'm starving."

"Sure."

As if on cue, a waitress strolled over with menus and

placed glasses of water in front of them. "I hope this place is acceptable," Callum said, moments later after taking a sip of his water.

"Trust me, it is," Gemma said smiling. "It's one of my favorites. The salads here are fabulous."

He chuckled. "Are they?"

"Yes."

"That might very well be, but I'm not a salad man. I prefer something a lot heavier. Like a steak and the French fries I hear this place is famous for."

"No wonder you and Ramsey get along. Now that he's married to Chloe, I'll bet he's in hog heaven with all those different meals she likes to prepare."

"I'm sure he is. It's hard to believe he's married," Callum said.

"Yes, four months tomorrow and I don't recall my brother ever being happier."

"And his men are happy, too, now that Nellie's been replaced as cook," he said. "She never could get her act together and it worked out well for everyone when she decided to move closer to her sister when her marriage fell apart."

Gemma nodded. "I hear the new cook is working out wonderfully, although most of the guys still prefer Chloe's cooking. But she is happy just being Ramsey's wife and a mother-in-waiting. She doesn't have long now and I'm excited about becoming an aunt.

"Are you an uncle yet?"

It was his turn to smile. "Yes. My two older brothers and one sister are married with a child each. I'm used to being around kids. And I also have a goddaughter who will be celebrating her first birthday soon."

At that moment the waitress returned. Callum resented the interruption.

* * *

Gemma appreciated the interruption. Although she had been around Callum plenty of times, she'd never noticed just how powerfully built he was. Her brothers and male cousins were all big men, but Callum was so much more manly.

And she had to listen carefully to what he said and stop paying so much attention to how he said it. His thick Australian accent did things to her. It sent a warm, sensual caress across her skin every time he opened his mouth to speak. Then there were his looks, which made her understand perfectly why Jackie Barnes and quite a number of other women had gone bonkers over him. In addition to being tall, with a raw, masculine build, he had thick chestnut-brown hair that fell to his shoulders. Most days he wore it pulled back into a ponytail. He'd made today an exception and it cascaded around his shoulders.

Gemma had once overheard him mention to her sister, Megan, that his full lips and dark hair came from his African-American mother and his green eyes and his square jaw from his father. She'd also heard him say that his parents had met on an airplane. His mother had been a flight attendant on his father's flight from the United States back to Australia. He'd told Megan it had been love at first sight, which made her wonder if he believed in such nonsense. She knew there was no such thing.

"So what do you think of Dillon and Pamela's news?"

Callum's question cut into her thoughts and she glanced up to meet his green eyes. She swallowed. Was there a hint of blue in their depths? And then there was his dimpled smile that took her breath away.

"I think it's wonderful," she said, suddenly feeling the need to take a sip of cold water. "There haven't been babies in our family in a long time. With Chloe expecting and now Pamela, that's two babies to spoil and I can't wait."

"You like children?"

She chuckled. "Yes, unfortunately, I'm one of those people who take to the precious darlings a little too much. That's why my friends call on me more often than not to babysit for them."

"You could always marry and have your own."

She made a face. "Thanks, but no thanks. At least no time soon, if ever. I'm sure you've heard the family joke about me never wanting to get serious about a man. Well, it's not a joke—it's the truth."

"Because of what you witnessed with your brothers while growing up?"

So he *had* heard. Any one of her brothers could have mentioned it, especially because she denounced their behavior every chance she got. "I guess you can say I saw and heard too much. My brothers and cousins had a reputation for fast cars and fast women. They thought nothing about breaking hearts. Ramsey usually had a steady girl, but Zane and Derringer were two of the worst when it came to playing women. As far as I'm concerned, they still are." Unfortunately, she'd overheard one of Zane's phone calls that very morning when she had stopped by to borrow some milk.

"I can clearly recall the times when Megan and I, and sometimes even Bailey, who was still young enough to be playing with her dolls, would be the ones to get the phone calls from love-stricken girls in tears after being mercilessly dumped by one of my brothers or cousins."

And they were females determined to share their teary-eyed, heart-wrenching stories with anyone willing to listen. Megan and Bailey would get them off the phone really quickly, but Gemma had been the bleeding heart. She would ease into a chair and take the time to listen to their sob stories, absorbing every heartbreaking detail like a sponge. Even to the point at which she would end up crying a river of tears right along with them.

She'd decided by the time she had begun dating that no man alive would make her one of those weeping women. And then there was this inner fear she'd shared with no one, the fear of falling in love and having the person abandon her one day…the way she felt whenever she thought about her parents. She knew she had no logical reason for feeling abandoned by them because she was certain if they'd had a choice they would have survived that plane crash. But still, as illogical as it might be, the fear was there for her and it was real. She was convinced there was no man worth a single Gemma Westmoreland tear or her fears, and intended to make sure she never shed one by never giving her heart to anyone. She would be celebrating her twenty-fifth birthday in a few months and so far she'd managed to keep both her heart and her virginity intact.

"And because of that you don't ever plan to get seriously involved with a man?"

She drew in a deep breath. She and her sisters had had this conversation many times and she was wondering why she was sitting here having it with Callum now. Why was he interested? It dawned on her that he probably wasn't; he was just asking to fill the time. "As far as I'm concerned that's a good enough reason. Those girls were in love with my brothers and cousins and assumed they loved them back. Just look what that wrong assumption did to them."

Callum took a sip of his water, deciding not to respond by saying that as far as he was concerned her brothers' behavior was normal for most men, and in some cases women. Granted, he hadn't been around Zane and Derringer while they had been in their teens and could just imagine some of the things they had gotten in to. Now, as grown men, he knew they enjoyed women, but then most hot-blooded men did. And just because a man might be considered a "player" somewhat before finally settling down with one woman— the one he chose to spend the rest of his life with—that didn't necessarily mean he was a man who totally disrespected women. In fairness to Zane and Derringer, they treated women with respect.

He wondered what she would think if she knew how his behavior had been before he'd met her. He hadn't considered himself a womanizer, although he'd dated a slew of woman. He merely thought of himself as a man who enjoyed life and wanted to have a good time with the opposite sex while waiting for the girl destined to share his life to come along. Once she had, he'd had no trouble bringing his fun-loving, footloose and fancy-free bachelor lifestyle to an end. Eventually, the same thing would happen to her brothers and cousins.

No wonder her brothers thought she was a lost cause, but he refused to accept that. He was determined to show her how things could be if she were to fall in love with a man committed to making her happy.

In a way, he felt he knew Gemma. He believed that beneath her rough and tough "I'll never fall in love" exterior was the heart of a woman who not only loved children but loved life in general. He also believed that she was a passionate woman. And that she was unknowingly reserving that passion for the one man capable of tapping into it. The same man destined to spend the rest of his life with her. Him.

The waitress delivered their food, and they engaged in chitchat while they ate their meal.

After they had finished eating and the waitress removed their plates, Gemma leaned back in her chair and smiled at Callum. "Lunch was wonderful. Now, about that business proposition?"

He chuckled, reached over and picked up the folder he

had placed on an empty chair. He handed it to her. "This is information on the home I purchased last year. I would love you to decorate it for me."

Callum saw how her eyes lit up. She loved her work and it showed in her face. She opened the folder and carefully studied every feature, every detail of the house. He knew exactly what he was doing. He was giving her 9,200 feet of house to do with as she pleased. It was an interior designer's dream.

She lifted her gaze with a look of awe on her face. "This place is beautiful. And it's huge. I didn't know you had purchased a house."

"Yes, but it's still empty and I want to turn it into a home. I like what you did with Ramsey's place and thought you would be the ideal person for the job. I'm aware that because of the size of the house it will take up a lot of your time. I'm willing to pay you well. As you can see I haven't picked out any furniture or anything. I wouldn't know where to begin."

Now that much was true, Callum thought. What he didn't tell her was that other designers had volunteered to decorate his new house, but he had bought it with her in mind.

She glanced back down at the papers in front of her. "Umm, eight bedrooms, six bathrooms, a huge kitchen, living room, dining room, family room, theater, recreation room and sauna. That's quite a lot of space for a single man."

He laughed. "Yeah, but I don't plan on staying single forever."

Gemma nodded, thinking that evidently Callum had decided to settle down and send for that girl back home. She glanced down at the papers again. She would love taking on this project, and he was right in thinking it would take up a lot of her time. But then she definitely needed the money.

"So, what do you think, Gemma?"

She glanced back up at him and smiled. "I think you just hired yourself an interior designer."

The smile that touched his face sent a tingling sensation flowing through her stomach. "I can't wait to see it."

"No problem. When can you get away?"

She pulled out her cell phone to check her calendar and her schedule for this week. Once she saw the place and gave him an official estimate, she could ask for a deposit, which would make up some of what Niecee had taken from her. "What about tomorrow around one?"

"That might be a bit of a problem."

"Oh." She figured he would probably be tied up at Ram's ranch doing something at that time, so without looking up she advanced her calendar another day. "What about Wednesday around noon."

He chuckled. "Twelve noon on Monday would be the earliest availability for me."

She nodded when she saw that time was free for her, although she wished she could see it sooner. "Monday at noon will be fine."

"Great, I'll make the necessary flight arrangements."

She put her phone back into her purse and glanced over at him. "Excuse me?"

"I said that I will make the necessary flight arrangements if we want to see the house Monday at noon. That means we'll need to fly out no later than Thursday morning."

Gemma frowned. "Thursday morning? What are you talking about? Just where is this house located?"

Callum leaned back in his chair and gave her a one kilowatt smile. "Sydney, Australia."

Chapter 2

Gemma didn't have to look in the mirror to know there was a shocked look on her face. And her throat felt tight, as if sound would barely pass through it if she tried to speak. To prove the point, she tried to utter a word and couldn't. So she just sat there and stared across the table at Callum like he had lost his ever-loving mind.

"Now that that's all settled, let's order some dessert," Callum said, picking up the menu.

She reached out, touched his hand and shook her head.

"What's the matter?" he asked. "You don't want dessert?"

She drew in a deep breath, made an attempt to speak once more and was glad when sound came out. But to be absolutely sure he understood, she held up her hands in the shape of a T. "Time out."

He lifted an eyebrow. "Time out?"

She nodded. "Yes, time out. You lost me between the flight on Thursday and Sydney, Australia. Are you saying this house that you want me to decorate is in Sydney, Australia?"

"Of course. Where else would it be?"

She fought hard not to glare at him; after all, he was a potential client. "I thought possibly in the Denver area," she said in what she hoped was a neutral tone.

"Why would you think that?"

She couldn't hold back her glare any longer. "Well, you've been in this country for almost three years now."

"Yes, but I've never said or insinuated to anyone that I wouldn't return home. I was here helping Ramsey out and now that he has the hang of things, I'm no longer needed. Now I can get back home and—"

"Get married," Gemma supplied.

He chuckled. "As I said earlier, I don't plan on staying single forever."

"And when do you plan on marrying her?"

"Her who?"

Gemma wondered why some men suddenly went daft when their girlfriends were mentioned. "The woman waiting for you back in Australia."

"Umm, I didn't know there was such a creature."

Gemma stared at him in disbelief. "Are you saying you don't have a fiancée or a sweetheart back in Australia?"

He smiled. "That's exactly what I'm saying. Where did you hear something like that?"

Normally Gemma wouldn't divulge her sources, but typically, Jackie knew what she was talking about, and that wouldn't be anything the woman would have made up. "Jackie Barnes. And everyone figured she got the information from you."

Callum shook his head. "She didn't get that from me, but I have an idea where it came from. Your brother, Zane. I complained about Jackie making a nuisance of herself and he figured the best way to get rid of a woman like Jackie was just to let her believe I was already taken."

"Oh." She could see Zane doing something like that. If for no other reason than to shift Jackie's interest from Callum to him. Her brother was a womanizer to the nth degree. And Derringer wasn't any better. It was a blessing that the twins, Adrian and Aidan, were away at college, where the only thing on their minds was making the grade. "I assume Zane's plan worked."

"It did."

"In that case you were lucky," Gemma decided to say. "Some women would not have cared that you were spoken for. They would have taken it as a challenge to swing your interest their way."

Callum couldn't help but think of just where his interest had been for the past three years and knew no one could have succeeded in doing that. The woman sitting across the table was the one he intended to marry.

"And you actually assumed I have someone of interest back home?"

She shrugged. "Hey, that's what we all heard and I had no reason to assume differently. As far as I knew, you weren't dating anyone and whenever we had events you always came alone."

And tried hanging around you every chance I got, he thought.

"You were almost as much of a loner as Ramsey," Gemma added. "If your goal was to keep the women away, then it evidently worked for you."

He took a sip of his drink, wondering if the reason she had yet to pick up on his interest in her was because she figured he was already taken.

"Callum, about this trip to Australia?"

He knew where she was about to take the discussion and was prepared with a spiel to reel her in. "What about it? If you're having second thoughts, I understand. No sweat. I've already contacted a backup in case you couldn't do it. Jeri Holliday at Jeri's Fashion Designs has indicated she would love the job and will have her bags packed for Australia before I can blink an eye."

Over my dead body, Gemma thought as she sat up

straight in her chair. Jeri Holliday had been trying to steal clients from her for years.

"I think she liked the fact that I'm offering $50,000, and half of that upfront."

His words froze her thoughts. "Come again?"

He smiled. "I said, considering that I'm asking the decorator to give up at least six weeks, I'm offering $50,000, just as a starting price."

Gemma could only stare at him once again in disbelief. She leaned closer to the table and spoke in a hushed tone, as if anyone sitting in close range could overhear their top-secret conversation. "Are you saying that you're paying $25,000 on acceptance of the job and the other half on completion; and that $50,000 does not include any of the materials? That's just for labor?"

"Yes, that's what I'm saying."

Gemma began nibbling on her bottom lip. The $25,000 would definitely boost her bank account, replacing what Niecee had stolen. And then to think there would be another $25,000 waiting when she completed everything. However, as good as it sounded there were a few possible conflicts.

"What do you see as the time line for this project, Callum?" she decided to ask him.

He shrugged wide shoulders. "I'll tell you the same thing I told Jeri. I think it will take a month to six weeks to take down all the measurements and get things ordered. I'd also like that person there to coordinate the selection of all the furniture. However, there's no rush on that."

Gemma began nibbling on her lips again. "The reason I asked is because there are two babies who will be born within a few months of each other and I'd like to be here for both births. If I can't make it back at the time of delivery then at least within a few days."

"No problem. In fact, I'll spring for the flight."

Gemma couldn't help but wonder why he was being so generous and decided to ask him.

"I've always believed in being fair when it came to those who worked for me," he said.

"In any case, I'm going to need to return myself to help out because Ramsey will be busy with Chloe and the baby," he continued. "I don't want him to worry about the ranch during that time, so I've already promised him that I would return. And although Dillon probably won't need me to do anything, he and Pamela are like family and I want to be here for their baby's arrival, too."

Gemma felt relieved. But still—Australia? That was such a long way from home. And for a month, possibly six weeks. The only other time she'd been away from home for so long was when she left for college in Nebraska. Now she was considering trekking off to another country. Heck, it was another continent.

She was suddenly filled with an anticipation she'd never felt before. She'd never been a traveler, but if she took Callum's job offer, she would get to see a part of the world she'd only read about. That was exciting.

"So are you still interested or do you want me to go with Jeri Holliday?"

She didn't hesitate. "I don't have a problem traveling to Australia and will be ready to fly out on Thursday. I just need to get my business in order. I'll be gone for a while and I'll need to let my family know."

It then occurred to her that her family might not like the idea of her going so far away. Ramsey had a tendency to be overprotective. But he had his hands full with Chloe expecting their baby at the end of November. He would be too busy to try to micromanage her life…thank goodness.

"Terrific. I'll make flight arrangements and will let you know when I have everything in order."

"All right."

Callum lifted up his soda glass in a toast. "Here's to adventures awaiting you in the outback."

Gemma chuckled as she lifted her glass in a toast, as well. "Yes, here's to adventures in the outback."

A few hours later back at her house, despite her outer calm, Gemma was trying to keep things together on the inside while she explained everything to her sisters, Megan and Bailey, as they sat together at the kitchen table. Megan was the oldest at twenty-six and Bailey was twenty-two.

"And why didn't you file a police report? Twenty thousand dollars isn't a little bit of money, Gem," an angry Megan wanted to know.

Gemma drew in a deep breath. "I'm working with the bank's security team in trying to recover the funds. The main reason I didn't get Sheriff Harper involved is because he's close friends with both Dillon and Ramsey. He'll probably get a report of the incident from the bank, eventually, but I think he'd be more inclined to keep his mouth shut about it. It would appear more of an official matter then."

"Oh."

From the look on her sisters' faces and their simultaneous responses, she knew they had forgotten that one important piece of information. There wasn't too much a Westmoreland did in these parts that Dillon and Ramsey didn't know about. Sheriff Harper, who had gone to high school with Dillon and Ramsey, made sure of that.

"And I didn't want to hear, 'I told you so' from those two. Neither of them wanted me to start my own business when I did. So there was no way I was going to tell them what Niecee had done. Hiring her was my mistake and I'll have to deal with it in my own way."

"But will you make sure she doesn't get away with her crime? I'd hate for her to steal from some other unsuspecting soul."

"Yes, I'm going to make sure she doesn't do this again. And to think that I trusted her," Gemma said with a nod.

"You're too trusting," Megan said. "I've always warned you about that."

And she had, Gemma thought. So had her older brothers. "So what do you think about me going to Australia?" She needed to change the subject.

Megan smiled. "Personally, I think it's cool and wish I could go with you, but I'm saving my time off at the hospital for that trip to visit Delaney in Tehran."

"I think that's cool, as well," Bailey said. "I'm still reeling over the fact that there's no woman waiting for Callum back in Sydney. If that's true, then why isn't he dating? I don't ever recall him having a girlfriend while he's been here in the States. He's nothing like Zane and Derringer."

"And he's such a cutie-pie," Megan added.

Gemma couldn't help smiling as she recalled how sexy he looked sitting across from her at lunch. "He'd already mentioned the job to Jeri Holliday, but it was contingent on whether or not I would accept his offer."

"And I'm sure she was ready to grab it," Bailey said with a frown.

"Of course she was. I wish the two of you could see the size of his house. I can't believe he'd buy such a place as a single man. Now that I've made up my mind about going to Australia, I need to let Ramsey know."

Gemma inhaled sharply at the thought of doing that, but knew it needed to be done. However, under no circumstances did Ramsey need to know that Niecee had embezzled $20,000 from her. She would let the bank's security team handle things.

"You don't have any appointments or projects scheduled for the next six weeks?" Megan asked as they helped her pack.

"No. This job offer came at a good time. I had thought

about taking a well-deserved vacation anyway, but now it's back to work for me. I'll take some time off during the holidays."

"If Callum bought a house in Australia, does that mean he's moving back home?"

Gemma glanced over at Bailey. That thought hadn't occurred to her. "I guess so."

"What a bummer. I've gotten used to seeing him," Bailey said with a pout. "I'd begun thinking of him as another big brother."

Gemma drew in a deep breath. For some reason she'd never thought of him as another big brother.

She'd never felt the need to become as friendly with him as Megan and Bailey had, but she never knew why she'd been standoffish with him. She'd only accepted that that was the way things were. Why now, all of a sudden, did the thought of him returning to Australia to live and her not seeing him ever again seem like such a big deal?

The very thought made her uneasy.

Chapter 3

"Are you okay, Gemma?"

Gemma turned her head to glance over at Callum. What had the pilot just said? They were now cruising at an altitude of 36,000 feet. Was Callum inquiring as to how she felt because she'd suddenly turned green?

Now was not the time to tell him that she had an aversion to flying. Although she'd flown before, that didn't mean she liked it. In fact, she didn't. She'd told herself while packing that she could handle the eighteen hours it would take to get to Australia. Now she was having some pretty serious doubts about that.

"Gemma?"

She drew in a deep breath. "Yes, I'm fine."

"You sure?"

No, she wasn't sure, but he would be the last person to know. "Yes."

She turned her head to look out the window and wondered if asking for a window seat had been a wise choice. All she could see were clouds and Callum's reflection. He smelled good, and she couldn't help wondering what cologne he was wearing. And he looked good, too. He had arrived to pick her up wearing a pair of jeans, a blue chambray shirt and Western boots. She'd seen him in similar outfits plenty of times, but for some odd reason he seemed different to her today.

"The attendant is about to serve snacks. Are you hungry?"

She turned and met his eyes. They were a beautiful green and she could swear that a strange expression shone in their dark depths. "No, I ate a good breakfast this morning with Ramsey and Chloe."

He lifted a brow. "You got up at five this morning to do that?"

She smiled. "Yes. All I had to do was set the alarm. I figured if I got up early, then by the time this plane leveled off in the sky I would be ready to take a nap."

He chuckled. "Does flying bother you?"

"Let's just say it's not one of my favorite things to do," she answered. "There're other things I prefer doing more. Like getting a root canal or something else equally as enjoyable."

He threw his head back and laughed, and she liked the sound of it. She'd known him for almost three years and this was the first time she recalled hearing him laugh. He'd always seemed so serious, just like Ramsey. At least that was how Ramsey used to be. She would be one of the first to say that marriage had changed her brother for the better.

"And then," she added in a soft, thoughtful tone. "My parents were killed in a plane crash and I can't help but think of that whenever I'm in the air." She paused a moment. "There was a time after their deaths that I swore I'd never get on a plane," she said quietly.

Callum did something at that moment she hadn't expected. He reached out and took her hand in his. His was warm and large and completely covered hers. "How did you overcome that fear?"

She shifted her gaze away from their joined hands to his face and sighed deeply. "I refused to live my life in fear of the unknown. So one day I went to Ramsey and told him I was ready to take my first plane ride. He was working with Dillon at Blue Ridge Land Management at the time and made arrangements to take me on his next business trip. I was fourteen."

A bright smile touched her lips. "He signed me out of school for a few days and I flew with him to New Mexico. My first encounter with turbulence almost sent me through the roof. But he talked me through it. He even made me write an essay on my airplane experience."

The flight attendant came around serving drinks and snacks, but Gemma declined everything. Callum took a pack of peanuts and ordered a beer. Gemma had asked for a pillow earlier and adjusted it against her neck as she reclined comfortably in her seat. She had to admit that the first-class seats on this international flight were spacious. And Callum had booked a double-seat row for just the two of them.

Gemma noticed that the attendant had given Callum one or two smiles more than was necessary. The attendant's obvious interest in her passenger made Gemma think of something. "Is it true that your parents met on a flight to Australia?"

He inclined his head to look at her. "Yes, that's true. Dad was actually engaged to someone else at the time and was returning home to Australia to help plan his wedding."

"And he fell for someone else when he was already engaged?"

Callum heard the shock in her voice. Considering what she thought about men deliberately breaking women's hearts, he decided to explain. "From what I was told, he had asked this woman to marry him and it was to be a marriage of convenience."

She lifted a brow. "A marriage of convenience for whom?"

"The both of them. She wanted a rich husband and he wanted a wife to start a family. They saw it as the perfect union."

Gemma nodded. "So love had nothing to do with it?"

"No. He didn't think such a thing could exist for him until he saw my mother. He was hit between the eyes with a ton of bricks." Callum chuckled. "Those are his words, not mine."

"And what happened to the other woman? The one he'd been engaged to at the time?"

He could hear pity in her voice. "Not sure. But I know what didn't happen to her."

Gemma lifted a curious brow. "What?"

A smile touched his lips. "She didn't get the wedding she planned."

"And you find that amusing?"

"Actually, yes, because it was discovered months later that she was pregnant with another man's child."

Gemma gasped sharply and leaned her head closer to Callum's. "Are you serious?"

"Very much so."

"The same thing almost happened to Ramsey, but Danielle stopped the wedding," Gemma said.

"So I heard."

"And I liked her."

"I heard that, too. I understand that your entire family did. But then that goes to show."

She looked over at him. "What?"

"Men aren't the only ones who can be heartbreakers."

Surprise swept across her face at his remark. Gemma leaned back against her seat and released her breath in a slow sigh. "I never said they were."

"You didn't?" he asked smiling.

"No, of course not."

Callum decided not to argue with her about it. Instead, he just smiled. "It's time for that nap. You're beginning to sound a bit grouchy."

To Callum's surprise, she took one, which gave him the opportunity to watch her while she slept. As he gazed at her, he experienced the same intense desire that he'd always felt whenever he was close to her. At the moment, he was close, but not close enough. He couldn't help but study her features and thought her moments of peaceful bliss had transformed her already beautiful face into one that was even more striking.

He would be the first to admit that she no longer looked like the young girl he'd seen that first day. In three years, her features had changed from that of a girl to a woman and it all started with the shape of her mouth, which was nothing short of sensuous. How could lips be that full and inviting, he wondered, as his gaze moved from one corner of her mouth to the other.

Callum's gaze drifted upward from her mouth to her closed eyes and the long lashes covering them. His gaze then moved to her cheekbones and he was tempted to take the back of his hand and caress them, or better yet, trace their beautiful curves with the tip of his tongue, branding her as his. And she *was* his, whether she knew it or not, whether she accepted it or not. She belonged to him.

He then noticed how even her breathing was, and how every breath drew his attention to the swell of her breasts that were alluringly hidden inside a light blue blouse. He'd always found her sexy, too sexy, and it had been hard not to want her, so he hadn't even bothered fighting the temptation. He had lusted after her from afar, which was something he couldn't help, since he hadn't touched another woman in almost three years. Once her place in his life had become crystal clear, his body had gone into a disciplined mode, knowing she would be the one and only woman he would make love to for the rest of his life. Now, the thought of that made his body go hard. He breathed in her scent, he closed the book he had been reading and adjusted his pillow. He closed his eyes and allowed his fantasies of her to do what they always did, take over his mind and do in his dreams what he couldn't yet do in reality.

Gemma slowly opened her eyes at the same moment she shifted in her seat. She glanced over at Callum and saw that he had fallen asleep. His head was tilted close to hers.

She would have to admit that at first his close proximity had bothered her because she assumed they would have to make a lot of unnecessary conversation during the flight. She wasn't very good at small talk or flirting. She'd dated before, but rarely, because most men had a tendency to bore her. She'd discovered that most liked talking about themselves, tooting their own horn and figured they were God's gift to women.

She pushed all thoughts of other men aside and decided to concentrate on this one. He was sitting so close that she could inhale his masculine scent. She had enough brothers and male cousins to know that just as no two women carried the same scent, the same held true for men. Each person's fragrance was unique and the one floating through her nostrils now was making funny feelings flutter around in her stomach.

Gemma found it odd that nothing like this had ever happened to her before, but then she couldn't recall Callum ever being this close to her. Usually they were surrounded by other family members. Granted, they weren't exactly alone now, but, still, there was a sense of intimacy with him sitting beside her. She could just make out the soft sounds of his even breathing.

She had been ready to go when he had arrived at her place. When she opened the door and he had walked in, her breath had gotten caught in her throat. She'd seen him in jeans more times than not, but there was something about the pair he was wearing now that had caused her to do a double take. When he'd leaned down to pick up her luggage, his masculine thighs flexed beneath starched denim. Then there were those muscled arms beneath the Western shirt. Her gaze had lingered longer than it should have on his body. She had followed him out the door while getting an eyeful of his make-you-want-to-drool tush.

She studied him now, fascinated by just what a good-looking man he was and how he'd managed to keep women at bay for so long. A part of her knew it hadn't just been the story Zane had fabricated about a woman waiting for him back in Australia. That tale might have kept some women like Jackie away, but it would not have done anything to hold back the bolder ones. It was primarily the way he'd carried himself. Just like Ramsey. In his pre-Chloe days, most women would have thought twice before approaching her brother. He radiated that kind of "I'm not in the mood" aura whenever it suited him.

But for some reason, she'd never considered Callum as unapproachable as Ramsey. Whenever they had exchanged words, he'd been friendly enough with her. A part of her was curious about why if he wasn't already taken; he'd held himself back from engaging in a serious relationship with a woman. Perhaps he wanted a wife who was from his homeland. That wouldn't be surprising, although it was ironic that his mother was American.

"Oh." The word slipped through her lips in a frantic tone when the plane shook from the force of strong turbulence. She quickly caught her breath.

"You okay?"

She glanced over at Callum. He was awake. "Yes. I hadn't expected that just then. Sorry if I woke you up."

"No problem," he said, straightening up in his seat.

"We've been in the air about four hours now, so we were bound to hit an air pocket sooner or later."

She swallowed when the airplane hit a smaller, less forceful pocket of turbulence. "And they don't bother you?"

"Not as much as they used to. When I was younger, my siblings and I would fly with Mom back to the States to visit our grandparents. I used to consider turbulence as exciting as a roller-coaster ride. I thought it was fun."

Gemma rolled her eyes. "There's nothing fun about the feel of an airplane shaking all over the place like it's about to come apart."

He released a soft chuckle. "You're safe, but let me check your seat belt to be sure."

Before she could pull in her next breath, he reached out to her waist and touched her seat belt. She felt his fingers brush against her stomach in the process. At that precise moment, sensations rushed all through her belly and right up her arms.

She glanced over at Callum and found her gaze ensnared by the deep green of his eyes and those sensations intensified. She knew at that moment that something was happening between them, and whatever it was, she wasn't quite prepared for it.

She'd heard about sexual awareness, but why would it affect her now, and why with someone who was almost a total stranger to her? It wasn't as if this was the first time she and Callum had been around each other. But then... as she'd acknowledged to herself earlier, this was the first time they had been alone to this degree. She wondered if her new feelings were one-sided, or if he'd felt it, as well.

"You're belted tight," he said, and to her his voice seemed a bit huskier...or perhaps she was just imagining things.

"Thanks for checking."

"No problem."

Since they were both wide awake now, Gemma decided

it was probably a good idea to engage in conversation. That would be safer than just sitting here and letting all kinds of crazy thoughts race through her mind, like what would happen if she were to check on his seat belt as he'd checked on hers. She felt heat infuse her face and her heart rate suddenly shot up.

Then her anxiety level moved up a notch when she thought his gaze lingered on her lips a little longer than necessary. Had that really been the case? "Tell me about Australia," she said quickly.

Evidently talking about his homeland was something he enjoyed doing if the smile tilting his lips was anything to go by. And they were a gorgeous pair. She'd noticed them before, but this was the first time she'd given those lips more than a passing thought.

Why all of a sudden was there something so compelling about Callum? Why did the thought of his lips, eyes and other facial features, as well as his hands and fingers, suddenly make her feel hot?

"You're going to love Australia," he said, speaking in that deep accent she loved hearing. "Especially Sydney. There's no place in the world quite like it."

She lifted a brow and folded her arms across her chest. She didn't want to get into a debate, but she thought Denver was rather nice, as well. "Nicer than Denver?"

He chuckled, as understanding lit his eyes. "Yes. Denver has its strong points—don't get me wrong—but there's something about Sydney that's unique. I'm not saying that just because it's where I was born."

"So what's so nice about it?"

He smiled again and, as if on cue, those sensations in her stomach fluttered and spread through her entire midsection.

"I hate to sound like a travel ad, but Australia is a cosmopolitan place drenched in history and surrounded by some of the most beautiful beaches imaginable. Close your eyes for a moment and envision this, Gemma."

She closed her eyes and he began talking in a soft tone, describing the beaches in detail. From his description, she could all but feel a spray of ocean water on her lips, a cool breeze caressing her skin.

"There're Kingscliff Beach, Byron Bay, Newcastle and Lord Howe, just to name a few. Each of them is an aquatic paradise, containing the purest blue-green waters your eyes can behold."

"Like the color of your eyes?" Her eyes were still closed.

She heard his soft chuckle. "Yes, somewhat. And speaking of eyes, you can open yours now."

She slowly lifted her lids to find his eyes right there. He had inched his head closer to hers and not only were his eyes right there, so were his lips. The thoughts that suddenly went racing through her mind were crazy, but all she would have to do was to stick out her tongue to taste his lips. That was a temptation she was having a hard time fighting.

Her breathing increased and she could tell by the rise and fall of his masculine chest, that so had his. Was there something significantly dangerous about flying this high in the sky that altered your senses? Zapped them real good and sent them reeling off course? Filled your mind with thoughts you wouldn't normally entertain?

If the answer to all those questions was a resounding yes, then that explained why her mind was suddenly filled with the thought of engaging in a romantic liaison with the man who was not only her client, but also her oldest brother's best friend.

"Gemma…" It seemed he had inched his mouth a little closer; so close she could feel his moist breath on her lips as he said her name in that deep Australian accent of his.

Instead of responding, she inched her mouth closer, too,

as desire, the intensity of which she'd never felt before, made her entire body shiver with a need she didn't know she was capable of having. The green eyes locked on hers were successfully quashing any thoughts of pulling her mouth back before it was too late.

"Would either of you like some more snacks?"

Callum jumped and then quickly turned his face away from Gemma to glance up at the smiling flight attendant. He drew in a deep breath before responding. "No, thanks. I don't want anything."

He knew that was a lie the moment he'd said it. He *did* want something, but what he wanted only the woman sitting beside him could give.

The flight attendant then glanced over at Gemma and she responded in a shaky voice. "No, I'm fine."

It was only after the attendant had moved on that Callum glanced at Gemma. Her back was to him while she looked out the window. He suspected that she was going to pretend nothing had happened between them a few moments ago. There was no doubt in his mind that they would have kissed if the flight attendant hadn't interrupted them.

"Gemma?"

It took her longer than he felt was necessary to turn around and when she did, she immediately began talking about something that he couldn't have cared less about. "I was able to pack my color samples, Callum, so that you'll get an idea of what will best suit your home. I'll give you my suggestions, but of course the final decision will be yours. How do you like earth-tone colors? I'm thinking they will work best."

He fought the urge to say that what would work best would be to pick up where they'd left off, but instead he nodded and decided to follow her lead for now. In a way he felt good knowing that at least something had been accomplished today. She had finally become aware of him as a man. And he was giving her time to deal with that. He wouldn't push her, nor would he rush things for now. He would let nature take its course and with the degree of passion they exhibited a short while ago, he had no reason to think that it wouldn't.

"I happen to like earth-tone colors, so they will probably work for me," he said, although he truly didn't give a royal damn. The bottom line was whatever she liked would work for him because he had every intention of her sharing that house with him.

"That's good, but I intend to provide you with a selection of vibrant colors, as well. Reds, greens, yellows and blues are the fashionable hues now. And we can always mix them up to create several bold splashes. Many people are doing that now."

She continued talking, and he would nod on occasion to pretend he was listening. If she needed to feel she was back in control of things, then so be it. He relaxed in his seat, tilted his head and watched ardently as her mouth moved while thinking what he would love doing to that mouth if given the chance. He decided to think positive and concentrated on what he would do with that mouth *when* he got the chance.

A few moments after Callum closed his eyes, Gemma stopped talking, satisfied that she had talked him to sleep. She had discussed some of everything with him regarding the decorating of his home to make sure they stayed on topic. The last thing she wanted was for him to bring up what almost happened between them. Just the thought of how close they'd come to sharing a kiss, right here on this airplane, had her pulse racing something awful.

She had never behaved inappropriately with a client before and wasn't sure exactly what had brought it on today.

She would chalk it up as a weak moment when she'd almost yielded to temptation. When she had noticed just how close their mouths were, it had seemed a perfectly natural thing to want to taste his lips. Evidently, he'd felt the same way about hers, because his mouth had been inching toward hers with as much enthusiasm as hers had moved toward his. She was grateful for the flight attendant's timely interruption.

Had the woman suspected what they had been about to do? The thought had made Gemma's head heat up with embarrassment. Her heart was racing and the palms of her hands felt damp just thinking about it. She readjusted the pillow behind her head, knowing she would have to regain control of senses jolted by too much turbulence. Callum was just a man. He was a client. A friend of her family. He was not someone she should start thinking about in a sexual way.

She had gone twenty-four years without giving any man a second thought and going another twenty-four the same way suited her just fine.

Chapter 4

Gemma glanced around the spacious hotel where she and Callum would be staying for the night—in separate rooms, of course. Once their plane had landed, she had given herself a mental shake to make sure all her senses were back under control. Fortunately, the rest of the flight had been uneventful. Callum had kept his lips to himself and she had kept hers where they belonged. After a while, she had begun feeling comfortable around him again.

They'd taken a taxi from the airport. Callum had informed her that a private car service would arrive the next morning to take them to his parents' home. Gemma assumed they would be staying with his parents for the duration of the trip.

She thought this hotel was beautiful and would rival any of the major chains back home. The suite was spacious with floor-to-ceiling windows that looked out onto Sydney, which at this hour was dotted with bright lights.

Because she had slept a lot on the plane, she wasn't sleepy now. In fact, she was wide awake, although the clock on the nightstand by the bed indicated that it was after midnight. It was hard to believe that on the other side of the world in Denver they were trailing a day behind and it was eight in the morning.

She strolled to the window and looked out. She missed Denver already, but she couldn't help being fascinated by all the things she'd already seen. Although their plane had landed during the night hours, the taxi had taken them through many beautiful sections of the city that were lit up, and showed just how truthful Callum had been when he'd said that there was no place in the world quite like Sydney.

Gemma drew in a deep breath and tried to ignore a vague feeling of disappointment. Even though she was glad Callum hadn't mentioned their interrupted kiss, she hadn't expected him to completely ignore her. Although they'd shared conversation since, most of it had been with him providing details about Sydney and with her going over information about the decorating of his home. The thought that he could control his emotions around her so easily meant that, although he had been drawn to her for that one quick instant, he didn't think she was worth pursuing. If those were his thoughts, she should be grateful, instead of feeling teed off. Her disappointment and irritation just didn't make any sense.

She left the window and crossed the hotel room to the decorative mirror on the wall to study her features. Okay, so she hadn't looked her best after the eighteen-hour plane flight, but she had taken a shower and had freshened up since then. Too bad he couldn't see her now. But overall, she hadn't looked awful.

Gemma couldn't help wondering what kind of woman would interest Callum. She was totally clueless. She'd never seen him with a woman before. She knew the types Zane and Derringer preferred dating—women who were all legs, beautiful, sophisticated, shallow, but easy to get into bed. For some reason she couldn't see Callum attracted to that type of woman.

There were times she wished she had a lot of experience with men and was not still a twenty-four-year-old virgin. There had been a number of times during her college days when guys had tried, although unsuccessfully, to get her into bed. When they had failed, they'd dubbed her "Ice Princess Gemma." That title hadn't bothered her in the least. She'd rather be known as an ice princess than an easy lay. She smiled, thinking that more than one frustrated stud had given up on seducing her. Giving up on her because she refused to put out was one thing, but ignoring her altogether was another.

A part of her knew the best thing to do was to relegate such thoughts to the back of her mind. It was better that he hadn't followed up on what had almost happened between them. But another part of her—the one that was a woman with as much vanity as any other female—hadn't liked it one bit and couldn't let it go.

A smile swept across her lips. Callum had suggested that they meet in the morning for breakfast before the car arrived to take them to his parents' home. That was fine with her, because she would be meeting his parents and she wanted to look her best. The last thing she wanted was for them to think he'd hired someone who didn't know how to dress professionally. So tomorrow she would get rid of her usual attire of jeans and a casual top and wear something a little more becoming.

She would see just how much Callum could ignore her then.

Callum got up the next morning feeling as tired as he'd been when he went to bed past midnight. He had tossed and turned most of the night, frustrated that he hadn't taken the opportunity to taste Gemma's lips when the chance to do so had been presented to him.

Every part of his body hardened with the memory of a pair of luscious lips that had been barely a breath away from his. And when she had tilted her head even more to him, placing her lips within a tongue reach, he had felt the lower part of his body throb.

The desire that had flowed between them had been anything but one-sided. Charged sensations as strong as any electrical current had surged through both their bodies and he had fought back the urge to unsnap her seat belt and pull her into his lap while lapping her mouth with everything he had.

He remembered the conversations they'd shared and how she'd tried staying on course by being the consummate professional. While she'd been talking, his gaze had been fixated on her mouth. He couldn't recall a woman who could look both sexy and sweet at the same time, as well as hot and cool when the mood suited her. He loved all the different facets of Gemma, and he planned on being a vital part of each one of them. How could any man not want to?

Minutes later, after taking a shower and getting dressed, he left his hotel room to walk a few doors down to where Gemma had spent the night. Just the thought that she had been sleeping so close had done something to him. He wondered if she had gotten a good night's sleep. Or had she tossed and turned most of the night, as he had? Probably not. He figured she had no idea what sexual frustration was all about. And if she did, he didn't want to know about it, especially if some other man ruled her thoughts.

The possibility of that didn't sit well with him, since he couldn't handle the thought of Gemma with any other man but him. He pulled in a deep breath before lifting his hand to knock on her door.

"Who is it?"

"Callum."

"Just a moment."

While waiting, he turned to study the design of the wallpaper that covered the expanse of the wall that led to the elevator. It was a busy design, but he had to admit that it matched the carpet perfectly, pulling in colors he would not have normally paid attention to.

He shook his head, remembering that Gemma had gone on and on about different colors and how her job would be to coordinate them to play off each other. He was surprised that he could recall any of her words when the only thoughts going through his mind had been what he'd like doing to her physically.

"Come on in, Callum. I just need to grab a jacket," she said upon opening the door.

He turned around and immediately sucked in a deep breath. He had to lean against the doorframe to keep from falling. *His* Gemma wasn't wearing jeans and a top today. Instead, she was dressed in a tan-colored skirt that flowed to her ankles, a pair of chocolate-suede, medium-heeled shoes and a printed blouse. Seeing her did something to every muscle, every cell and every pore of his body. And his gut twisted in a knot. She looked absolutely stunning. Even her hair was different. Rather than wearing it in a ponytail she had styled it to hang down to her shoulders.

He'd only seen her a few other times dressed like this, and that had been when they'd run into each other at church. He entered the room and closed the door behind him, feeling a gigantic tug in his chest as he watched her move around the room. He became enmeshed in her movements and how graceful and fluid they were.

"Did you get a good night's sleep, Callum?"

He blinked when he noticed that she stood staring at him, smiling. Was he imagining things or did he see amusement curving her lips? "I'm sorry, what did you ask?"

"I wanted to know if you got a good night's sleep. I'm sure it felt good being back home."

He thought about what she said and although he could agree that it was good being back home, it felt even better having her here with him. He'd thought about this a number of times, dreamed that he would share his homeland with her. He had six weeks and he intended to make every second, minute and hour count.

Apparently, she was waiting for his response. "Sleep didn't come easy. I guess I'm suffering from jet lag. And, yes, I'm glad to be home," he said, checking his watch. "Ready to go down for breakfast?"

"Yes, I'm starving."

"I can imagine. You didn't eat a whole lot on the plane."

She chuckled. "Only because I wasn't sure I could keep it down. There was a lot of turbulence."

And he'd known how much that bothered her. He was glad when she'd finally been able to sleep through it. He had watched her most of the time while she'd done so.

"I'm ready now, Callum."

He was tempted to reach out and take her hand in his, but he knew that doing such a thing would not be a smart move right now. He needed her to get to know him, not as her brother's best friend, but as the man who would always be a part of her life.

"Hey, don't look at my plate like that. I told you I was hungry," Gemma said, laughing. Her stack of pancakes was just as high as Callum's. He had told her this particular hotel, located in downtown Sydney, was known to serve the best pancakes. They not only served the residents of the hotel but locals who dropped in on their way to work. From where Gemma sat, she could see the Sydney Harbour Bridge in the distance. It was a beautiful sight.

"Trust me, I understand. I remember my mom bringing me here as a kid when I did something good in school," he said while pouring syrup onto his pancakes.

"Wow, you mean this hotel is *that* old?" Her eyes twinkled with mischief.

He glanced over at her as amusement flickered in his gaze. "Old? Just what are you trying to say, Gemma?"

"Umm, nothing. Sorry. I have to remember that you're my client and I have to watch what I say. The last thing I want to do is offend you."

"And be careful that you don't," he warned, chuckling. "Or all that information you provided yesterday on colors and designs would have been for naught. How you can keep that stuff straight in your head is beyond me."

He paused a moment. "And I talked to Ramsey last night. Everything is fine back in Denver and I assured him all was well here."

Gemma smiled as she took a sip of her coffee. "Did you tell him we were on the flight from hell getting here?"

"Not quite in those words, but I think he got the idea. He asked me if you fainted when the plane hit the first pocket of turbulence."

She made a face. "Funny. Did he mention how Chloe is doing?"

"Yes, she's fine, just can't wait for November to roll around." He smiled. "She has two more months to go."

"I started to call them last night when we got in, but after I took a shower and went to bed that did it for me. I hadn't thought I'd be able to sleep so soundly, but I did."

During the rest of their meal, Gemma explained to him how they managed to pull off a surprise baby shower for Chloe last month right under her sister-in-law's nose, and how, although Ramsey and Chloe didn't want to know the sex of the baby before it was born, Megan, Bailey and she were hoping for a girl, while Zane, Derringer and the twins were anticipating a boy.

Sipping coffee and sharing breakfast with Callum seemed so natural. She hadn't ever shared breakfast with him before…at least not when it had been just the two of them. Occasionally, they would arrive at Ramsey's place for breakfast at about the same time, but there had always been other family members around. She found him fun to talk to and felt good knowing he had noticed her outfit and even complimented her on how she looked. She had caught him staring at her a few times, which meant he couldn't ignore her so easily after all.

They had finished breakfast and were heading back toward the elevators when suddenly someone called out.

"Callum, it's you! I can't believe you're home!"

Both Callum and Gemma glanced around at the same time a woman threw herself at him and proceeded to wrap her arms around his waist while placing a generous smack on his lips.

"Meredith! It's good to see you," Callum said, trying to pry himself from the woman's grip. Once that was accomplished, he smiled pleasantly at the dark-haired female who was smiling up at him like an adoring fan. "What are you doing in town so early?"

The woman laughed. "I'm meeting some friends for breakfast." It was then that she turned and regarded Gemma. "Oh, hello."

The first thought that came into Gemma's mind was that the woman was simply beautiful. The second was that if it was the woman's intent to pretend she was just noticing Gemma's presence, then she had failed miserably, since there was no way she could have missed her, when she'd nearly knocked her down getting to Callum.

"Meredith, I'd love you to meet a good friend of mine," he said, reaching out, catching Gemma's hand and pulling her closer to his side. "Gemma Westmoreland. Gemma, this is Meredith Kenton. Meredith's father and mine are old school chums."

Gemma presented her hand to the woman when it became obvious the woman was not going to extend hers. "Meredith."

Meredith hesitated a second before taking it. "So, you're from the States, Gemma?"

"Yes."

"Oh."

She then turned adoring eyes on Callum again, and Gemma didn't miss the way the woman's gaze lit up when Callum smiled at her. "Now that you're back home, Callum, what about us doing dinner at the Oasis, going sailing and having a picnic on the beach."

For crying out loud. Will you let the man at least catch his breath, Gemma wanted to scream, refusing to consider that she was feeling a bit jealous. *And besides, for all you know, I might be his woman and if I were I wouldn't let him do any of those things with you. Talk about blatant disrespect.*

"I'm going to be tied up this visit," Callum said, easing Gemma closer to his side. Gemma figured he was trying to paint a picture for Meredith that really wasn't true—that they were a twosome. Any other time she might have had a problem with a man insinuating such a thing, but in this case she didn't mind. In fact, she welcomed the opportunity to pull the rug right out from under Miss Disrespect. Meredith was obviously one of those "pushy" women.

"And I'm only back home for a short while," he added.

"Please don't tell me you're going back over there."

"Yes, I am."

"When are you coming home for good?" Meredith pouted, her thin lips exuding disappointment.

Gemma looked up at Callum, a questioning look in her eyes. Was this the woman waiting for him that he told her didn't exist? He met her gaze and as if he read the question lingering there, he pulled her even closer to his side. "I'm not sure. I kind of like it over there. As you know, Mom is an American, so I'm fortunate to have family on both continents."

"Yes, but your home is here."

He smiled as he glanced down at Gemma. He then looked back at Meredith. "Home is where the heart is."

The woman then turned a cold, frosty gaze on Gemma. "And he brought you back with him."

Before Gemma could respond, Callum spoke up. "Yes, I brought her back with me to meet my parents."

Gemma knew the significance of that statement, even if it was a lie. To say he had brought her home to meet his parents meant there was a special relationship between them. In truth, that wasn't the case but for some reason he didn't want Meredith to know that, and in a way she didn't want Meredith to know it, either.

"Well, I see my friends have arrived now," she said in a cutting tone. "Gemma, I hope you enjoy your time here in Sydney and, Callum, I'll talk to you later." The woman then beat a hasty retreat.

With his hand on her arm, Callum steered Gemma toward the elevator. Once they were alone inside the elevator, Gemma spoke. "Why did you want Meredith to assume we were an item?"

He smiled down at her. "Do you have a problem with that?"

Gemma shook her head. "No, but why?"

He stared at her for a few moments, opened his mouth to say something, then closed it. He seemed to think for a minute. "Just because."

She lifted a brow. "Just because?"

"Yes, just because."

She frowned up at him. "I'd like more of a reason than that, Callum. Is Meredith one of your former girlfriends?"

"Not officially. And before you assume the worst about me, I never gave her a reason to think anything between us was official or otherwise. I never led her on. She knew where she stood with me and I with her."

So it was one of those kinds of relationships, Gemma mused. The kind her brothers were notorious for. The kind that left the woman broken down and brokenhearted.

"And before you start feeling all indignant on Meredith's behalf, don't waste your time. Her first choice of the Austells was my brother, Colin. They dated for a few years and one day he walked in and found her in bed with another man."

"Oh." Gemma hadn't liked the woman from the first, and now she liked her even less.

The elevator stopped. They stepped off and Callum turned to her and placed his hand on her arm so she wouldn't go any farther. She hadn't expected the move and sensations escalated up her rib cage from his touch.

"I want to leave you with something to think about, Gemma," he said in that voice she loved hearing.

"What?"

"I know that watching your brothers and cousins operate with girls has colored your opinion of men in general. I think it's sad that their exploits have left a negative impression on you and I regret that. I won't speak for your brothers, because they can do that for themselves, but I can speak for myself. I'd never intentionally hurt any woman. It's my belief that I have a soul mate out there somewhere."

She lifted a brow. "A soul mate?"

"Yes."

Gemma couldn't help but wonder if such a thing really existed. She would be the first to admit that her cousin Dillon's first wife hadn't blended in well with the family, nor had she been willing to make any sacrifices for the man she loved. With his current wife, Pam, it was a different story. From the moment the family had met Pam, they'd known she was a godsend. The same thing held true for Chloe. Gemma, Megan and Bailey had bonded with their sister-in-law immediately, even before she and Ramsey had married. And just to see the two couples together, you would know they were meant for each other and loved each other deeply.

So Gemma knew true love worked for some people, but she wasn't willing to suffer any heartbreak while on a quest to find Mr. Right or her soul mate. But as far as Callum was concerned, she was curious about one thing. "And you really believe you have a soul mate?"

"Yes."

She noted that he hadn't hesitated in answering. "How will you know when you meet her?"

"I'll know."

He sounded pretty confident about that, she thought. She shrugged. "Well, good luck in finding her," she said as they exited the building and headed toward the parking garage.

She noted that Callum appeared to have considered her comment, and then he tilted his head and smiled at her. "Thanks. I appreciate that."

Chapter 5

"Wow, this car is gorgeous, but I thought a private car was coming for us."

Callum looked over at Gemma and smiled as they walked toward the car parked in the hotel's parking garage. "I decided to have my car brought to me instead."

"This is your car?" Gemma studied the beautiful, shiny black two-seater sports car.

He chuckled as he opened the door for her. "Yes, this baby is mine." *And so are you,* he wanted to say as he watched her slide her legs into the car, getting a glimpse of her beautiful calves and ankles. "I've had it now for a few years."

She glanced up at him. "Weren't you ever tempted to ship it to Denver?"

"No," he said with a smile. "Can you imagine me driving something like this around Ramsey's sheep farm?"

"No, I can't," she said, grinning when he got in on the other side and snapped his seat belt into place. "Is it fast?"

"Oh, yes. And you'll see that it has a smooth ride."

Callum knew she was sold on the car's performance moments later when they hit the open highway and she settled back in her seat. He used to imagine things being just like this, with him driving this car around town with the woman he loved sitting in the passenger seat beside him.

He glanced over at her for a second and saw how closely she was paying attention to everything they passed, as if she didn't want to miss anything. He drew in a deep breath, inhaling her scent right along with it, and felt desire settle into his bones. Nothing new there; he'd wanted Gemma since the first time he'd seen her and knew she would be his.

"This place is simply beautiful, Callum."

He smiled, pleased that she thought so. "More so than Denver?"

She threw her head back and laughed. "Hey, there's no place like home. I love Denver."

"I know." Just as he knew it would be hard getting her to leave Denver to move to Sydney with him. He would have returned home long ago, but he'd been determined not to until he had her with him.

"We're on our way to your parents' home?" she asked, interrupting his thoughts.

"Yes. They're looking forward to meeting you."

Surprise swept across her face. "Really? Why?"

He wished he could tell her the truth, but decided to say something else equally true. "You're Ramsey's sister. Your brother made an impression on them during the six months he lived here. They consider him like another son."

"He adores them, as well. Your family is all he used to write us about while he was here. I was away at college and his letters used to be so full of adventure. I knew then that he'd made the right decision to turn over the running of the family's real-estate firm to Dillon and pursue his dream of becoming a sheep rancher. Just as my father always wanted to do."

He heard the touch of pain in her voice and sensed that mentioning her father had brought back painful memories. "You were close to him, weren't you?"

When they came to a snag in traffic, he watched her moisten her lips before replying to his question. "Yes. I was definitely a daddy's girl, but then so were Megan and

Bailey. He was super. I can still recall that day Dillon and Ramsey showed up to break the news to us. They had been away at college, and when I saw them come in together I knew something was wrong. But I never imagined the news they were there to deliver."

She paused a moment. "The pain wouldn't have been so great had we not lost our parents and Uncle Adam and Aunt Clarisse at the same time. I'll never forget how alone I felt, and how Dillon and Ramsey promised that, no matter what, they would keep us together. And they did. Because Dillon was the oldest, he became the head of the family and Ramsey, only seven months younger, became second in charge. Together they pulled off what some thought would be impossible."

Callum recalled hearing the story a number of times from Ramsey. He had hesitated about going to Australia because he hadn't wanted to leave everything on Dillon's shoulders, so he'd waited until Bailey had finished high school and started college before taking off for Australia.

"I'm sure your parents would be proud of all of you," he said.

She smiled. "Yes, I'm sure they would be, as well. Dillon and Ramsey did an awesome job and I know for sure we were a handful at times, some of us more than others."

He knew she was thinking about her cousin, Bane, and all the trouble he used to get into. Now Brisbane Westmoreland was in the Navy with dreams of becoming a SEAL.

Callum checked his watch. "We won't be long now. Knowing Mom, she'll have a feast for lunch."

A smile touched Gemma's lips. "I'm looking forward to meeting your parents, especially your mother, the woman who captured your father's heart."

He returned her smile, while thinking that his mother was looking forward to meeting her—the woman who'd captured his.

* * *

Surprise swept across Gemma's face when Callum brought his car to the marker denoting the entrance to his family's ranch. She leaned forward in her seat to glance around through the car's windows. She was spellbound, definitely at a loss for words. The ranch, the property it sat on and the land surrounding it were breathtaking.

The first thing she noticed was that this ranch was a larger version of her brother's, but the layout was identical. "I gather that Ramsey's design of the Shady Tree Ranch was based on this one," she said.

Callum nodded. "Yes, he fell in love with this place and when he went back home he designed his ranch as a smaller replica of this one, down to every single detail, even to the placement of where the barns, shearing plants and lambing stations are located."

"No wonder you weren't in a hurry to return back here. Being at the Shady Tree Ranch was almost home away from home for you. There were so many things to remind you of this place. But then, on the other hand, if it had been me, seeing a smaller replica of my home would have made me homesick."

He keyed in the code that would open the electronic gate while thinking that the reason he had remained in Denver after helping Ramsey set up his ranch, and the reason he'd never gotten homesick, were basically the same. Gemma. He hadn't wanted to leave her behind and return to Australia, and he hadn't, except for the occasional holiday visit. And he truly hadn't missed home because, as he'd told Meredith, home is where the heart is and his heart had always been with Gemma, whether she knew it or not.

He put the car in gear and drove down the path leading to his parents' ranch house. The same place where he'd lived all his life before moving into his own place at twenty-three, right out of college. But it hadn't been unusual to sleep over while working the ranch with his father and brothers. He had many childhood memories of walks along this same path, then bicycle rides, motorcycle rides and finally rides behind the wheel of a car. It felt good to be home—even better that he hadn't come alone.

He fully expected not only his parents to be waiting inside the huge ranch house, but his brothers and their wives, and his sister and brother-in-law as well. Everyone was eager to meet the woman whose pull had kept him working in North America as Ramsey's ranch manager for three years. And everyone was sworn to secrecy, since they knew how important it was for him to win Gemma's heart on his turf.

She was about to start getting to know the real Callum Austell. The man she truly belonged to.

When Callum brought the car to a stop in front of the sprawling home, the front door opened and a smiling older couple walked out. Gemma knew immediately that they were his parents. They were a beautiful couple. A perfect couple. Soul mates. Another thing she noted was that Callum had the older man's height and green eyes and had the woman's full lips, high cheekbones and dimpled smile.

And then, to Gemma's surprise, following on the older couple's heels were three men and three women. It was easy to see who in the group were Callum's brothers and his sister. It was uncanny just how much they favored their parents.

"Seems like you're going to get to meet everyone today, whether you're ready to do so or not," Callum said.

Gemma released a chuckle. "Hey, I have a big family, too. I remember how it was when I used to come home after being away at college. Everyone is glad to see you come home. Besides, you're your parents' baby."

He threw his head back and laughed. "Baby? At thirty-four, I don't think so."

"I do. Once a baby always a baby. Just ask Bailey."

Just a look into his green eyes let her know he still wasn't buying it. He smiled as he opened the door to get out and said, "Just get ready for the Austells."

By the time Callum had rounded the car to open the door for her to get out, his parents, siblings and in-laws were there and she could tell that everyone was glad to see him. Moments later she stood, leaning against the side of his car, and watched all the bear hugs he was receiving, thinking there was nothing quite like returning home to a family who loved you.

"Mom, Dad, everyone, I would like you to meet Gemma Westmoreland." He reached out his hand to her and she glanced over at him a second before moving away from the car to join him where he stood with his family.

"So you're Gemma," Le'Claire Austell said, smiling after giving Gemma a hug. "I've heard quite a lot about you."

Surprise lit up Gemma's features. "You have?"

The woman smiled brightly. "Of course I have. Ramsey adores his siblings and would share tales with us about you, Megan, Bailey and your brothers, as well as all the other Westmorelands all the time. I think talking about all of you made missing you while he was here a little easier."

Gemma nodded and then she was pulled into Callum's dad's arms for a hug and was introduced to everyone present. There was Callum's oldest brother, Morris, and his wife, Annette, and his brother, Colin, and his wife, Mira. His only sister Le'Shaunda, whom everyone called Shaun, and her husband, Donnell.

"You'll get to meet our three grands at dinner," Callum's mom was saying.

"I'm looking forward to it," Gemma replied warmly.

While everyone began heading inside the house, Callum touched Gemma's arm to hold her back. "Is something wrong?" He looked at her with concern in his green eyes.

"I saw the way you looked at me when I called you over to meet everyone."

Gemma quickly looked ahead at his family, who were disappearing into the house and then back at Callum. "You didn't tell your family why I'm here."

"I didn't have to. They know why you're here." He studied her features for a moment. "What's going on in that head of yours, Gemma Westmoreland? What's bothering you?"

She shrugged, suddenly feeling silly for even bringing it up. "Nothing. I just remember what you insinuated with Meredith and hoped you weren't going to give your family the same impression."

"That you and I have something going on?"

"Yes."

He watched her for a moment and then touched her arm gently. "Hey, relax. My family knows the real deal between us, trust me. I thought you understood why I pulled that stunt with Meredith."

"I do. Look, let's forget I brought it up. It's just that your family is so nice."

He chuckled and pulled her to him. "We're Aussies, eight originals and one convert. We can't help but be nice."

She tossed him a grin before easing away. "So you say." She then looked over at the car as she headed up the steps to the house. "Do you need help getting our luggage?"

"No. We aren't staying here."

She turned around so quickly she missed her step and he caught her before she tumbled. "Be careful, Gemma."

She shook her head, trying to ignore how close they were standing and why she suddenly felt all kinds of sensations flooding her insides. "I'm okay. But why did you say we're not staying here?"

"Because we're not."

She went completely still. "But—but you said we were staying at your home."

He caught her chin in his fingers and met her gaze. "We are. This is not my home. This is my parents' home."

She swallowed, confused. "I thought your home is what I'm decorating. Isn't it empty?"

"*That* house is, but I also own a condo on the beach. That's where we're staying while we're here. Do you have a problem with that, Gemma?"

Gemma forced herself to breathe when it became clear that she and Callum would be sharing living space while she was here. Why did the thought of that bother her?

She had to admit for the first time she was noticing things about him she'd never noticed before. And she was experiencing things around him that she hadn't experienced before. Like the way she was swept up in heated desire and the sensuous tickling in the pit of her stomach whenever he was within a few feet of her, like now...

"Gemma?"

She swallowed again as she met his gaze and the green eyes were holding hers with an intensity that she wasn't used to. She gave her head a mental shake. His family had to be wondering why they were still outside. She had to get real. She was here to do a job and she would do it without having these crazy thoughts that Callum was after her body, just because she'd begun having crazy fantasies about him.

"No, I don't have a problem with that." She pulled away from him and smiled. "Come on, your parents are probably wondering why we're still out here," she said, moving ahead and making an attempt to walk up the steps again.

She succeeded and kept walking toward the door, fully aware that he was watching every step she took.

Callum glanced around his parents' kitchen and drew in a deep breath. So far, things were going just as he'd hoped. From the masked smiles and nods he'd gotten from his family, he knew they agreed with his assessment of Gemma— that she was a precious gem. Even his three nephews, ages six, eight and ten, who were usually shy with strangers, had warmed up to her.

He knew that, for a brief moment, she had been confused as to why his family had taken so readily to her. What he'd told her hadn't been a lie. They knew the reason she was here and decorating that house he had built was only part of it. In fact, a minor part.

"When are you getting a haircut?"

Callum turned and smiled at his father. "I could ask you the same thing." Todd Austell's hair was just as long as his son's and Callum couldn't remember him ever getting his hair cut. In fact, it appeared longer now than the last time he'd seen it.

"Don't hold your breath for that to happen," his father said with joking amusement in his green gaze. "I love my golden locks. The only thing I love more is your mother."

Callum leaned against the kitchen counter. His mother, sister and sisters-in-law had Gemma in a corner and from their expressions he knew they were making *his woman* feel right at home. His brother and brothers-in-law were outside manning the grills, and his nephews were somewhere playing ball. His parents had decided to have a family cookout to welcome him and Gemma home.

"Gemma is a nice girl, Callum. Le'Claire and Shaun like her."

He could tell. He glanced up at his father. "And you?"

A smile crossed Todd Austell's lips. "I like her."

As if she felt Callum's gaze, she glanced over in his direction and smiled. His muscles tightened in desire for her.

"Dad?"

"Yes?"

"After you met Mom and knew she was the woman for you, how long did it take you to convince her of it?"

"Too long."

Callum chuckled. "How long was too long?"

"A few months. Remember, I had an engagement to

break off and then your mother assumed that flying was her life. I had to convince her that she was sorely mistaken about that, and that I was her life."

Callum shook his head. His father was something else. Callum's was one of the wealthiest families in Sydney; the Austells had made their millions not only in sheep farming but also in the hotel industry. The hotel where he and Gemma had stayed last night was part of just one of several hotel chains that Colin was in charge of. Morris was vice president of the sheep-farm operation.

When Callum was home, he worked wherever he was needed, but he enjoyed sheep farming more. In fact, he was CEO of his own ranching firm, which operated several sheep ranches in Australia. Each was run by an efficient staff. He also owned a vast amount of land in Australia. He'd never been one to flaunt his wealth, although in his younger days he'd been well aware money was what had driven a lot of women to him. He had frustrated a number of them by being an elusive catch.

He glanced again at the group of women together and then at his father. "I guess it worked."

The older man lifted a brow. "What worked?"

"You were able to convince Mom that you were her life."

A deep smile touched his father's lips. "Four kids and three grandsons later, what can I say?"

A smile just as deep touched Callum's lips. "You can say that in the end Mom became your life as well. Because I think it's obvious that she has."

Chapter 6

The moment Gemma snapped her seat belt in place, a bright smile curved her lips. "Your family is simply wonderful, Callum, and I especially like your mom. She's super."

"Yes, she is," Callum agreed as he started the car's engine to leave his parents' home.

"And your dad adores her."

Callum chuckled. "You can tell?"

"How could I not? I think it's wonderful."

She was quiet for a moment. "I recall my parents being that way, having a close relationship and all. As I got older, although I missed them both, I couldn't imagine one living without the other, so I figured that if they had to die, I was glad they at least went together," she said.

Gemma forced back the sadness that wanted to cloud what had been a great day. She glanced over at Callum. "And I love your parents' home. It's beautiful. Your mother mentioned that she did all the decorating."

"She did."

"Then why didn't you get her to decorate yours?"

"Mine?"

"Yes, the one you've hired me to do. I'm grateful that

you thought of me, mind you, but your mother could have done it."

"Yes, she could have, but she doesn't have the time. Taking care of my dad is a full-time job. She spoils him rotten."

Gemma laughed. "Appears he likes spoiling her as well."

She had enjoyed watching the older couple displaying such a warm, loving attitude toward each other. It was obvious that their children were used to seeing them that way. Gemma also thought Callum's three nephews were little cuties.

"Is it far to the condo where you live?" she asked him, settling back against the car seat. When they walked out of Callum's parents' house, she noted that the evening temperature had dropped and it was cool. It reminded her of Denver just weeks before the first snowfall in late September. She then remembered that Australia's seasons were opposite the ones in North America.

"No, we'll be there in around twenty minutes. Are you tired?"

"Umm. Jet lag I think."

"Probably is. Go ahead and rest your eyes for a while."

Gemma took him up on his offer and closed her eyes for a moment. Callum was right, the reason she wanted to rest had to do with jet lag. She would probably feel this way until she adjusted to the change in time zone.

She tried to clear her mind of any thoughts, but found it impossible to do when she was drawn back to the time she had spent at Callum's parents' home. What she'd told him was true. She had enjoyed herself and thought his family was wonderful. They reminded her of her siblings.

She was close to her siblings and cousins, and they teased each other a lot. She'd picked up on the love between Callum and his siblings. He was the youngest and it was obvious that they cared deeply about him and were protective of him.

More than once, while talking to Callum's mom, she had felt his eyes on her and had glanced across the room to have her gaze snagged by his. Had she imagined it or had she seen male interest lurking in their green depths?

There had been times when the perfection of Callum's features had nearly stopped her in her tracks and she found herself at several standstills today. Both of his brothers were handsome, but in her book, Callum was gorgeous, and was even more so for some reason today. She could understand the likes of Meredith trying to come on to him. Back in Denver on the ranch, he exuded the air of a hardworking roughneck, but here in Sydney, dressed in a pair of slacks and a dress shirt and driving a sports car, he passed the test as the hot, sexy and sophisticated man that he was. If only all those women back in Denver could see him now.

She slowly opened her eyes and studied his profile over semi-lowered lashes as he drove the car. Sitting in a perfect posture, he radiated the kind of a strength most men couldn't fabricate, even on their best days. His hair appeared chestnut in color in the evening light and hung around his shoulders in fluid waves.

There was something about him that infused a degree of warmth all through her. Why hadn't she felt it before? Maybe she had, but had forced herself to ignore it. And then there was the difference in their ages. He was ten years her senior. The thought of dating a man in close proximity to her age was bad enough; to consider one older, she'd thought, would be asking for trouble, definitely way out of her league.

Her gaze moved to his hands. She recalled on more than one occasion seeing those hands that were now gripping the steering wheel handle the sheep on her brother's ranch. There was an innate strength about them that extended all the way to his clean and short fingernails.

According to Megan, you could tell a lot about a man

by his hands. That might be true, but Gemma didn't have a clue what she should be looking for. It was at times like this that her innocence bothered her. For once—maybe twice—she wouldn't mind knowing how it felt to get lost in the depth of a male's embrace, kissed by him in a way that could curl her toes and shoot sparks of pleasure all threw her. She wanted to be made love to by a man who knew what he was doing. A man who would make her first time special, something she would remember for the rest of her life and not forget when the encounter was over.

She closed her eyes again and remembered that moment on the plane when Callum had awakened and found her there, close to his face and staring at him. She remembered how he had stared back, how she had actually felt a degree of lust she hadn't thought she could feel and a swell of desire that had nearly shaken her to the core. She had felt mesmerized by his gaze, had felt frozen in a trance, and the only thing that would break it would be a kiss. And they had come seconds, inches from sharing one.

She knew it would have to be one of those kisses she'd always dreamed of sharing with a man. The kind that for some reason she believed only Callum Austell could deliver. Yes, the mind-blowing, toe-curling kind. A ripple of excitement sent shivers up her spine at the thought of being swept up in Callum's embrace, kissed by him, made love to by him.

She sucked in a quick breath, wondering what was making her think such things. What was causing her to have such lurid thoughts? And then she knew. She was attracted to her brother's best friend in the worst possible way. And as the sound of the car's powerful engine continued to roar under Callum's skillful maneuvering on the roadway, she felt herself fall deeper and deeper into a deep sleep with thoughts of Callum Austell getting embedded thoroughly into her mind.

* * *

Callum settled comfortably in the driver's seat as he drove the road with the power and ease he had missed over the years. Three in fact. Although he had returned home on occasion and had taken the car on the road for good measure whenever he did, there was something different about it this time. Because he had his future wife sitting beside him.

He smiled when he quickly glanced at her before returning his gaze to the road. She was *sleeping* beside him. He couldn't wait for the time when she would be sleeping with him. The thought of having her in his arms, making love to every inch of her body, filled him with a desire he didn't know it was possible to feel. But then Gemma had always done that to him, even when she hadn't known she was doing it.

Over the years he'd schooled himself well, and very few knew how he felt. Ramsey and Dillon knew, of course, and he figured Zane and Derringer suspected something as well. What had probably given Callum away was his penchant for watching Gemma the way a fox watched the henhouse, with his eye on one unsuspecting hen. It wasn't surprising that Gemma was totally clueless.

So far things were going as planned, although there had been a few close calls with his family when he thought one of them would slip and give something away. He wanted Gemma to feel comfortable around him and his family, and the last thing he wanted was for her to feel as if she'd deliberately been set up in any way. He wanted her to feel a sense of freedom here that he believed she wouldn't feel back in Denver.

For her to want to try new and different things, to embrace herself as a woman, topped his list. And for the first time, he would encourage her to indulge all her desires with a man. But not just any man. With him. He wanted her to see that not all men had only one thing in mind when it came to a woman, and for two people to desire each other wasn't a bad thing.

He wanted her to understand and accept that no matter what happened between them, it would be okay because nothing they shared would be for the short term. He intended to make this forever.

Callum pulled into the gated condo community and drove directly to his home, which sat on a secluded stretch of beach, prized for the privacy he preferred. He planned to keep this place even after their home was fully decorated and ready to move in. But first he had to convince Gemma that he was worth it for her to leave the country where she'd been born, the country in which her family resided, and move here with him, to his side of the world.

He brought his car to a stop and killed the ignition. It was then that he turned toward her, keeping one hand on the steering wheel and draping the other across the back of the passenger seat. She looked beautiful, sleeping as if she didn't have a care in the world—and in a way she didn't. He would shoulder whatever problems she had from here on out.

With an analytical eye he studied her features. She was smiling while she slept and he wondered why. What pleasing thoughts were going through her mind? It had gotten dark, and the lights from the fixtures in front of his home cast a glow on her face at an angle that made it look even more beautiful. He could imagine having a little girl with her mouth and cheekbones, or a son with her ears and jaw. He thought she had cute ears.

With a tentative hand he reached out and brushed his fingers gently across her cheeks. She shifted and began mumbling something. He leaned closer to catch what she was saying and his gut tightened in a ball of ravenous desire when she murmured in her sleep, "Kiss me, Callum."

* * *

Gemma felt herself drowning in a sea of desire she'd never felt before. She and Callum were not on the ranch in Denver, but were back on the plane. This time the entire plane was empty. They were the only two people onboard.

He had adjusted their seats to pull her into his arms, but instead of kissing her he was torturing her mouth inside, nibbling from corner to corner, then taking his tongue and licking around the lines of her lips.

She moaned deep in her throat. She was ready for him to take her mouth and stop toying with it. She needed to feel his tongue sucking on hers, tasting it instead of teasing it, and then she wanted their tongues to tangle in a delirious and sensual duel.

She began mumbling words, telling him to stop toying with her and asking that he finish what he'd started. She wanted the kiss she'd almost gotten before—a kiss to lose herself in sensual pleasure. Close to her ear she heard a masculine growl, sensed the passion of a man wanting to mate and breathed in the scent of a hot male.

Then suddenly she felt herself being gently shaken. "Gemma. Wake up, Gemma."

She lifted drowsy lids only to find Callum's face right there in front of hers. Just as it had been on the plane. Just as it had been moments earlier in her dream. "Callum?"

"Yes," he replied in a warm voice that sent delicious shivers up her spine. His mouth was so close she could taste his breath on her lips. "Do you really want me to kiss you, Gemma? You are one Westmoreland that I'll give whatever you want."

Chapter 7

Gemma forced the realization into her mind that she wasn't dreaming. This was the real deal. She was awake in Callum's car and he was leaning over her with his face close to hers and there wasn't a flight attendant to interrupt them if he decided to inch his mouth even closer. Would he?

That brought her back to his question. Did she want him to kiss her? Evidently, she had moaned out the request in her sleep and he'd heard it. From the look in the depth of his green eyes, he was ready to act on it. Is that what she wanted? He did say he would give her whatever she wanted.

More than anything, she wanted to be kissed by him. Although it wouldn't be her first kiss, she believed it would be the first one she received with a semblance of passion and desire on both sides. Before guys had wanted to kiss her, but she hadn't really cared if she kissed them or not.

This time she would act first and worry about the consequences of her actions later.

Holding his gaze, she whispered against his lips, "Yes, I want you to kiss me." She saw him smiling and giving a small nod of satisfaction before he leaned in closer. Before she could catch her next breath, he seized her mouth with his.

The first thing he did was seek out her tongue and the

moment he captured it in his, she was a goner. He started off slow, plying her with a deep, thorough kiss as if he wanted to get acquainted with the taste and texture of her mouth, flicking the tip of his tongue all over the place, touching places she hadn't known a tongue could reach, while stirring up even more passion buried deep within her bones.

For a timeless moment, heat flooded her body in a way it had never done before, triggering her breasts to suddenly feel tender and the area between her thighs to throb. How could one man's kiss deliver so much pleasure? Elicit things from her she never knew existed?

Before she could dwell on any answers to her questions, he deepened the kiss and began mating with her mouth with an intensity and hunger that made her stomach muscles quiver. It was a move she felt all the way to her toes. She felt herself becoming feverish, hot and needy. When it came to a man, she'd never been needy.

He slanted his head, taking the kiss deeper still, while tangling with her tongue in a way she had dreamed about only moments earlier. But now she was getting the real thing and not mere snippets of a fantasy. He wasn't holding back on anything and his tongue was playing havoc with her senses in the process. It was a work of art, a sensuous skill. The way he'd managed to wrap his tongue around hers, only letting it go when it pleased him and capturing it again when he was ready to dispense even more pleasurable torture.

She had asked for this kiss and wasn't disappointed. Far from it. He was taking her over the edge in a way that would keep her falling with pleasure. His mouth seemed to fit hers perfectly, no matter what angle he took. And the more it plowed her mouth hungrily, the more every part of her body came alive in a way she wasn't used to.

She moaned deep in her throat when she felt the warmth of his fingers on her bare thigh and wondered when had he slid his hand under her skirt. When those fingers began inching toward her center, instinctively she shifted her body closer to his. The move immediately parted her thighs.

As if his fingers were fully aware of the impact they were having on her, they moved to stake a claim on her most intimate part. As his fingers slid beneath the waistband of her panties, she released another moan when his hand came into contact with her womanly folds. They were moist and she could feel the way his fingertips were spreading her juices all over it before he dipped a finger inside her.

The moment he touched her there, she pulled her mouth away from his to throw back her head in one deep moan. But he didn't let her mouth stay free for long. He recaptured it as his fingers caressed her insides in a way that almost made her weep, while his mouth continued to ply her with hungry kisses.

Suddenly she felt a sensation that started at her midsection and then spread throughout her body like tentacles of fire, building tension and strains of sensuous pressure in its wake. Her body instinctively pushed against his hand just as something within her snapped and then exploded, sending emotions, awareness and all kinds of feeling shooting all through her, flooding her with ecstasy.

Although this was the first time she'd ever experienced anything like it, she knew what it was. Callum had brought her to her first earthshaking and shattering climax. She'd heard about them and read about them, but had never experienced one before. Now she understood what it felt like to respond without limitations to a man.

When the feelings intensified, she pulled her mouth from his, closed her eyes and let out a deep piercing scream, unable to hold it back.

"That's it. Come for me, baby," he slurred thickly against her mouth before taking it again with a deep erotic thrust of his tongue.

And he kept kissing her in this devouring way of his until she felt deliciously sated and her body ceased its trembling. He finally released her mouth, but not before his tongue gave her lips a few parting licks. It was then that she opened her eyes, feeling completely drained but totally satisfied.

He held her gaze and she wondered what he was thinking. Had their business relationship been compromised? After all, he was her client and she had never been involved with a client before. And whether she'd planned it or not, they were involved. Just knowing there were more kisses where that one came from sent shivers of pleasure down her spine.

Better yet, if he could deliver this kind of pleasure to her mouth, she could just imagine what else he could do to other parts of her body, like her breasts, stomach, the area between her legs. The man possessed one hell of a dynamic tongue and he certainly knew how to use it.

Heat filled her face from those thoughts and she wondered if he saw it. At least he had no idea what she was thinking. Or did he? He hadn't said anything yet. He was just staring at her and licking his lips. She felt she should say something, but at the moment she was speechless. She'd just had her very first orgasm and she still had her clothes on. Amazing.

Callum's nostrils flared from the scent of a woman who'd been pleasured in the most primitive way. He would love to strip her naked and taste the dewy essence of her. Brand his tongue with her intimate juices, lap her up the way he'd dreamed of doing more times than he could count.

She was staring at him as if she was still trying to figure out why and how this thing had happened. He would allow her time to do that, but what he wouldn't tolerate was her thinking that what they'd shared was wrong, because it wasn't. He would not accept any regrets.

The one thing he'd taken note of with his fingers was that she was extremely tight. With most men that would send up a red flag, but not him because her sexual experience, or lack thereof, didn't matter. However, if she hadn't been made love to before, he wanted to know it.

He opened his mouth to ask her, but she spoke before he could do so. "We should not have done that, Callum."

She could say that? While his hand was still inside of her? Maybe she had forgotten where his fingers were because they weren't moving. He flexed them, and when she immediately sucked in a deep breath as her gaze darkened with desire, he knew he'd succeeded in reminding her.

And while she watched, he slid his hand from inside of her and moments later he brought it to his lips and licked every finger that had been inside her. He then raked one finger across her lips before leaning down and tracing with his tongue where his finger had touched her mouth before saying, "With that I have to disagree." He spoke in a voice so throaty he barely recognized it as his own.

Her taste sent even more desire shooting through him. "Why do you feel that way, Gemma?"

He saw her throat move when she swallowed with her eyes still latched on his. "You're my client."

"Yes. And I just kissed you. One has nothing to do with the other. I hired you because I know you will do a good job. I just kissed you because—"

"I asked you to?"

He shook his head. "No, because I wanted to and because you wanted me to do it, too."

She nodded. "Yes," she said softly. "I wanted you to."

"Then there's no place for regrets and our attraction to each other has nothing to do with your decorating my home, so you can kill that idea here and now."

She didn't say anything for a moment and then she asked, "What about me being Ramsey's sister? Does that mean anything to you?"

A smile skidded across his lips. "I consider myself one of Ramsey's closest friends. Does that mean anything to you?"

She nervously nibbled on her bottom lip. "Yes. He will probably have a fit if he ever finds out we're attracted to each other."

"You think so?"

"Yes," she said promptly, without thinking much about his question. "Don't you?"

"No. Your brother is a fair man who recognizes you as the adult you are."

She rolled her eyes. "Are we talking about the same Ramsey Westmoreland?"

He couldn't help but grin. "Yes, we're talking about the same Ramsey Westmoreland. My best friend and your brother. You will always be one of his younger sisters, especially since he had a hand in raising you. Ramsey will always feel that he has a vested interest in your happiness and will always play the role of your protector, and understandably so. However, that doesn't mean he doesn't recognize that you're old enough to make your own decisions about your life."

She didn't say anything and he knew she was thinking hard about what he'd said. To reinforce the meaning of his words, he added. "Besides, Ramsey knows I would never take advantage of you, Gemma. I am not that kind of guy. I ask before I take. But remember, you always have the right to say no." A part of him hoped she would never say no to any direction their attraction might lead.

"I need to think about this some more, Callum."

He smiled. "Okay. That's fine. Now it's time for us to go inside."

He moved to open the door and she reached out and touched his hand. "And you won't try kissing me again?"

He reached out and pushed a strand of hair away from her face. "No, not unless you ask me to or give me an indication that's what you want me to do. But be forewarned, Gemma. If you ask, then I will deliver because I intend to be the man who will give you everything you want."

He then got out of the car and strolled to the other side to open the door for her.

He intended to be the man who gave her everything she wanted? A puzzled Gemma walked beside Callum toward his front door. When had he decided that? Before the kiss, during the kiss or after the kiss?

She shook her head. It definitely hadn't been before. Granted, they'd come close to kissing on the plane, but that had been the heat of the moment, due to an attraction that had begun sizzling below the surface. But that attraction didn't start until… When?

She pulled in a deep breath, really not certain. She'd always noticed him as a man from afar, but only in a complimentary way, since she'd assumed that he was taken. But she would be the first to admit that once he'd told her he wasn't, she'd begun seeing him in a whole different light. But she'd been realistic enough to know that, given the ten-year difference in their ages and the fact he was Ramsey's best friend, chances were that even if she was interested in him there was no way he would reciprocate that interest.

Or had it been during the kiss, when he had shown her just what a real kiss was like? Had he detected that this was her first real kiss? She'd tried following his lead, but when that lead began taking her so many different places and had made her feel a multitude of emotions and sensations she hadn't been used to, she just gave up following and let him take complete control. She had not been disappointed.

Her first orgasm had left every cell in her body feeling strung from one end to the other. She wondered just how many women could be kissed into an orgasm? She wondered how it would be if she and Callum actually made love. The pleasure just might kill her.

But then, he might have decided that he was the man to give her whatever she wanted after the kiss, when she was trying to regain control of her senses. Did he see her as a novelty? Did he want to rid her of her naiveté about certain things that happen between a man and a woman?

Evidently, he thought differently about how her oldest brother saw things. Well, she wasn't as certain as he was about Ramsey's reaction. She was well aware that she was an adult, old enough to call the shots about her own life. But with all the trouble the twins, Bane and Bailey had given everyone while growing up, she had promised herself never to cause Ramsey any unnecessary grief.

Although she would be the first to admit that she had a tendency to speak her mind whenever it suited her and she could be stubborn to a fault at times, she basically didn't cross people unless they crossed her. Those who'd known her great-grandmother—the first Gemma Westmoreland—who'd been married to Raphel, said she had inherited that attitude from her namesake. That's probably why so many family members believed there was more to the story about her great-grandfather Raphel and his bigamist ways that was yet to be uncovered. She wasn't as anxious about uncovering the truth as Dillon had been, but she knew Megan and some of her cousins were.

She stopped walking once they reached the door and Callum pulled a key from his pocket. She glanced around and saw that this particular building was set apart from the others on a secluded cul-de-sac. And it was also on a lot larger than the others, although, to her way of thinking, all of them appeared massive. "Why is your condo sitting on a street all by itself?" she asked.

"I wanted it that way for privacy."

"And they obliged you?"

He smiled. "Yes, since I bought all the other lots on this side of the complex as buffers. I didn't want to feel crowded. I'm used to a lot of space, but I liked the area because the beach is practically in my backyard."

She couldn't wait to see that, since Denver didn't have beaches. There was the Rocky Mountain Beach that included a stretch of sand but wasn't connected to an ocean like a real beach.

"Welcome to my home, Gemma."

He stood back and she stepped over the threshold at the same exact moment that he flicked a switch and the lights came on. She glanced around in awe. The interior of his home was simply beautiful and unless he had hidden decorating skills she wasn't aware of, she had to assume that he'd retained the services of a professional designer for this place, too. His colors, masculine in nature, were well-coordinated and blended together perfectly.

She moved farther into the room, taking note of everything—from the Persian rugs on the beautifully polished walnut floors, to the decorative throw pillows on the sofa, to the style of curtains and blinds that covered the massive windows. The light colors of the window treatments made each room appear larger in dimension and the banister of the spiral staircase that led to another floor gave the condo a sophisticated air.

When Callum crossed the room and lifted the blinds, she caught her breath. He hadn't lied when he'd said the beach was practically in his backyard. Even at night, thanks to the full moon overhead, she could see the beautiful waters of the Pacific Ocean.

Living away from home while attending college had

taken care of any wanderlust she might have had at one time. Seeing the world had never topped her list. She was more than satisfied with the one hundred acres she had acquired on her twenty-first birthday—an inheritance for each of the Westmorelands. The section of Denver most folks considered as Westmoreland Country was all the home she'd ever known and had ever wanted. But she would have to admit that all she'd seen of Sydney so far was making it a close second.

Callum turned back to her. "So what do you think?"

Gemma smiled. "I think I'm going to love it here."

Chapter 8

The next morning, after taking his shower, Callum dressed as he gazed out his bedroom window at the beautiful waters of the ocean. For some reason he believed it was going to be a wonderful day. He was back home and the woman he intended to share his life with was sleeping under his roof.

As he stepped into his shoes, he had to admit that he missed being back in Denver, working the ranch and spending time with the men he'd come to know over the past three years. During that time Ramsey had needed his help and they'd formed a close bond. Now Ramsey's life had moved in another direction. Ramsey was truly happy. He had a wife and a baby on the way and Callum was happy for his friend.

And more than anything he intended to find some of that same happiness for himself.

As he buttoned up his shirt, he couldn't help but think about the kiss he and Gemma had shared last night. The taste of her was still on his tongue. He'd told her that he wouldn't kiss her again until she gave the word, and he intended to do everything within his power to make sure she gave it—and soon.

The one thing he knew about Gemma was that she was stubborn. If you wanted to introduce an idea to her, you had to make her think that it had been *her* idea. Otherwise, she would balk at any suggestion you made. He had no problems doing that. When he put his seduction plan into motion, he would do it in such a way that she would think she was seducing him.

The thought of such a thing—her seducing him—had his manhood flexing. Although his feelings for Gemma were more than sexual, he couldn't help those nightly dreams that had plagued him since first meeting her. He'd seen her stripped bare—in his dreams. He'd tasted every inch of her body—in his dreams. And in his dreams he'd constantly asked what she wanted. What she needed from him to prove that she was his woman in every way.

Last night after he'd shown her the guestroom she would be using and had brought in their luggage, she had told him she was still suffering from jet lag and planned to retire early. She had quickly moved into her bedroom and had been sequestered there ever since. That was fine. In time she would find out that, when it came to him, she could run but she most certainly couldn't hide.

He would let her try to deny this thing that was developing between them, but she would discover soon enough that he was her man.

But what he wanted and needed right now was another kiss. He smiled, thinking his job was to make sure she felt that she needed another kiss as well. And as he walked out of his bedroom he placed getting another kiss at the top of his agenda.

Gemma stood in her bare feet in front of the window in Callum's kitchen as she gazed out at the beach. The view was simply amazing. She'd never seen anything like it.

One year while in college, during spring break weekend, she and a few friends had driven from Nebraska to Florida to spend the weekend on the beach in Pensacola.

There she had seen a real beach with miles and miles of the purest blue-green waters. She was convinced that the Pacific Ocean was even more breathtaking and she'd come miles and miles away from home to see it.

Home.

Although she did miss home, she considered being in Australia an adventure as well as a job. Because of the difference in time zones, when she'd retired last night, she hadn't made any calls, but she intended to try to do so today. Megan was keeping tabs on the bank situation involving Niecee. With the money Callum had advanced her, her bank account was in pretty good shape, with more than enough funds to cover her debts. But she had no intention of letting Niecee get away with what she'd done. She had yet to tell anyone else in the family, other than Megan and Bailey, about the incident and planned on keeping things that way until the funds had been recovered and were back in her bank account.

She took another sip of her coffee, thinking about the kiss she and Callum had shared last night. Okay, she would admit it had been more than off the chain and the climax was simply shocking. Just the thought gave her sensuous shivers and was making her body tingle all over. What Callum had done with his tongue in her mouth and his fingers between her legs made her blush.

It had been hard getting to sleep. More than once she had dreamed of his tongue seeking hers and now that she was fully aware of what he could do with that tongue and those fingers, she wanted more.

She drew in a deep breath, thinking there was no way she would ask for a repeat performance. She could now stake a claim to knowing firsthand what an orgasm was about with her virginity still intact. Imagine that.

She couldn't imagine it when part of her dream last night dwelled on Callum making love to her and taking away her innocence, something she'd never thought of sharing with another man. The thought of being twenty-four and a virgin had never bothered her. What bothered her was knowing that there was a lot more pleasure out there that she was missing out on. Pleasure she was more than certain Callum could deliver, with or without a silver platter.

All she had to do was tell him what she wanted.

"Good morning, Gemma."

She turned around quickly, surprised that she had managed to keep from spilling her coffee. She hadn't heard Callum come down the stairs. In fact, she hadn't heard him moving around upstairs. And now he stood in the middle of his kitchen, dressed in a way she'd never seen before.

He was wearing an expensive-looking gray suit. Somehow he had gone from being a sheep-ranch manager to a well-groomed, sophisticated and suave businessman. But then the chestnut-brown hair flowing around his shoulders gave him a sort of rakish look. She wasn't sure what to make of the change and just which Callum Austell she most preferred.

"Good morning, Callum," she heard herself say, trying not to get lost in the depths of his green eyes. "You're already dressed and I'm not." She glanced down at herself. In addition to not wearing shoes, she had slipped into one of those cutesy sundresses Bailey had given as a gift for her birthday.

"No problem. The house isn't going anywhere. It will be there when you're ready to see it. I thought I'd go into the office today and let everyone know that I'm back for a while."

She lifted a brow. "The office?"

"Yes, Le'Claire Developers. It's a land development company similar to Blue Ridge Land Management. But also under the umbrella of Le'Claire are several smaller sheep ranches on the same scale as Ramsey's."

"And you are…"

"The CEO of Le'Claire," he said.

"You named it after your mother?"

He chuckled. "No, my father named it after my mother. When we all turned twenty-one, according to the terms of a trust my great-grandfather established, all four of us were set up in our own businesses. Morris, being the firstborn, will inherit the sheep farms that have been in the Austell family for generations as well as stock in all the businesses his siblings control. Colin is CEO of the chain of hotels my family owns. The one we stayed in the other night is one of them. Le'Shaunda received a slew of supermarket chains, and I was given a land development company and several small sheep ranches. Although I'm CEO, I have a staff capable of running things in my absence."

Gemma nodded, taking all this in. Bailey had tried telling her and Megan that she'd heard that Callum was loaded in his own right, but she really hadn't believed her. Why would a man as wealthy as Bailey claimed Callum was settle for being the manager of someone else's sheep ranch? Granted, he and Ramsey were close, but she couldn't see them being *so* close that Callum would give up a life of wealth and luxury for three years to live in a small cabin on her brother's property.

"Why did you do it?" she heard herself asking.

"Why did I do what?"

"It's obvious that you have money, so why would you give all this up for three years and work as the manager of my brother's sheep ranch?"

This, Callum thought, would be the perfect time to sit Gemma down and explain things to her, letting her know the reason he'd hung around Denver for three years. But he had a feeling just like when his father had tried explaining to his mother about her being his soul mate and it hadn't gone over well, it wouldn't go over well with Gemma, either.

According to Todd Austell, trying to convince Le'Claire Richards it had been love at first sight was the hardest thing he ever had to do. In fact, she figured he wanted to marry her to rebel against his parents trying to pick out a wife for him and not because he was truly in love with her.

Callum was sure that over the years his mother had pretty much kissed that notion goodbye, because there wasn't a single day that passed when his father didn't show his mother how much he loved her. Maybe that's why it came so easily to Callum to admit that he loved a woman. His father was a great role model.

But still, when it came to an Austell falling in love, Callum had a feeling that Gemma would be just as skeptical as his mother had been. So there was no way he could tell her the full truth of why he had spent three years practically right in her backyard.

"I needed to get away from my family for a while," he heard himself saying, which really wasn't a lie. He had been wild and reckless in his younger years, and returning home from college hadn't made things any better. The death of his grandfather had.

He had loved the old man dearly and he would have to say that his grandfather had spoiled him rotten. With the old man gone, there was no one to make excuses for him, no one to get him out of the scrapes he got into and no one who would listen to whatever tale he decided to fabricate. His father had decided that the only way to make him stand on his own was to make him work for it. So he had.

He had worked on his parents' ranch for a full year, right alongside the other ranch hands, to prove his worth. It had only been after he'd succeeded in doing that that his father had given him Le'Claire to run. But by then Callum had decided he much preferred a ranch-hand bunk to a glamorous thirty-floor high rise overlooking the harbor. So he had hired the best management team money could buy to run his corporation while he returned to work on his parents' ranch. That's when he'd met Ramsey and the two had quickly become fast friends.

"I understand," said Gemma, cutting into his thoughts.

He lifted a brow. He had expected her to question him further. "You do?"

"Yes. That's why Bane left home to join the Navy. He needed his space from us for a while. He needed to find himself."

Brisbane was her cousin Dillon's baby brother. From what Callum had heard, Bane had been only eight when his parents had been killed. He had grieved for them in a different way than the others, by fighting to get the attention he craved. When he'd graduated from high school, he had refused to go to college. After numerous brushes with the law and butting heads with the parents of a young lady who didn't want him to be a part of their daughter's life, Dillon had convinced Bane to get his life together. Everyone was hoping the military would eventually make a man of him.

Callum decided that he didn't want to dig himself in any deeper than he'd be able to pull himself out of when he finally admitted the truth to Gemma. "Would you like to go into the office with me for a while today? Who knows? You might be able to offer me a few decorating suggestions for there as well."

Her face lit up and he thought at that moment, she could decorate every single thing he owned if it would get him that smile.

"You'd give me that opportunity?"

He held back from saying, *I'll give you every single thing you want, Gemma Westmoreland.* "Yes, but only if it's within my budget," he said instead.

She threw her head back and laughed, and the hair that

went flying around her shoulders made his body hard. "We'll see if we can work something out," she said, moving toward the stairs. "It won't take long for me to dress. I promise."

"Take your time," he said to her fleeting back. He peeped around the corner and caught a glimpse of long, shapely legs when she lifted the hem of her outfit to rush up the stairs. His body suddenly got harder with a raw, primitive need.

He went over to the counter to pour a cup of the coffee she'd prepared, thinking he hadn't gotten that kiss yet, but he was determined to charm it out of her at some point today.

"Welcome back, Mr. Austell."

"Thanks, Lorna. Is everyone here?" Callum asked the older woman sitting behind the huge desk.

"Yes, sir. They are here and ready for today's meeting."

"Good. I'd like you to meet Gemma Westmoreland, one of my business associates. Gemma this is Lorna Guyton."

The woman switched her smile over to Gemma, who was standing by Callum's side. "Nice meeting you, Ms. Westmoreland," the woman said, offering Gemma her hand.

"Same here, Ms. Guyton." Gemma couldn't help but be pleased with the way Callum had introduced her. Saying she was a business associate sounded a lot better than saying she was merely the woman decorating one of his homes.

She glanced around, taking mental note of the layout of this particular floor of the Le'Claire Building. When they had pulled into the parking garage, she had definitely been impressed with the thirty-floor skyscraper. So far, the only thing she thought she would change with respect to the interior design, if given the chance, was the selection of paintings on the various walls.

"You can announce us to the team, Lorna," Callum said,

and placing his hand on Gemma's arm, he led her toward the huge conference room.

Gemma had caught the word *us* the moment Callum touched her arm and wasn't sure which had her head suddenly spinning more—him including her in his business meeting or the way her body reacted to his touch.

She had assumed that since he would be talking business he would want her to wait in the reception area near Lorna's desk. But the fact that he had included her sent a degree of pleasure up her spine and filled her with an unreasonable degree of importance.

Now if she could just stop the flutters from going off in her stomach with the feel of his hand on her arm. But then she'd been getting all kinds of sensations—more so than ever—since they had kissed. When he'd walked into the kitchen this morning looking like he should be on the cover of *GQ* magazine, a rush of blood had shot to her head and it was probably still there. She'd had to sit beside him in the car and draw in his scent with every breath she took. And it had been hard sitting in that seat knowing what had happened last night while she'd been sitting there. On the drive over, her body had gone through some sort of battle, as if it was craving again what it once had.

"Good morning, everyone."

Gemma's thoughts were interrupted when Callum swept her into the large conference room where several people sat waiting expectantly. The men stood and the women smiled and gave her curious glances.

Callum greeted everyone by name and introduced Gemma the same way he had in speaking to Lorna. When he moved toward the chair at the head of the table, she stepped aside to take a chair in the back of the room. However, he gently tightened his grip on her arm and kept her moving toward the front with him.

He then pulled out the empty chair next to his for her to

sit in. Once she had taken her seat, he took his and smiled over at her before calling the meeting to order in a deep, authoritative voice.

She couldn't help but admire how efficient he was and had to remind herself several times during the course of the business meeting that this was the same Callum who'd managed her brother's sheep farm. The same Callum who would turn feminine heads around town when he wore tight-fitting jeans over taut hips and an ultrafine tush, and sported a Western shirt over broad shoulders.

And this was the same Callum who had made her scream with pleasure last night…in his car of all places. She glanced over at his hand, the same one whose fingers were now holding an ink pen, and remembered just where that hand had been last night and what he'd been doing with those fingers.

Suddenly, she felt very hot and figured that as long as she kept looking at his hands she would get even hotter. Over the course of the hour-long meeting, she tried to focus her attention on other things in the room like the paintings on the wall, the style of window treatments and carpeting. Given the chance, she would spruce things up in here. Unlike the other part of the office, for some reason this particular room seemed a little drab. In addition to the boring pictures hanging on the walls, the carpeting lacked any depth. She wondered what that was all about. Evidently, no one told the prior interior designer that the coloring of carpet in a business often set the mood of the employees.

"I see everyone continues to do a fantastic job for me in my absence and I appreciate that. This meeting is now adjourned," Callum said.

Gemma glanced up to see everyone getting out of their seats, filing out of the room and closing the door behind them. She turned to find Callum staring at her. "What's wrong? You seemed bored," he said.

She wondered how he'd picked up on it when his full attention should have been on the meeting he was conducting. But since he had noticed...

"Yes, but I couldn't help it. This room will bore you to tears and I have a bucket full of them." She glanced around the room. "Make that *two* buckets."

Callum threw his head back and laughed. "Do you always say whatever suits you?"

"Hey, you did ask. And yes, I usually say whatever suits me. Didn't Ramsey warn you that I have no problem giving my opinion about anything?"

"Yes, he did warn me."

She gave him a sweet smile. "Yet you hired me anyway, so, unfortunately, you're stuck with me."

Callum wanted nothing more than to lean over and plant a kiss firmly on Gemma's luscious lips and say that being stuck with her was something he looked forward to. Instead, he checked his watch. "Do you want to grab lunch before we head over to the house you'll be decorating? Then while we eat you can tell me why you have so many buckets of tears from this room."

She chuckled as she stood up. "Gladly, Mr. Austell."

Chapter 9

"Well, here we are and I want you to tell me just what you can do with this place."

Gemma heard Callum's words, but her gaze was on the interior of a monstrosity of a house. She was totally in awe. There weren't too many homes that could render her speechless, but this mansion had before she'd stepped over the threshold. The moment he'd pulled into the driveway, she'd been overwhelmed by the architecture of it. She'd known when she'd originally seen the design of the home on paper that it was a beauty, but actually seeing it in all its grandiose splendor was truly a breathtaking moment.

"Give me the history of this house," she said, glancing around at the elegant staircase, high sculptured ceilings, exquisite crown molding and gorgeous wood floors. And for some reason she believed Callum knew it. Just from her observation of him during that morning's meeting, she'd determined that he was an astute businessman, sharp as a tack, although he preferred sporting jeans and messing with sheep to wearing a business suit and tweaking mission statements.

Over lunch she'd asked how he'd managed to keep up with his business affairs with Le'Claire while working for Ramsey. He'd explained that he had made trips back home several times when his presence had been needed on important matters. In addition, the cottage he occupied in Denver had a high-speed Internet connection, a fax machine and whatever else was needed to keep in touch with his team in Australia. And due to the difference in time zones, six in the evening in Denver was ten in the morning the next day in Sydney. He'd been able to call it a day with Ramsey around five, go home and shower and be included in a number of critical business meetings by way of conference call by seven.

"This area is historic Bellevue Hills and this house was once owned by one of the richest men in Australia. Shaun told me about it, thought I should take a look at it and make the seller an offer. I did."

"Just like that?" she asked, snapping her fingers for effect.

He met her gaze. "Just like that," he said, snapping his.

She couldn't help but laugh. "I like the way you think, Callum, because, as I said, this place is a beauty."

He shifted his gaze away from her to look back at the house. "So, it's a place where you think the average woman would want to live?"

She placed her hands on her hips. "Callum, the average woman would die to live in a place like this. This is practically a mansion. It's fit for a queen. I know because I consider myself the average woman and I would."

"You would?"

"Of course. Now, I'm dying to take a look around and make some decorating suggestions."

"As extensive as the ones you made at lunch regarding that conference room at Le'Claire?"

"Probably," she said with a smile. "But I won't know until I go through it and take measurements." She pulled her tape measure out of her purse.

"Let's go."

He touched her arm and the moment he did so, she felt that tingling sensation that always came over her when he touched her, but now the sensations were even stronger than before.

"You okay, Gemma? You're shivering."

She drew in a deep breath as they moved from the foyer toward the rest of the house. "Yes, I'm fine," she said, refusing to look at him. *If only he knew the truth about how she was feeling.*

Callum leaned against the kitchen counter and stared over at Gemma as she stood on a ladder taking measurements of a particular window. She had long ago shed her jacket and kicked off her shoes. He looked down at her feet and thought she had pretty toes.

They had been here a couple of hours already and there were still more measurements to take. He didn't mind if he could continue to keep her up there on a ladder. Once in a while, when she moved, he'd get a glimpse of her gorgeous legs and her luscious-looking thighs.

"You're quiet."

Her observation broke into his thoughts. "What I'm doing is watching you," he said. "Having fun?"

"The best kind there is. I love doing this and I'm going to love decorating this house for you." She paused a second. "Unfortunately, I have some bad news for you."

He lifted a brow. "What bad news?"

She smiled down at him. "What I want to do in here just might break you. And, it will take me longer than the six weeks planned."

He nodded. Of course, he couldn't tell her he was counting on that very thing. "I don't have a problem with that. How is your work schedule back in Denver? Will remaining here a little longer cause problems for you?"

"No. I finished all my open projects and was about to

take a vacation before bidding on others, so that's fine with me if you think you can handle a houseguest for a little while longer."

"Absolutely."

She chuckled. "You might want to think about it before you give in too easily."

"No, you might want to think about it before you decide to stay."

She glanced down at him and went perfectly still and he knew at that moment she was aware of what he was thinking. Although they had enjoyed each other's company, they had practically walked on eggshells around each other all day. After lunch he'd taken her on a tour of downtown and showed her places like the Sydney Opera House, the Royal Botanic Gardens and St. Andrew's Cathedral. And they had fed seagulls in Hyde Park before coming here. Walking beside her seemed natural, and for a while they'd held hands. Each time he had touched her she had trembled.

Did she think he wasn't aware of what those shivers meant? Did she not know what being close to her was doing to him? Could she not see the male appreciation as well as the love shining in his eyes whenever he looked at her?

Breaking eye contact, he looked at his watch. "Do you plan to measure all the windows today?"

"No, I'd planned to make this my last one for now. You will bring me back tomorrow, though, right?"

"Just ask. Whatever you want, it's yours."

"In that case, I'd like to come back to finish up this part. Then we'll need to decide on what fabrics you want," she said, moving to step down from the ladder. "The earlier the better, especially if it's something I need to backorder."

He moved away from the counter to hold the ladder steady while she descended. "Thanks," she said, when her bare feet touched the floor. He was standing right there in front of her.

"Don't mention it," he said. "Ready to go?"

"Yes."

Instead of taking her hand, he walked beside her and said nothing. He felt her looking over at him, but he refused to return her gaze. He had promised that the next time they kissed she would ask for it, but she'd failed to do that, which meant that when they got back to his place he would turn up the heat.

"You all right, Callum?"

"Yes, I'm fine. Where would you like to eat? It's dinnertime."

"Doesn't matter. I'm up for anything."

He smiled when an idea popped into his head. "Then how about me preparing dinner tonight."

She lifted a brow. "Can you cook?"

"I think I might surprise you."

She chuckled. "In that case, surprise me."

Whatever you want, it's yours.

Gemma stepped out of the Jacuzzi to dry herself while thinking that Callum had been saying that a lot lately. She wondered what he would think of her if she were to tell him that what she wanted more than anything was another dose of the pleasure he'd introduced her to last night.

Being around him most of the day had put her nerves on edge. Every time he touched her or she caught him looking at her, she felt an overwhelming need to explore the intense attraction between them. His mouth and fingers had planted a need within her that was so profound, so incredibly physical, that certain parts of her body craved his touch.

She'd heard of people being physically attracted to each other to the point of lust consuming their mind and thoughts, but such a thing had never happened to her. Until now. And why was it happening at all? What was there about Callum—other than the obvious—that had her in such a tizzy? He made her want things she'd never had before. She was tempted to go further with him than she had with any other man.

In a way she had already done that last night. There was no other man on the face of this earth who could ever lay a claim to fingering her. But Callum had done that while kissing her senseless, stirring a degree of passion within her that even now made her heart beat faster just thinking about it.

She shook her head, and tried to get a grip but failed to do so. She couldn't let go of the memories of how her body erupted in one mind-shattering orgasm. Now she knew what full-blown pleasure was about. But she knew that she hadn't even reached the tip of the iceberg and her body was aching to get pushed over that turbulent edge. The thought that there was something even more powerful, more explosive to experience sent sensual shivers through her entire being.

There were a number of reasons why she should not be thinking of indulging in an affair with Callum. And yet, there were a number of reasons why she should. She was a twenty-four-year-old virgin. To give her virginity to Callum was a plus in her book, because, in addition to being attracted to him, he would know what he was doing. She'd heard horror stories about men who didn't.

And if they were to have an affair, who would know? He wasn't the type to kiss and tell. And he didn't seem bothered by the fact that his best friend was her brother. Besides, since he would be returning to Australia to live, she didn't have the worry about running into him on a constant basis, seeing him and being reminded of what they'd done.

So what was holding her back?

She knew the answer to that question. It was the same reason she was still a virgin. She was afraid the guy she would give her virginity to would also capture her heart.

And the thought of any man having her heart was something she just couldn't abide. What if he were to hurt her, break her heart the way her brothers had done to all those girls?

She nibbled on her bottom lip as she slipped into her dress to join Callum for dinner. Somehow she would have to find a way to experience pleasure without the possibility of incurring heartache. She should be able to make love with a man without getting attached. Men did it all the time. She would enter into the affair with both eyes open and not expect any more than what she got. And when it was over, her heart would still be intact. She wouldn't set herself up like those other girls who'd fancied themselves in love with a Westmoreland, only to have their hearts broken.

It should be a piece of cake. After all, Callum had told her he was waiting to meet his soul mate. So there would be no misunderstanding on either of their parts. She wasn't in love with him and he wasn't in love with her. He would get what he wanted and she would be getting what she wanted.

More of last night.

A smile of anticipation touched her lips. She mustn't appear too eager and intended to play this out for all it was worth and see how long it would last. She was inexperienced when it came to seduction, but she was a quick study.

And Callum was about to discover just how eager she was to learn new things.

Callum heard Gemma moving around upstairs. He had encouraged her to relax and take a bubble bath in the huge Jacuzzi garden tub while he prepared dinner.

Since they'd eaten a large lunch at one of the restaurants downtown near the Sydney Harbour, he decided to keep dinner simple—a salad and an Aussie meat pie.

He couldn't help but smile upon recalling her expression when she'd first seen his home, and her excitement about decorating it just the way she liked. He had gone along with every suggestion she made, and although she had teased him about the cost, he knew she was intentionally trying to keep prices low, even though he'd told her that doing so wasn't necessary.

His cell phone rang and he pulled it off his belt to answer it. "Hello."

"How are you doing, Callum?"

He smiled upon hearing his mother's voice. "I'm fine, Mom. What about you?"

"I'm wonderful. I hadn't talked to you since you were here yesterday with Gemma, and I just want you to know that I think she's a lovely girl."

"Thanks, Mom. I think so, too. I just can't wait for her to figure out she's my soul mate."

"Have patience, Callum."

He chuckled. "I'll try."

"I know Gemma is going to be tied up with decorating that house, but Shaun and I were wondering if she'll be free to do some shopping with us next Friday," his mother said. "Annette and Mira will be joining us as well."

The thought of Gemma being out of his sight for any period of time didn't sit well with him. He knew all about his mother, sister and sisters-in-law's shopping trips. They could be gone for hours. He felt like a possessive lover. A smile touched his lips. He wasn't Gemma's lover yet, but he intended to be while working diligently to become a permanent part of her life—namely, her husband.

"Callum?"

"Yes, Mom. I'm sure that's something Gemma will enjoy. She's upstairs changing for dinner. I'll have her call you."

He conversed with his mother for a little while longer before ending the call. Pouring a glass of wine, he moved to the window that looked out over the Pacific. His decision to keep this place had been an easy one. He loved the view as well as the privacy.

The house Gemma was decorating was in the suburbs, sat on eight acres of land and would provide plenty of room for the large family he wanted them to have. He took a sip of wine while his mind imagined a pregnant Gemma, her tummy round with his child.

He drew in a deep breath, thinking that if anyone would have told him five years ago that he would be here in this place and in this frame of mind, he would have been flabbergasted. His mother suggested that he have patience. He'd shown just how much patience he had for the past three years. Now it was time to make his move.

"Callum?"

The sound of her voice made him turn around. He swallowed deeply, while struggling to stay where he was, not cross the room, pull her into his arms and give her the greeting that he preferred. As usual, she looked beautiful, but there was something different about her this evening. There was a serene glow to her face that hadn't been there before. Had just two days in Australia done that to her? Hell, he hoped so. More than anything, he wanted his native land to grow on her.

"You look nice, Gemma," he heard himself saying.

"Thanks. You look nice yourself."

He glanced down at himself. He had changed out of his suit, and was now wearing jeans and a pullover shirt. She was wearing an alluring little outfit—a skirt that fell a little past her knees, a matching top and a cute pair of sandals. He looked at her and immediately thought of one word. *Sexy.* Umm, make that two words. *Super sexy.* He knew of no other woman who wore her sexuality quite the way Gemma did.

His gaze roamed the full length of her in male appreciation, admiring the perfection of her legs, ankles and calves. He had to have patience, as his mother suggested and tamp down his rising desire. But all he had to do was breathe in, take a whiff of her scent and know that would not be an easy task.

"What are you drinking?"

Her words pulled his attention from her legs back to her face. "Excuse me? I missed that."

A smile curved her lips. "I asked what you're drinking."

He held up his glass and glanced at it. "Wine. Want some?"

"Sure."

"No problem. I'll pour you a glass," he said.

"No need," she said, walking slowly toward him. He felt his pulse rate increase and his breathing get erratic with every step she took.

"I'll just share yours," she said, coming to a stop in front of him. She reached out, slid the glass from his hand and took a sip. But not before taking the tip of her tongue and running it along the entire rim of the glass.

Callum sucked in a quick breath. Did she know how intimate that gesture was? He watched as she then took a sip. "Nice, Callum. Australia's finest, I assume."

He had to swallow before answering, trying to retain control of his senses. "Yes, a friend of my father owns a winery. There's plenty where that came from. Would you like some more?"

Her smile widened. "No, thank you. But there is something that I do want," she said, taking a step closer to him.

"Is there?" he said, forcing the words out of a tight throat. "You tell me what you want and, as I said yesterday and again today, whatever you want I will deliver."

She leaned in closer and whispered. "I'm holding you to your word, Callum Austell, because I've decided that I want you."

Chapter 10

Gemma half expected Callum to yank her down and take her right there on the living room floor. After all, she'd just stated that she wanted him, and no one would have to read between the lines to figure out what that meant. Most men would immediately act on her request, not giving her the chance to change her mind.

Instead, Callum deliberately and slowly put his glass down. His gaze locked with hers and when his hands went to her waist he moved, bringing their bodies in close contact. "And what you want, Gemma, is just what you will get."

She saw intense heat in the depths of his eyes just seconds before he lowered his mouth to hers. The moment she felt his tongue invade her mouth, she knew he would be kissing her senseless.

He didn't disappoint her.

The last time they'd kissed, he had introduced her to a range of sensations that she'd never encountered before. Sensations that started at her toes and worked their way up to the top of her head. Sensations that had lingered in her lower half, causing the area between her legs to undergo all kinds of turbulent feelings and her heart all kinds of unfamiliar emotions.

This kiss was just as deadly, even more potent than the last, and her head began swimming in passion. She felt that drowning would soon follow. Blood was rushing, fast and furiously, through her veins with every stroke of his tongue. He was lapping her up in a way that had her entire body shuddering from the inside out.

Callum had encouraged her to ask for what she wanted and was delivering in full measure. He wasn't thinking about control of any kind and neither was she. He had addressed and put to rest the only two concerns she had—his relationship with her brother and her relationship with him as a client. Last night, he'd let her know that those two things had nothing to do with this—the attraction between them—and she was satisfied with that.

And now she was getting satisfied with this—his ability to deliver a kiss that was so passionate it was nearly engulfing her in flames. He was drinking her as if she were made of the finest wine, even finer than the one he'd just consumed.

She felt the arms around her waist tighten and when he shifted their positions she felt something else, the thick hardness behind the zipper of his jeans. When she moved her hip and felt his hard muscles aligned with her curves, the denim of his jeans rubbing against her bare legs, she moaned deep in her throat.

Callum released Gemma's mouth and drew in a deep breath and her scent. She smelled of the strawberry bubble bath she had used and whatever perfume she had dabbed on her body.

He brushed kisses across her forehead, eyebrows, cheeks and temples while giving her a chance to breathe. Her mouth was so soft and responsive, and it tasted so damn delicious. The more he deepened the kiss, the more responsive she became and the more accessible she made her mouth.

His hands eased from her waist to smooth across her

back before cupping her backside. He could feel every inch of her soft curves beneath the material of her skirt and top, and instinctively, he pulled her closer to the fit of him.

"Do you want more?" he whispered against her lips, tasting the corners of her mouth while moaning deep in his throat from how good she tasted.

"Yes, I want more," she said in a purr that conveyed a little catch in her breathing.

"How much more?" He needed to know. Any type of rational thought and mind control was slipping away from him big time. It wouldn't take much to strip her naked right now.

He knew for a fact that she'd rarely dated during the time he'd been in Denver. And although he wasn't sure what she did while she was in college, he had a feeling his Gemma was still a virgin. The thought of that filled him with intense pride that she would give him the honor of being her first.

"I want all you can give me, Callum," she responded in a thick slur, but the words were clear to his ears.

He sucked a quick gulp of air into his lungs. He wondered if she had any idea what she was asking for. What he could give was a whole hell of a lot. If he had his way, he would keep her on her back for days. Stay inside her until he'd gotten her pregnant more times than humanly possible.

The thought of his seed entering her womanly channel, made the head of his erection throb behind his zipper, begging for release, practically pleading for the chance to get inside her wet warmth.

"Are you on any type of birth control?" He knew that she was. He had overheard a conversation once that she'd had with Bailey and knew she'd been taking oral contraceptives to regulate her monthly cycle.

"Yes, I'm on the pill," she acknowledged. "But not because I sleep around or anything like that. In fact, I'm…"

She stopped talking in midsentence and was gazing up at him beneath her long lashes. Her eyes were wide, as if it just dawned on her what she was about to reveal. He had no intention of letting her stop talking now.

"You're what?"

He watched as she began nervously nibbling on her bottom lip and he almost groaned, tempted to replace her lip with his and do the nibbling for her.

He continued to brush kisses across her face, drinking in her taste. And when she didn't respond to his inquiry, he pulled back and looked at her. "You can tell me anything, Gemma. Anything at all."

"I don't know," she said in a somewhat shaky voice. "It might make you want to stop."

Not hardly, he thought, and knew he needed to convince her of that. "There's nothing you can tell me that's going to stop me from giving you what you want. Nothing," he said fervently.

She gazed up into his eyes and he knew she believed him. She held the intensity in his gaze when she leaned forward and whispered. "I'm still a virgin."

"Oh, Gemma," he said, filled with all the love any man could feel for a woman at that particular moment. He had suspected as much, but until she'd confessed the truth, he hadn't truly been certain. Now he was, and the thought that he would be the man who carried her over the threshold of womanhood gave him pause, had him searching for words to let her know just how he felt.

He hooked her chin with his fingers as he continued to hold her gaze. "You trust me enough with such a precious gift?"

"Yes," she said promptly without hesitation.

Filled with both extreme pleasure and profound pride, he bent his head and kissed her gently while sweeping her off her feet into his arms.

* * *

When Callum placed her on his bed and stepped back to stare at her, one look at his blatantly aroused features let Gemma know that he was going to give her just what she had asked for. Just what she wanted.

Propped up against his pillow, she drank him in from head to toe as he began removing his shoes. Something—she wasn't sure just what—made her bold enough to ask. "Will you strip for me?"

He lifted his head and looked over at her. If he was shocked by her request, he didn't show it. "Is that what you want?"

"Yes."

He smiled and nodded. "No problem."

Gemma shifted her body into a comfortable position as a smile suffused her face. "Be careful or I'll begin to think you're easy."

He shrugged broad shoulders as he began removing his shirt. "Then I guess I'll just have to prove you wrong."

She chuckled. "Oooh, I can't wait." She stared at his naked chest. He was definitely built, she thought.

He tossed his shirt aside and when his hand went to the zipper of his jeans, a heated sensation began traveling along Gemma's nerve endings. When he began lowering the zipper, she completely held her breath.

He slid the zipper halfway down and met her gaze. "Something I need to confess before I go any further."

Her breath felt choppy. "What?"

"I dreamed about you last night."

Gemma smiled, pleased with his confession. "I have a confession of my own." He lifted his brows. "I dreamed about you, too. But, then, I think it was to be expected after last night."

He went back to slowly easing his zipper down. "You could have come to my bedroom. I would not have minded."

"I wasn't ready."

He didn't move as he held her gaze. "And now?"

She grinned. "And now I'm a lady-in-waiting."

He threw his head back and laughed as he began sliding his pants down his legs. She scooted to the edge of the bed to watch, fascinated when he stood before her wearing a skimpy pair of black briefs. He had muscular thighs and a nice pair of hairy legs. The way the briefs fit his body had her shuddering when she should have been blushing.

All her senses suddenly felt hot-wired, her heart began thumping like crazy in her chest and a tingling sensation traveled up her nerve endings. She felt no shame in staring at him. The only thing she could think of at that moment was that *her* Aussie was incredibly sexy.

Her Aussie?

She couldn't believe her mind had conjured up such a thought. He wasn't hers and she wasn't his. At least not in *that* way. But tonight, she conceded, and whenever they made love, just for that moment, they would belong to each other in every way.

"Should I continue?"

She licked her lips in anticipation. "I might hurt you if you don't."

He chuckled as he slid his hands into the waistband of his briefs and slowly began easing them down his legs. "Oh my…" She could barely get the words past her throat.

Her breasts felt achy as she stared at that part of his anatomy, which seemed to get larger right before her eyes. She caught a lip between her teeth and tried not to clamp down too hard. But he had to be, without a doubt, in addition to being totally aroused and powerfully male, the most beautiful man she'd ever seen. And he stood there, with his legs braced apart, his hands on his hips and with a mass of hair flowing around his face, fully exposed to her. This was a man who could make women drool. A man who would get a second look whenever he entered a room, no matter what he was wearing. A man whose voice alone could make woman want to forget about being a good girl and just enjoy being bad.

She continued to stare, unable to do anything else, as he approached the bed. She moved into a sitting position to avoid being at eye level with his erection.

Gemma couldn't help wondering what his next move would be. Did he expect her to return the favor and strip for him? When he reached the edge of the bed, she tilted her head back and met his gaze. "My turn?"

He smiled. "Yes, but I want to do things differently."

She lifted a confused brow. "Differently?"

"Yes, instead of you stripping yourself, I want to do it."

She swallowed, not sure she understood. "You want to take my clothes off?"

He shook his head as a sexy smile touched his lips. "No, I want to strip your clothes off you."

And then he reached out and ripped off her blouse.

The surprised look on her face was priceless. Callum tossed her torn blouse across the room. And now his gaze was fixed on her chest and her blue satin push-up bra. Fascinated, he thought she looked sexy as hell.

"You owe me for that," she said when she found her voice.

"And I'll pay up," he responded as he leaned forward to release the front clasp and then eased the straps down her shoulders, freeing what he thought were perfect twin mounds with mouth-watering dark nipples.

His hand trembled when he touched them, fondled them between his eager fingers, while watching her watch him, and seeing how her eyes darkened, and how her breath came out in a husky moan.

"Hold those naughty thoughts, Gemma," he whispered

when he released her and reached down to remove her sandals, rubbing his hands over her calves and ankles, while thinking her skin felt warm, almost feverish.

"Why do women torture their feet with these things?" His voice was deep and husky. He dropped the shoes by the bed.

"Because we know men like you enjoy seeing us in them."

He continued to rub her feet when he smiled. "I like seeing *you* in them. But then I like seeing you out of them, too."

His hand left her feet and began inching up her leg, past her knee to her thigh. But just for a second. His hand left her thigh and shifted over to the buttons on her skirt and with one tug sent them flying. She lifted her hips when he began pulling the skirt from her body and when she lay before him wearing nothing but a pair of skimpy blue panties, he felt blood rush straight to his heads. Both of them.

But it was the one that decided at that moment to almost double in size that commanded his attention. Without saying a word, he slowly began easing her panties down her thighs and her luscious scent began playing havoc with his nostrils as he did so.

He tossed her panties aside and his hands eased back between her legs, seeing what he'd touched last night and watching once again as her pupils began dilating with pleasure.

And to make sure she got the full Callum Austell effect, he bent his head toward her chest, captured a nipple in his mouth and began sucking on it.

"Callum!"

"Umm?" He released that nipple only to move to the other one, licking the dark area before easing the tip between his lips and sucking on it as he'd done to the other one. He liked her taste and definitely liked the sounds she was making.

Moments later he began inching lower down her body and when his mouth came to her stomach, he traced a wet path all over it.

"Callum."

"I'm right here. You still sure you want me?" His fingers softly flicked across her womanly folds while he continued to lick her stomach.

"Oh, yes."

"Are there any limitations?" he asked.

"No."

"Sure?"

"Positive."

He took her at her word and moved his mouth lower. Her eyes began closing when he lifted her hips and wrapped her legs around his neck, lowered his head and pressed his open mouth to her feminine core.

Pleasure crashed over Gemma and she bit down to keep from screaming. Callum's tongue inside her was driving her crazy, and pushing her over the edge in a way she'd never been pushed before. Her body seemed to fragment into several pieces and each of those sections was being tortured by a warm, wet and aggressive tongue that was stroking her into a stupor.

Her hands grabbed tight to the bedspread as her legs were nudged further apart when his mouth burrowed further between her thighs and his tongue seem to delve inside her deeper.

She continued to groan in pleasure, not sure she would be able to stop moaning even when he ceased doing this to her. She released a deep moan when the pressure of his mouth on her was too much, and the erotic waves she was drowning in gave her little hope for a rescue.

And then, just like the night before, she felt her body jackknife into an orgasm that had her screaming. She was grateful for the privacy afforded by the seclusion of Callum's condo.

"Gemma."

Callum's deep Australian voice flowed through her mind as her body shuddered nearly uncontrollably. It had taken her twenty-four years to share this kind of intimacy with a man and it was well worth the wait.

"Open your eyes. I want you to be looking at me the moment I make you mine."

She lifted what seemed like heavy lids and saw that he was over her, his body positioned between her legs, and her hips were cupped in the palms of his hands. She pushed the thought out of her mind that she would never truly be his, and what he'd said was just a figure of speech, words just for the moment, and she understood because at this moment she wanted to be his.

As she gazed up into his eyes, something stirred deep in her chest around her heart and she forced the feeling back, refusing to allow it to gain purchase there, rebuffing the very notion and repudiating the very idea. This was about lust, not love. He knew it and she knew it as well. There was nothing surprising about the way her body was responding to him; the way he seemed to be able to strum her senses the same way a musician strummed his guitar.

And then she felt him, felt the way his engorged erection was pressed against her femininity and she kept her gaze locked with his when she felt him make an attempt to slide into her. It wasn't easy. He was trying to stretch her and it didn't seem to be working. Sweat popped on his brow and she reached up and wiped his forehead with the back of her hand.

He saw her flinch in pain and he went still. "Do you want me to stop?"

She shook her head from side to side. "No. I want you to make it happen, and you said you'll give me what I want."

"Brat," he said. When she chuckled, he thrust forward. When she cried out he leaned in and captured her lips.

You truly belong to me now and I love you, Callum wanted to say, but knew that he couldn't. Instead, after her body had adjusted to his, he began moving. Every stroke into her body was a sign of his love whether she knew it or not. One day when she could accept it, she would know and he would gladly tell her everything.

He needed to kiss her, join his mouth to hers the same way their bodies were joined. So he leaned close and captured her mouth, kissing her thoroughly and hungrily, and with a passion he felt through every cell in his body. When she instinctively began milking his erection, he deepened the kiss.

And when he felt her body explode, which triggered his to do likewise, he pulled his mouth from hers to throw his head back to scream her name. *Her name.* No other woman's name but hers, while he continued to thrust in and out of her.

His body had ached for this for so long, his body had ached for her. And as a climax continued to rip through them, he knew that, no matter what, Gemma Westmoreland was what he needed in his life and there was no way he would ever give her up.

Chapter 11

Sunlight flitting across her face made Gemma open her eyes and she immediately felt the hard muscular body sleeping beside her. Callum's leg was thrown over hers and his arms were wrapped around her middle. They were both naked—that was a given—and the even sound of his breathing meant he was still asleep.

The man was amazing. He had made love to her in a way that made her first time with a man so very special. He'd also fed her last night the tasty meal he'd prepared, surprising her and proving that he was just as hot in the kitchen as he was in the bedroom.

She drew in a deep breath, wondering which part of her was sorer, the area between her legs or her breasts. Callum had given special attention to both areas through most of the night. But with a tenderness that touched her deeply, he had paused to prepare a warm, soothing soak for her in his huge bathtub. He hadn't made love to her since then. They'd eaten a late dinner, and returning to bed, he had cuddled her in his arms, close to his warm, masculine body. His hands had caressed her all over, gently stroking her to sleep.

And now she was awake and very much aware of everything they'd done the night before. Everything she'd asked him for, he had delivered. Even when he had wanted to stop because last night was her first time, she had wanted to experience more pleasure and he had ended up making it happen, giving her what she wanted. And although her body felt sore and battered today, a part of her felt that last night had truly been worth it.

Deciding to get a little more sleep, she closed her eyes and immediately saw visions of them together. But it wasn't a recent image. She looked older and so did he and there were kids around. Whose kids were they? Certainly not theirs. Otherwise that would mean…

Her eyes sprang open, refusing to let such an apparition enter her mind. She would be the first to admit that what they'd shared last night had overwhelmed her, and for a moment she'd come close to challenging everything she believed about relationships between men and women. But the last thing she needed to do was get offtrack. Last night was what it was—no more, no less. It was about a curious, inexperienced woman and a horny, experienced man. And both had gotten satisfied to the nth degree. They had both gotten what they wanted.

"You're awake?"

Callum's voice sent sensations running across her skin. "Who wants to know?"

"The man who made love to you last night."

She shifted her body, turned to face him and immediately wished she hadn't. Fully awake he was sexy as sin. A half asleep Callum, with a stubble chin, drowsy eyes and long eyelashes, could make you come just looking at him.

"You're the one who did that to me last night, aren't you?"

A smile curved his lips. "I'm the one who plans to do that to you every night."

She chuckled, knowing he only meant every night she remained in Australia. She was certain he knew that when they returned to Denver things would be different. Although she had her own little place, he would not be making late-night booty calls on her Westmoreland property.

"You think you have the stamina to do it every night?"

"Don't you?"

She had to admit that the man's staying power was truly phenomenal. But she figured, in time, when she got the hang of it, she would be able to handle him. "Yes, I do."

She then reached out and rubbed a hand across his chin. "You need a shave."

He chuckled. "Do I?"

"Yes." Then she grabbed a lock of his hair. "And…"

"Don't go there. I get my hair trimmed, never cut."

She smiled. "That must be an Austell thing, since I see your father and brothers evidently feel the same way. Don't be surprised if I start calling you Samson."

"And I'll start calling you Delilah, the temptress."

She couldn't help but laugh. "I wouldn't know how to tempt a man."

"But you know how to tempt me."

"Do I?"

"Yes, but don't get any ideas," he said. "Last night you made me promise to get you to your new office by ten o'clock."

Yes, she had made him promise that. He'd told her she could set up shop in the study of the house. He would have a phone installed as well as a fax machine and a computer with a high-speed Internet connection. The sooner she could get the materials she needed ordered, the quicker she could return to Denver. For some reason, the thought of returning home tugged at her heart. This was her third day here and she already loved this place.

"You do want to be on the job by ten, right?"

A smile touched her lips. "Yes, I do. Have you decided when and if you're returning to Denver?" She just had to know.

"Yes, I plan to return with you and will probably stay

until after Ramsey and Chloe's baby is born to help out on the ranch. When things get pretty much back to normal for Ramsey, then I'll leave Denver for good and return here."

She began nibbling on her bottom lip. This was September, and Chloe was due to deliver in November, which meant Callum would be leaving Denver a few months after that. Chances were there would be no Callum Austell in Denver come spring.

"Umm, let me do that."

She lifted her gaze to his eyes when he interrupted her thoughts. "Let you do what?"

"This."

He leaned closer and began gently nibbling on her lips, then licking her mouth from corner to corner. When her lips parted on a breathless sigh, he entered her mouth to taste her fully. The kiss grew deeper, hotter and moments later, when he pulled his mouth away, he placed his fingers to her lips to stop the request he knew she was about to make.

"Your body doesn't need me that way, Gemma. It needs an adjustment period," he whispered against her lips.

She nodded. "But later?"

His lips curved in a wicked smile. "Yes, later."

Callum was vaguely aware of the information the foreman of one of his sheep ranches was giving to him. The report was good, which he knew it would be. During the time he'd been in Denver, he'd pretty much kept up with things here as well as with Le'Claire. He'd learned early how to multitask.

And he smiled, thinking how well he'd multi-tasked last night. There hadn't been one single part of Gemma he hadn't wanted to devour—and all at the same time. He'd been greedy, and so had she. His woman had more passion in her body than she knew what to do with, and he was more than willing to school her in all the possibilities. But he also knew that he had to be careful. He didn't want her to start thinking that what was between them was more lust than love. His goal was to woo her every chance he got, which is why he'd hung up with the florist a few moments ago.

"So as you can see, Mr. Austell, everything is as it should be."

He smiled at the man who'd been talking for the past ten minutes, going over his sheep-herding records. "I figured they would be. I appreciate the job you and your men have done in my absence, Richard."

A huge grin covered the man's face. "We appreciate working for the Austells."

Richard Vinson and his family had worked on an Austell sheep ranch for generations. In fact, upon Callum's grandfather's death, Jack Austell had deeded over five hundred acres of land to the Vinson family in recognition of their loyalty, devotion and hard work.

A few minutes later, Callum was headed back to his car when his phone rang. A quick check showed it was a call from the States, namely Derringer Westmoreland. "Yes, Derringer?"

"Just calling to see if you've given any more thought to becoming a silent partner in our horse-breeding venture?"

Durango Westmoreland, part of those Atlanta Westmorelands, had teamed up with a childhood friend and cousin-in-law named McKinnon Quinn, and bought a very successful horse-breeding and -training operation in Montana. They had invited their cousins, Zane, Derringer and Jason, to become part of their outfit as Colorado partners. Callum, Ramsey and Dillon had expressed an interest in becoming silent partners. "Yes. I'm impressed with all I've heard about it, so count me in."

"Boy, you're easy," Derringer teased.

His words made Callum think about Gemma. She had said the same thing to him last night, but during the course of the night he'd shown her just how wrong she was. "Hey, what can I say? Are you behaving yourself?"

Derringer laughed. "Hey, now what can I say? And speaking of behaving, how is that sister of mine? She hasn't driven you crazy yet?"

Callum smiled. Gemma had driven him crazy but in a way he'd rather not go into with her brother. "Gemma is doing a great job decorating my place."

"Well, watch your wallet. I heard her prices can sometimes get out of sight."

"Thanks for the warning."

He talked to Derringer a few moments longer before ending the call. After he married Gemma, Ramsey, Zane, Derringer, the twins, Megan and Bailey would become his in-laws, and those other Westmorelands, including Dillon, his cousins-in-law. Hell, he didn't want to think about all those other Westmorelands, the ones from Atlanta that Ramsey and his siblings and cousins were just beginning to get to know. It didn't take the Denver Westmorelands and the Atlanta Westmorelands long to begin meshing as if they'd had a close relationship all their lives.

Callum's father had been an only child and so had his father before him. Todd Austell probably would have been content having one child, but Le'Claire had had a say in that. His father had known that marrying the American beauty meant fathering at least three children. Callum chuckled, remembering that, according to his father, his birth had been a surprise. Todd had assumed his daddy days were over, but Le'Claire had had other ideas about that, and Todd had decided to give his wife whatever she wanted. Callum was using that same approach with Gemma. Whatever this particular Westmoreland wanted is what she would get.

After Callum snapped his seat belt in place, he checked his watch. It was a little past three and he would be picking Gemma up around five. He'd wanted to take her to lunch, but she'd declined, saying she had a lot of orders to place if he wanted the house fully decorated and ready for him to move in by November.

He really didn't care if he was in that house, still living in his condo on the beach or back in Denver. All that mattered to him was that Gemma was with him—wherever he was. And as he turned the ignition to his car, he knew that making that happen was still his top priority.

"Will there be anything else, Ms. Westmoreland?"

Gemma glanced up at the older woman Callum had introduced her to that morning, Kathleen Morgan. "No, Kathleen. That's it. Thanks for all you did today."

The woman waved off her words. "I didn't do anything but make a lot of phone calls to place those orders. I can just imagine how this place is going to look when you finish with it. I think Mr. Austell's decision to blend European and Western styles will be simply beautiful. One day this house will be a showplace for Mr. Austell and his future wife. Goodbye."

"Goodbye." Gemma tried letting the woman's words pass, but couldn't. The thought of Callum sharing this house with a woman—one he would be married to—bothered her.

She tossed her pencil on the desk and glanced over at the flowers that had been delivered not long after he'd dropped her off here. A dozen red roses. Why had he sent them? The card that accompanied them only had his signature. They were simply beautiful, and the fragrance suffused her office.

Her office.

And that was another mystery. She had assumed she would have an empty room on the main floor of the house with a table and just the bare essentials to operate as a temporary place to order materials and supplies. But when she'd stepped through the door with Callum at her back, she had seen that the empty room had been transformed into a work place, equipped with everything imaginable, including a live administrative assistant.

She pushed her chair back and walked across the room to the vase of flowers she'd placed on a table in front of a window. That way she could pause while working to glance over at them and appreciate their beauty. Unfortunately, seeing them also made her think of the man who'd sent them.

She threw her head back in frustration. She had to stop thinking of Callum and start concentrating on the job he'd hired her to do. Not only had he hired her, he had brought her all the way from Denver to handle her business.

But still, today she'd found herself remembering last night and this morning. True to his word, he had not made love to her again, but he had held her, tasted her lips and given her pleasure another way. Namely with his mouth. He had soothed her body and brought it pleasure at the same time. Amazing.

She turned when her cell phone rang and quickly crossed the room to pick it up. It was her sister, Megan. "Megan, how are you doing?" She missed her sisters.

"I'm fine. I have Bailey here with me and she says hello. We miss you."

"And I miss you both, too," she said honestly. "What time is it there?" She placed her cell phone on speaker to put away the files spread all over her desk.

"Close to ten on Monday night. It's Tuesday there already, right?"

"Yes, Tuesday afternoon around four. Today was my first day on the job. Callum set a room up at the house for me to use as an office. I even have an administrative assistant. And speaking of administrative assistants, has the bank's security team contacted you about Niecee?"

"Yes, in fact I got a call yesterday. It seems she deposited the check in an account in Florida. They are working with that bank to stop payment. What's in your favor is that you acted right away. Most businesses that are the victims of embezzlement don't find out about the thefts until months later, and then it's too late to recover the funds. Niecee gave herself away when she left that note apologizing the next day. Had she been bright she would have called in sick a few days, waited for the check to clear and then confessed her sins. Now it looks like she'll be getting arrested."

Gemma let out a deep sigh. A part of her felt bad, but then what Niecee had done was wrong. The woman probably figured that because Gemma was a Westmoreland she had the money to spare. Well, she was wrong. Dillon and Ramsey had pretty much drilled into each of them to make their own way. Yes, they'd each been given one hundred acres and a nice trust fund when they'd turned twenty-one, but making sure they used that money responsibly was up to them. So far all of them had. Luckily, Bane had turned his affairs over to Dillon to handle. Otherwise, he would probably be penniless by now.

"Well, I regret that, but I can't get over what she did. Twenty thousand dollars is not small change."

A sound made Gemma turn around and she drew in a deep breath when she saw Callum standing there, leaning in the doorway. And from the expression on his face, she knew he'd been listening to her and Megan's conversation. How dare he! She wondered if he would mention it to Ramsey.

"Megan, I'll call you back later," she said, placing her phone off speaker. "Tell everyone I said hello and give them my love."

She ended the call and placed the phone back on her desk. "You're early."

"Yes, you might say that," he said, crossing his arms across his chest. "What's this about your administrative assistant embezzling money from you?"

Gemma threw her head back, sending hair flying over her shoulders. "You were deliberately eavesdropping on my conversation."

"You placed the call on speaker and I just happened to arrive while the conversation was going on."

"Well, you could have let me know you were here."

"Yes, I could have. Now answer the question about Niecee."

"No. It's none of your business," she snapped.

He strolled into the room toward her. "That's where you're wrong. It *is* my business, on both a business and a personal level."

A frown deepened her brow. "And how do you figure that?"

He came to a stop in front of her. "First of all, on a business level, before I do business with anyone I expect the company to be financially sound. In other words, Gemma, I figured that you had enough funds in your bank account to cover the initial outlay for this decorating job."

She placed her hands on her hips. "I didn't have to worry about that since you gave me such a huge advance."

"And what if I hadn't done that? Would you have been able to take the job here?"

Gemma didn't have to think about the answer to that. "No, but—"

"No buts, Gemma." He didn't say anything for a minute and it seemed as if he was struggling not to smile. That only fueled her anger. What did he find so amusing?

Before she could ask, he spoke. "And it's personal, Gemma, because it's you. I don't like the idea of anyone taking advantage of you. Does Ramsey know?"

Boy, that did it! "I own Designs by Gems—not Ramsey. It's my business and whatever problems crop up are *my* problems. I know I made a mistake in hiring Niecee. I see that now and I should have listened to Ramsey and Dillon and done a background check on her, as they suggested. I didn't and I regret it. But at least I'm—"

"Handling your business." He glanced at his watch. "Ready to go?" he asked, walking away and heading for the door, turning off the light switch in the process. "There's a nice restaurant not far from here that I think you'll like."

Gemma spun around to face him. "I'm not going anywhere with you. I'm mad."

Callum flashed her a smile. "Then get over it."

Gemma was too undone…and totally confused. "I won't be getting over it."

He nodded. "Okay, let's talk about it then."

She crossed her arms over her chest. "I don't want to talk about it, because it's none of your business."

Callum threw his head back and laughed. "We're back to that again?"

Gemma glared at him. "We need to get a few things straight, Callum."

He nodded. "Yes, we do." He walked back over to her. "I've already told you why it's my business and from a business perspective you see that I'm right, don't you?"

It took her a full minute, but she finally said, "Yes, all right. I see that. I'll admit that you are right from a business perspective. That's not the way I usually operate but…"

"You were robbing Peter to pay Paul, I know. However, I don't like being Peter or Paul. Now, as far as it being personal, *you* were right."

She lifted a brow. "I was?"

"Yes. It was your business and not Ramsey's concern. I admitted it and told you that you handled it. That was the end of it," he said.

She gave herself a mental shake, trying to keep up with him. He had scolded her on one hand, but complimented her way of handling things on the other. "So you won't mention it to Ramsey?"

"No. It's not my place to do that…unless your life is in danger or something equally as dire, and it's not." He looked down at her and smiled. "As I said, from the sound of the conversation you just had with Megan, you handled this matter in an expeditious manner. By all accounts, you will be getting your money back. Kudos for you."

A smile crossed Gemma's lips. She was proud of herself. "Yes, kudos for me." Her eyes narrowed. "And just what did you find amusing earlier?"

"How quickly you can get angry just for the sake of doing so. I'd heard about your unique temperament but never experienced it before."

"Did it bother you?"

"No."

Gemma frowned, not sure how she felt about that. In a way she liked that Callum didn't run for cover when her temper exploded, as it did at times. Zane, Derringer and the twins were known to have had a plate aimed at their heads once or twice, and knew to be ready to duck if they gave her sufficient cause.

"However, I would like you to make me a promise," he said, breaking into her thoughts.

She lifted a curious brow. "What?"

"Promise that if you ever find yourself in a bind again, financial or otherwise, you'll let me know."

She rolled her eyes. "I don't need another older brother, Callum."

He smiled and his teeth flashed a bright white against his brown skin. "There's no way you can think we have anything close to a brother-sister relationship after last night. But just in case you need a little reminder…"

He pulled her into his arms, lowered his head and captured her mouth with his.

Chapter 12

Gemma's face blushed with anticipation as she walked into Callum's condo. Dinner was fantastic, but she liked being back here alone with him.

"Are you tired, Gemma?"

He had to be kidding. She glanced over her shoulder and gave him a wry look. He was closing the door and locking it. "What makes you think that?"

"You were kind of quiet at dinner."

She chuckled. "Not hardly. I nearly talked your ears off."

"And I nearly talked yours off, too."

She shook her head. "No, you didn't. You were sharing how your day went, and basically, I was doing the same." *While sitting there nearly drooling over you from across the table.* Now that they were alone, she wondered if she would have to tell him what she wanted or if he already had a clue.

"So Kathleen worked out well for you?"

"Yes," she said, easing out of her shoes. "She's a sweetheart and so efficient. She was able to find all the fabric I need and the cost of shipping won't be bad. I really hadn't expected you to set up the office like that. Thanks again for the roses. They were beautiful."

"You thanked me already for the flowers, and I'm glad

you liked them. I plan to take you to the movies this weekend, but how would you like to watch a DVD now?"

She studied his features as he walked into the living room. Was that what he really wanted to do? "A movie on DVD sounds fine."

"You got a favorite?"

She chuckled as she dropped down on the sofa. "And if I do, should I just assume you have it here?"

He sat in the wingback chair across from her. "No, but I'm sure it can be ordered through my cable company. As I said, whatever you want, I will make it happen."

In that case. She stood from the sofa and in bare feet she slowly crossed the room and came to a stop between his opened legs. "Make love to me, Callum."

Callum didn't hesitate to pull Gemma down into his lap. He had been thinking about making love to her all day. That kiss in her office had whetted his appetite and now he was about to be appeased. But first he had to tell her something before he forgot.

"Mom called. She's invited you to have lunch and go shopping with her, my sister and my sisters-in-law next Friday."

Surprise shone on Gemma's face. She twisted around in his arms to look up at him. "She did?"

"Yes."

"But why? I'm here to decorate your house. Why would they want to spend time with me?"

Callum chuckled. "Why wouldn't they? You've never been to Australia and I gather from the conversations the other day they figured you like to shop like most other women."

"The same way men like watching sports. I understand that sports are just as popular here in this country as in the States."

"Yes, I played Australian rules football a lot growing

up. Not sure how my body would handle it now, though," he said, adjusting her in his lap to place the top of his chin on the crown of her head. "I also like playing cricket. One day I'm going to teach you how to play."

"Well, you must have plans to do that during the time I'm here, because once I return home it's back to tennis for me."

Callum knew Gemma played tennis and that she was good at it. But what stuck out more than anything was her mentioning returning home. He didn't intend for that to happen, at least not on a permanent basis. "How can you think of returning to Denver when you still have so much to do here?"

She smiled. "Hey, give me a break. Today was my first full day on the job. Besides, you hired Kathleen for me. She placed all the orders and I even hired the company to come in and hang the drapes and pictures. Everything is moving smoothly. Piece of cake. I'll have that place decorated and be out of here in no time."

He didn't say anything for a moment, thinking he definitely didn't like the sound of that. Then he turned her in his arms. "I think we got sidetracked."

She looked up at him. "Did we?"

"Yes. You wanted to make love."

She tilted her head. "Umm, did I?"

"Yes."

She shook her head, trying to hide a grin, which he saw anyway. "Sorry, your time is up."

He stood with her in his arms. "I don't think so."

Callum carried her over to the sofa and sat down with her in his arms. "We have more room here," he said, adjusting her body in his lap to face him. "Now tell me what you want again."

"I don't remember," she said, amusement shining in her gaze.

"Sounds like you need another reminder," he said, standing.

She wrapped her arms around his neck. "Now where are you taking me?"

"To the kitchen. I think I'd like you for dessert."

"What! You're kidding, aren't you?"

"No. Watch me."

And she did. Gemma sat on the kitchen counter, where he placed her, while he rummaged through his refrigerator looking for God knows what. But she didn't mind, since she was getting a real nice view of his backside.

"Don't go anywhere. I'll have everything I need in a sec," he called out, still bent over, scouring his fridge.

"Oh, don't worry, I'm not going anywhere. I'm enjoying the view," she said, smiling, her gaze still glued to his taut tush.

"The view is nice this time of night, isn't it?" he asked over his shoulder.

She grinned as she studied how the denim of his jeans stretched over his butt. He thought she was talking about the view of the ocean outside the window. "I think this particular view is nice anytime. Day or night."

"You're probably right."

"I know I am," Gemma said, fighting to keep the smile out of her voice.

Moments later Callum turned away from the refrigerator and closed the door with his hands full of items. He glanced over at Gemma. She was smiling. He arched a brow. "What's so funny?"

"Nothing. What you got there?"

"See for yourself," he said, placing all the items on the counter next to her.

She picked up a jar. "Cherries?"

A slow smile touched his lips at the same time she saw a hint of heat fill his green eyes. "My favorite fruit."

"Yeah, I'll bet."

She picked up another item. "Whipped cream?"

"For the topping."

She shook her head as she placed the whipped cream back on the counter and selected another item. "Nuts?"

"They go well with cherries," he said, laughing.

"You're awful."

"No, I'm not.

She picked up the final item. "Chocolate syrup?"

"That's a must," he said, rolling up his sleeve.

Gemma watched as he began taking the tops off all the containers. "So what are you going to do with all that stuff?"

He smiled. "You'll see. I told you that you're going to be my dessert."

She blinked when she read his thoughts. He was serious.

"Now for my fantasy," he said, turning to her and placing his hands on her knees as he stepped between them, widening her legs as he did so. He began unbuttoning her shirt and when he took it off her shoulders he neatly placed it on the back of the kitchen chair.

He reached out to unsnap the front of her bra, lifting a brow at its peach color. He'd watched her put it on this morning and when he asked her about it, she told him she liked matching undies.

"Nice color."

"Glad you like it."

Gemma couldn't believe it a short while later when she was sitting on Callum's kitchen counter in nothing but her panties. He then slid her into his arms. "Where are we going now?"

"Out on the patio."

"More room?"

"Yes, more room, and the temperature tonight is unusually warm."

He carried her through the French doors to place her on the chaise longue. "I'll be back."

"Okay." Anticipation was flowing through her veins and she could feel her heart thudding in her chest. She'd never considered herself a sexual being, but Callum was proving just how passionate she could be. At least with him. She had a pretty good idea just what he planned to do and the thought was inciting every cell in her body to simmer with desire. The thought that couples did stuff like this behind closed doors, actually had fun being together, being adventurous while making love, had her wondering what she'd been missing all these years.

But she knew she hadn't been missing anything because the men she'd dated in the past hadn't been Callum. Besides being drop-dead gorgeous, the man certainly had a way with women. At least he had a way with her. He had made her first time memorable; not only in giving her pleasure but in the way he had taken care of her afterwards.

And then there were the flowers he'd sent today. And then at dinner, she had enjoyed their conversation where not only had he shared how his day had gone, but had given her a lot of interesting information about his homeland. This weekend he had offered to take her sailing on his father's yacht. She was looking forward to that.

While sitting across from him during dinner, every little thing had boosted up her desire for him. She couldn't wait to return here to be alone with him. It could be the way he would smile at her over the rim of his wineglass, or the way he would reach across the table and touch her hand on occasion for no reason at all. They had ordered different entrées and he had hand-fed her some of his when she was curious as to how his meal tasted.

Callum returned and she watched as he placed all the items on the small table beside her. The patio was dark, except for the light coming in from the kitchen and the moonlight overhead. They had eaten breakfast on the patio this morning and she knew there wasn't a single building on either side of them, just the ocean.

He pulled a small stool over to where she lay on her back, staring up at him. "When will you be my dessert?" she tried asking in a calm voice, but found that to be difficult when she felt her stomach churning.

"Whenever you want. Just ask. I'll give you whatever you want."

He'd been telling her that so much that she was beginning to believe it. "The ocean sounds so peaceful and relaxing. You'd better hope I don't fall asleep," she warned.

"If you do, I'll wake you."

She looked up at him, met his gaze and felt his heat. She'd told him last night there were no limitations. There still weren't. It had taken her twenty-four years to get to this point and she intended to enjoy it for all it was worth. Callum was making this a wonderful experience for her and she appreciated him for being fascinating as well as creative.

He moved off the stool just long enough to lean over her to remove her panties. "Nice pair," he said, while easing the silky material down her thighs and legs.

"Glad you like them."

"I like them off you even better," he said, balling them up and standing to put them into the back pocket of his jeans. "Now for my dessert."

"Enjoy yourself."

"I will, sweetheart."

It seemed that her entire body responded to his use of that endearment. He meant nothing by it—she was certain of it. But still, she couldn't help how rapidly her heart was beating from hearing it and how her stomach was fluttering in response to it.

While she lay there, she watched as Callum removed

his shirt and tossed it aside before returning to his stool. He leaned close and she was tempted to reach out and run her fingertips across his naked chest, but then decided she wouldn't do that. This was his fantasy. He'd fulfilled hers last night.

"Now for something sweet, like you," he said, and she nearly jumped when she felt a warm, thick substance being smeared over her chest with his fingers and hands in a sensual and erotic pattern. When he moved to her stomach the muscles tightened as he continued rubbing the substance all over her belly, as if he was painting a design on her.

"What is it?"

"My name."

His voice was husky and in the moonlight she saw his tense features, the darkness of the eyes staring back at her, the sexy line of his mouth. All she could do was lie there and stare up at him speechlessly, trying to make sense of what he said. He was placing his name on her stomach as if he was branding her as his. She forced the thought from her mind, knowing he didn't mean anything by it.

"How does it feel?" he asked as his hand continued spreading chocolate syrup all over her.

"The chocolate feels sticky, but your hands feel good," she said honestly. He had moved his hands down past her stomach to her thighs.

He didn't say anything for a long moment, just continued to do what he was doing.

"And this is your fantasy?" she asked.

His lips curved into a slow smile that seemed to heat his gaze even more. "Yes. You'll see why in a moment."

When Callum was satisfied that he had smeared enough chocolate syrup over Gemma's body, he grabbed the can of whipped cream and squirted some around her nipples, outlined her belly button, completely covered her feminine mound, and made squiggly lines on her thighs and legs.

"Now for the cherries and nuts," he said, still holding her gaze.

He then proceeded to sprinkle her with nuts and place cherries on top of the whipped cream on her breasts, navel and womanly mound. In fact, he placed several on the latter.

"You look beautiful," he said, taking a step back and looking down at her to see just what he'd done.

"I'll take your word for it," she said, feeling like a huge ice-cream sundae. "I just hope there isn't a colony of ants around."

He laughed. "There isn't. Now to get it off you."

She knew just how he intended to do that, but nothing prepared her for the feel of his tongue when he began slowly licking her all over. Every so often he would lean up and kiss her, giving her a taste of the concoction that was smeared all around his mouth, mingling his tongue with hers. At one point he carried a cherry with his teeth, placed it in her mouth and together they shared the taste.

"Callum…"

Callum loved the sound of his name on her lips and as he lowered his mouth back down to her chest, he could feel the softness of her breasts beneath his mouth. And each nipple tasted like a delicious pebble wrapped around his tongue. Every time he took one into his mouth she shivered, and he savored the sensation of sucking on them.

He kissed his way down her stomach and when he came to the area between her legs, he looked up at her, met her gaze and whispered, "Now I will devour you."

"Oh, Callum."

He dropped to his knees in front of her and homed in to taste her intimately. She cried out his name the moment his tongue touched her and she grabbed hold of his hair to hold his mouth hostage. There was no need, since he didn't plan to go anyplace until he'd licked his fill. Every time his tongue stroked her clitoris, her body would tremble beneath his mouth.

She began mumbling words he was certain had no meaning, but hearing her speak incoherently told him her state of mind. It was tortured, like his. She was the only woman he desired. The only woman he loved.

Moments later when she bucked beneath his mouth when her body was ripped by a massive sensual explosion, he kept his tongue planted deep inside her, determined to give her all the pleasure she deserved. All the pleasure she wanted.

When the aftershocks of her orgasm had passed, he pulled away and began removing his jeans. And then he moved his body in position over hers, sliding between her open legs and entering her in one smooth thrust.

He was home. And he began moving, stroking parts of her insides that his tongue hadn't been able to reach, but his manhood could. And this way he could connect with all of her now. This way. Mating with her while breathing in her delicious scent, as the taste of her was still embedded in his mouth.

The magnitude of what they were sharing sent him reeling over the top, and he felt his own body beginning to explode. He felt his release shoot straight into her the moment he called out her name.

Instinctively, her body began milking him again, pulling everything out of him, making him moan in pleasure. And he knew this was just a part of what he felt for her. And it wasn't lust. It was everything love was based on— the physical and the emotional. And he hoped she would see it. Every day she was here he would show her both sides of love. He would share his body with her. He would share his soul. And he would continue to make her his.

He was tempted to tell her right then and there how he felt, let her know she was his soul mate, but he knew he couldn't. Not yet. She had to realize for herself that there was more between them than this. She had to realize and believe that she was the only woman for him.

He believed that would happen and, thankfully, he had a little time on his side to break down her defenses, to get her to see that all men weren't alike, and that he was the man destined to love her forever.

"So what do you think of this one, Gemma?" Mira Austell asked, showing Gemma the diamond earrings dangling from her ears.

"They're beautiful," Gemma said, and truly meant it.

The Austell ladies had picked her up around ten and it was almost four in the afternoon and they were still at it. Gemma didn't want to think about all the stores they had patronized or how many bags they had between the five of them.

Gemma had seen this gorgeous pair of sandals she just had to buy and also a party dress, since Callum had offered to take her to a club on the beach when she mentioned that she enjoyed dancing.

This particular place—an upscale jewelry store—was their last stop before calling it a day. Le'Claire suggested they stop here, since she wanted a new pair of pearl earrings.

"Gemma, Mira, come look at all these gorgeous rings," Le'Shaunda was saying, and within seconds they were all crowded around the glass case.

"I really like that one," Annette said, picking out a solitaire with a large stone.

"Umm, and I like that one," Le'Claire said, smiling. "I have a birthday coming up soon, so it's time to start dropping hints."

Gemma thought Callum's mother was beautiful and could understand how his father had fallen in love so fast.

And no wonder Todd gave her anything she wanted. But then Callum gave her anything she wanted as well. Like father, like son. Todd had trained his offspring well. Last weekend Callum had treated her to a picnic on the beach, and another one was planned for this weekend as well. She had enjoyed her time with him and couldn't help but appreciate the time and attention he gave to her when he really didn't have to do so.

"Gemma, which of these do you like the best?" Le'Claire asked.

Gemma pressed her nose to the glass case as she peered inside. All the rings were beautiful and no doubt expensive. But if she had to choose...

"That one," she said, pointing to a gorgeous four-carat, white-gold, emerald-cut ring. "I think that's simply beautiful."

The other ladies agreed, and each picked out their favorites. The store clerk even let everyone try them on to see how each ring looked on their hands. Gemma was amused by how the others said they would remind their husbands about those favorites when it got close to their birthdays.

"It's almost dinnertime, so we might as well go somewhere to get something to eat," Le'Shaunda said. "I know a wonderful restaurant nearby."

Le'Claire beamed. "That's a wonderful idea."

Gemma thought it was a wonderful idea as well, although she missed seeing Callum. He had begun joining her for lunch every day at her office, always bringing good sandwiches for her to eat and wine to drink. They usually went out to a restaurant in town for dinner. Tonight they planned to watch a movie and make love. Or they would make love and then watch a movie. She liked the latter better, since they could make love again after the movie.

"Did Callum mention anything to you about a hunting trip in a couple of weeks?" Annette asked.

Gemma smiled over at her. "Yes, he did. I understand all the men are leaving for a six-day trip."

"Yes," Mira said as if she was eager for Colin to be gone. The other woman glanced over at Gemma and explained. "Of course I'm going to miss my husband, but that's when we ladies get to do another shopping trip."

Everyone laughed and Gemma couldn't keep from laughing right along with them.

Chapter 13

"Hello," Gemma mumbled into the telephone receiver.

"Wake up, sleepy."

A smile touched Gemma's lips as she slowly forced her eyes fully open. "Callum," she whispered.

"Who else?"

She smiled sleepily. He had left two days ago on a hunting trip with his father and brothers and would be gone for another four days. "I've been thinking about you."

"I've been thinking about you, too, sweetheart. I miss you already," he said.

"And I miss you, too," she said, realizing at that moment just how much. He had taken her to a party at his friend's home last weekend and she had felt special walking in with him. And he'd never left her side. It was nice meeting some of the guys he'd gone to college with. And the night before leaving to go hunting he'd taken her to the movies again. He filled a lot of her time when she wasn't working, so yes, she did miss him already.

"That's good to hear. You had a busy day yesterday, right?"

She pulled herself up in bed. "Yes, but Kathleen and I were able to make sure everything would be delivered as planned."

"Don't forget, you promised to take a break and let me fly you to India when I get back."

"Yes, and I'm looking forward to it, although I hope there isn't a lot of turbulence on that flight."

"You never know, but you'll be with me and I'll take care of you."

Her smile widened. "You always do."

A few moments later they ended the call, and she fluffed her pillow and stretched out in the bed. It was hard to believe that she had been in Australia four weeks already. Four glorious weeks. She missed her family and friends back home, but Callum and his family were wonderful and treated her like she was one of them.

She planned to go shopping with his mother, sister and sisters-in-law again tomorrow, and then there would be a sleepover at Le'Claire's home. She genuinely liked the Austell women and had had some rather amusing moments when they'd shared just how they handled their men. It had been hilarious when Le'Claire even gave pointers to Le'Shaunda, who claimed her husband could be stubborn at times.

But nothing, Gemma thought, could top all the times she'd spent with Callum. They could discuss anything. When she'd received the call that Niecee had been arrested, she had let him handle it so that her emotions wouldn't stop her from making sure the woman was punished for what she had done. And then there were the flowers he continued to send her every week, and the "I'm thinking of you" notes that he would leave around the house for her to find. She stared up at the ceiling, thinking that Callum was definitely not like other men. The woman he married would be very lucky.

At that moment a sharp pain settled around her heart at the thought of any other woman with Callum, sharing anything close to what they had shared this past month. To know that another woman, his soul mate, would be living with him in the house she was decorating almost made her ill.

She eased to the edge of the bed, knowing why she felt that way. She had fallen in love with him. "Oh, no!"

She dropped back on the bed and covered her face with her hands. How did she let that happen? Although Callum wouldn't intentionally break her heart, he would break it just the same. How could she have fallen in love with him? She knew the answer without much thought. Callum was an easy man to love. But it wasn't meant for her to be the one to love him. He had told her about his soul mate.

She got out of bed and headed for the bathroom, knowing what she had to do. There was no way she would not finish the job she came here to do, but she needed to return home for at least a week or two to get her head screwed back on straight. Kathleen could handle things until she returned. And when she got back, she'd be capable of handling a relationship with Callum the way it should be handled. She would still love him, but at least she would have thought things through and come to the realization she couldn't ever be the number one woman in his life. She'd have to be satisfied with that.

A few hours later she had showered, dressed and packed a few of her things. She had called Kathleen and given her instructions as to what needed to be done in her absence, and assured the older woman that she would be back in a week or so.

Gemma decided not to call Callum to tell him she was leaving. He would wonder why she was taking off all of a sudden. She would think of an excuse to give him when she got home to Denver. She wiped the tears from her eyes. She had let the one thing happen to her that she'd always sworn would never happen.

She had fallen in love with a man who didn't love her.

Callum stood on the porch of the cabin and glanced all around. Nothing, he thought, was more beautiful than the Australian outback. He could recall the first time he'd come to this cabin as a child with his brothers, father and grandfather.

His thoughts drifted to Gemma. He knew for certain that she was his soul mate. The last month had been idyllic. Waking up with her in his arms every morning, making love with her each night, was as perfect as perfect could get. And he was waiting patiently for her to realize that she loved him, too.

It would be then that they would talk about it and he would tell her that he loved her as well, that he'd known for a while that she was the one, but had wanted her to come to that realization on her own.

Callum took a sip of his coffee. He had a feeling she was beginning to realize it. More than once over the past week he'd caught her staring at him with an odd look on her face, as if she was trying to figure out something. And at night when she gave herself to him, it was as if he would forever be the only man in her life. Just as, when he made love to her, he wanted her to believe that she would forever be the only woman in his.

"Callum. You got a call. It's Mom."

Morris's voice intruded on his thoughts and he reentered the cabin and picked up the phone. "Yes, Mom?"

"Callum, it's Gemma."

His heart nearly stopped beating. He knew the ladies had a shopping trip planned for tomorrow. "What's wrong with Gemma? What happened?"

"I'm not sure. She called and asked me to take her to the airport."

"Airport?"

"Yes. She said she had to return home for a while, and I could tell she'd been crying."

He rubbed his forehead. That didn't make any sense. He'd just spoken to her that morning and she was fine. She had two pregnant sisters-in-law and he hoped nothing had happened. "Did she say why she was leaving, Mom? Did she mention anything about a family crisis?"

"No, in fact I asked and she said it had nothing to do with her family."

Callum pulled in a deep breath, not understanding any of this.

"Have you told her yet that you're in love with her, Callum?"

"No. I didn't want to rush her and was giving us time to develop a relationship before doing that. I wanted her to see from my actions that I loved her and get her to admit to herself that she loved me, too."

"Now I understand completely," Le'Claire said softly.

"You do?"

"Yes."

"Then how about explaining things to me because I'm confused."

He heard his mother's soft chuckle. "You're a man, so you would be. I think the reason Gemma left is because she realizes that she loves you. She's running away."

Callum was even more confused. "Why would she do something like that?"

"Because if she loves you and you don't love her back then—"

"But I do love her back."

"But she doesn't know that. And if you explained about waiting for a soul mate the way you explained it to me, she's probably thinking it's not her."

The moment his mother's words hit home, Callum threw his head back in frustration and groaned. "I think you're right, Mom."

"I think I'm right, too. So what are you going to do?"

A smile cascaded across Callum's lips. "I'm going after my woman."

Chapter 14

Ramsey Westmoreland had been in the south pasture most of the day, but when he got home he'd heard from Chloe that Gemma was back. She'd called for Megan to pick her up at the airport. And according to what Megan had shared with Chloe, Gemma looked like she'd cried during the entire eighteen-hour flight.

He was about to place a call to Callum to find out what the hell had happened when he received a call from Colin saying Callum was on his way to Denver. The last thing Ramsey needed in his life was drama. He'd had more than enough during his affair with Chloe.

But here he was getting out of his truck to go knock on the door to make sure Gemma was all right. Callum was on his way and Ramsey would leave it to his best friend to handle Gemma from here on out because his sister could definitely be Miss Drama Queen. And seeing that she was here at Callum's cabin and not at her own place spoke volumes, whether she knew it or not. However, for now he would play the dumb-ass, just to satisfy his curiosity. And Chloe's.

He knocked on the door and it was yanked open. For a moment he was taken aback. Gemma looked like a mess, but he had enough sense not to tell her that. Instead, he took off his hat, passed by her and said in a calm tone. "Back from Australia early, aren't you?"

"Just here for a week or two. I'm going back," she said in a strained voice, which he pretended not to hear.

"Where's Callum? I'm surprised he let you come by yourself, knowing how afraid you are of flying. Was there a lot of turbulence?"

"I didn't notice."

Probably because you were too busy crying your eyes out. He hadn't seen her look like this since their parents' funeral. Ramsey leaned against a table in the living room and glanced around. He then looked back at her. "Any reason you're here and not at your own place, Gemma?"

He knew it was the wrong question to ask when suddenly her mouth quivered and she started to sob. "I love him, but he doesn't love me. I'm not his soul mate. But that's okay. I can deal with it. I just didn't want to ever cry over a man the way those girls used to do when Zane and Derringer broke up with them. I swore that would *never* happen to me. I swore I would never be one of them and fall for a guy who didn't love me back."

Ramsey could only stare at her. She actually thought Callum didn't love her? He opened his mouth to tell her just how wrong she was, then suddenly closed it. It was not his place to tell her anything. He would gladly let Callum deal with this.

"Sorry, Ram, but I need to be alone for a minute." He then watched as she quickly walked into the bedroom and closed the door behind her.

Moments later Ramsey was outside, about to open the door to his truck to leave when a vehicle pulled up. He sighed in relief when he saw Callum quickly getting out of the car.

"Ramsey, I went to Gemma's place straight from the airport and she wasn't there. Where the hell is she?"

Ramsey leaned against his truck. Callum looked like he hadn't slept for a while. "She's inside and I'm out of here. I'll let you deal with it."

Callum paused before entering his cabin. Ramsey had jumped into his truck and left in a hurry. Had Gemma trashed his place or something? Drawing in a deep breath, he removed his hat before slowly opening the door.

He strolled into the living room and glanced around. Everything was in order, but Gemma was nowhere in sight. Then he heard a sound coming from the bedroom. He perked up his ears. It was Gemma and she was crying. The sound tore at his heart.

Placing his hat on the rack, he quickly crossed the room and opened his bedroom door. And there she was, lying in his bed with her head buried in his pillows.

He quietly closed the door behind him and leaned against it. Although he loved her and she loved him, he was still responsible for breaking her heart. But, if nothing else, he'd learned over the past four weeks that the only way to handle Gemma was to let her think she was in control, even when she really wasn't. And even if you had to piss her off a little in the process.

"Gemma?"

She jerked up so fast he thought she was going to tumble out of the bed. "Callum! What are you doing here?" She stood quickly, but not before giving one last swipe to her eyes.

"I could ask you the same thing, since this is my place," he said, crossing his arms over his chest.

She threw her hair over her shoulder. "I knew you weren't here," she said as if that explained everything. It didn't.

"So you took off from Australia, left a job unfinished,

got on a plane although you hate flying to come here. For what reason, Gemma?"

She lifted her chin and glared at him. "I don't have to answer that, since it's none of your business."

Callum couldn't help but smile at that. He moved away from the door to stand in front of her. "Wrong. It is my business. Both business and personal. It's business because I hired you to do a job and you're not there doing it. And it's personal because it's you and anything involving you is personal to me."

She lifted her chin a little higher. "I don't know why."

"Well, then, Gemma Westmoreland, let me explain it to you," he said, leaning in close to her face. "It's personal because you mean everything to me."

"I can't and I don't," she snapped. "Go tell that to the woman you're going to marry. The woman who is your soul mate."

"I am telling that to her. You are her."

She narrowed her eyes. "No, I'm not."

"Yes, you are. Why do you think I hung around here for three years working my tail off? Not because I needed the job, but because the woman I love, the woman who's had my heart since the first day I saw her, was here. The woman I knew the moment I saw her that she was destined to be mine. Do you know how many nights I went to this bed thinking of you, dreaming of you, patiently waiting for the day when I could make you belong to me in every possible way?"

He didn't give her a chance to answer him. Figured she probably couldn't anyway with the shocked look on her face, so he continued. "I took you to Australia for two reasons. First, I knew you could do the job, and secondly, I wanted you on my turf so I could court you properly. I wanted to show you that I was a guy worth your love and trust. I wanted you to believe in me, believe that I would never break your heart because, no matter what you thought, I was always going to be there for you. To give you every single thing you wanted. I love you."

There, he had his say and he knew it was time to brace himself when she had hers. She shook her head as if to mentally clear her mind and then she glanced back up at him. And glared.

"Are you saying that I'm the reason you hung around here and worked for Ramsey and that you took me to Australia to decorate your house and to win me over?"

She had explained it differently, but it all came down to the same thing. "Yes, that about sums it all up, but don't forget the part about loving you."

She threw her hands up in the air and then began angrily pacing the room while saying, "You put me through all this for nothing! You had me thinking I was decorating that house for another woman. You had me thinking that we were just having an affair that would lead nowhere."

She stopped pacing and her frown deepened. "Why didn't you tell me the truth?"

He crossed the room to stand in front of her. "Had I told you the truth, sweetheart, you would not have been ready to hear it, nor would you have believed it. You would have given me more grief than either of us needed," he said softly.

A smile then crossed his lips. "I had threatened to kidnap you, but Ramsey thought that was going a little too far."

Her eyes widened. "Ramsey knew?"

"Of course. Your brother is a smart man. There's no way I could have hung around here for three years sniffing around his sister and he not know about it."

"Sniffing around me? I want you to know that I—"

He thought she'd talked enough and decided to shut her up by pulling her into his arms and taking her mouth. The moment his tongue slid between her lips he figured she would either bite it or accept it. She accepted it and it began tangling with hers.

Callum deepened the kiss and tightened his hold on Gemma and she responded by wrapping her arms around his neck, standing on tiptoes and participating in their kiss the way he'd shown her how to do. He knew they still had a lot to talk about, and he would have to go over it again to satisfy her, but he didn't care. He would always give her what she wanted.

Callum forced his mouth from hers, but not before taking a quick lick around her lips. He then rested his forehead against hers and pulled in a deep breath. "I love you, Gemma," he whispered against her temple. "I loved you from the moment I first saw you. I knew you were the one, my true soul mate."

Gemma dropped her head to Callum's chest and wrapped her arms around his waist, breathing in his scent and glowing in his love. She was still reeling from his profession of love for her. Her heart was bursting with happiness.

"Gemma, will you marry me?"

She snatched her head up to look into his eyes. And there she saw in their green depths what she hadn't seen before. Now she did.

"Yes, I'll marry you, but..."

Callum chuckled. "There's a but?"

"Yes. I want to be told every day that you love me."

He rolled his eyes. "You've hung around my mom, sister and sisters-in-law too much."

"Whatever."

"I don't have a problem doing that. No problem at all." He sat down on the bed and pulled her down into his lap. "You never answered my question. What are you doing here and not at your place?"

She lowered her head, began toying with the buttons on his shirt and then glanced up and met his gaze. "I know it sounds crazy, but I came home to get over you, but once I got here I had to come here to feel close to you. I was going to sleep in this bed tonight because I knew this is where you slept."

Callum tightened his arms around her. "I got news for you, Gemma. You're *still* sleeping in this bed tonight. With me."

He eased back on the bed and took her with him, covering her mouth with his, kissing her in a way that let her know how much love he had for her. He adjusted their bodies so he could remove every stitch of her clothing and then proceeded to undress himself.

He returned to the bed and pulled her into his arms, but not before taking a small box from the pocket of his jacket. He placed his knee on the bed and pulled her into his arms to slide a ring on her finger. "For the woman who took my breath away the moment I saw her. To the woman I love."

Tears clouded Gemma's eyes when she gazed down at the beautiful ring Callum had placed on her finger. Her breath nearly stopped. She remembered the ring. She had seen it that day when she'd gone shopping with the Austell women and they had stopped by that jewelry store. Gemma had mentioned to Le'Claire how much she'd liked this particular one.

"Oh, Callum. Even your mom knows?" She had to fight back tears as she continued to admire her ring.

"Sweetheart, everybody knows," he said, grinning. "I had sworn them to secrecy. It was important for me to court you the way you deserved. You hadn't dated a whole lot, and I wanted to show you that not all guys were heartbreakers."

She wrapped her arms around his neck. "And you did court me. I just didn't know that's what you were doing. I just figured you were being nice, sending me those flowers, taking me to the movies and those picnic lunches on the beach. I just thought you were showing me how much you appreciated me…"

"In bed?"

"Yes."

"And that's what I was afraid of," he said, pulling her closer to him. "I didn't want you to think it was all about sex, because it wasn't. When I told you I would give you anything and everything you wanted, Gemma, I meant it. All you had to do was ask for it, even my love, which is something you already had."

She rested her head on his bare chest for a moment and then she lifted her head to look back at him. "Do you think you wasted three years living here, Callum?"

He shook his head. "No. Being here gave me a chance to love you from afar while watching you grow and mature into the beautiful woman you are today. I saw you gain your independence and then wear it like a brand of accomplishment in everything you did. I was so proud of you when you landed that big contract with the city, because I knew exactly what you could do. That gave me the idea to buy that house for you to decorate. That will be our home and the condo will become our private retreat when we want to spend time at the beach."

He paused a moment. "I know you'll miss your family and all, and—"

Gemma reached up and placed a finger to his lips. "Yes, I will miss my family, but my home will be with you. We will come back and visit and that will be good enough for me. I want to be in Sydney with you."

Callum didn't say anything for a moment and then asked. "What about your business here?"

Gemma smiled. "I'm closing it. I've already opened another shop in Sydney, thanks to you. Same name but different location."

Her smile widened. "I love you, Callum. I want to be

your wife and have your babies and I promise to always make you happy."

"Oh, Gemma." He reached out and cupped her face with both hands, lightly brushing his lips against hers before taking it in a hard kiss, swallowing her breath in the process.

He shifted to lie down on the bed and took her with him, placing her body on top of his while he continued to kiss her with a need that made every part of his body feel sensitive.

He tore his mouth away from hers to pull in a much-needed breath, but she fisted her hands in his hair to bring his face closer, before nibbling on his lips and licking around the corners of his mouth. And when he released a deep moan, she slid her tongue into his mouth and begin kissing him the way she'd gotten used to him kissing her.

Callum felt his control slipping and knew this kiss would be imprinted on his brain forever. He deepened the kiss, felt his engorged sex press against the apex of her thighs, knowing just what it wanted. Just what it needed.

Just what it was going to get.

He pulled his mouth away long enough to adjust her body over his. While staring into her eyes, he pushed upward and thrust into her, immediately feeling her heat as he buried himself deep in her warmth. He pulled out and thrust in again while the hard nipples of her breasts grazed his chest.

And then she began riding him, moving her body on top of his in a way that had him catching his breath after every stroke. Together, they rode, they gave and took, mated in a way that touched everything inside of him; had him chanting her name over and over.

Then everything seemed to explode and he felt her body when it detonated. He soon followed, but continued hammering home, getting all he could and making her come again.

"Callum!"

"That's it, my love, feel the pleasure. Feel our love."

And then he leaned up and kissed her, took her mouth with a hunger that should already have been appeased. But he knew he would always want this. He would always want her, and he intended to never let her regret the day she'd given him her heart.

Totally sated, Gemma slowly opened her eyes and, like so many other times over the past weeks, Callum was in bed with her, and she was wrapped in his embrace. She snuggled closer and turned in his arms to find him watching her with satisfied passion in the depth of his green eyes.

She smiled at him. "I think we broke the bed."

He returned her smile and tightened his arms around her. "Probably did. But it can be fixed."

"If not, we can stay at my place," she offered.

"That will work."

At that moment the phone rang and he shifted their bodies to reach and pick it up. "That's probably Mom, calling to make sure things between us are all right."

He picked up the phone. "Hello."

He nodded a few times. "Okay, we're on our way."

He glanced over at Gemma and smiled. "That was Dillon. Chloe's water broke and Ramsey rushed her to the hospital. Looks like there's going to be a new Westmoreland born tonight."

It didn't take long for Callum and Gemma to get to the hospital, and already it was crowded with Westmorelands. It was almost 3:00 a.m. If anyone was curious as to why they were all together at that time of the morning, no one mentioned it.

"The baby is already here," Bailey said, excited. "We have a girl, just like we wanted."

Callum couldn't help throwing his head back and laughing. Good old Ram had a daughter.

"How's Chloe?" Gemma asked.

"Ramsey came out a few moments ago and said she's fine," Megan said. "The baby is a surprise."

"Yes, we didn't expect her for another week," Dillon said grinning. He glanced over at his pregnant wife, Pam, and smiled as he pulled her closer to him. "That makes me nervous."

"Has anyone called and told Chloe's father?"

"Yes," Chloe's best friend, Lucia, said smiling. "He's a happy grandpa and he'll be here sometime tomorrow."

"What's the baby's name?" Callum asked.

It was Derringer who spoke up. "They are naming her Susan after Mom. And they're using Chloe's mom's name as her middle name."

Gemma smiled. She knew Chloe had lost her mother at an early age, too. "Oh, that's nice. Our parents' first grand. They would be proud."

"They *are* proud," Dillon said, playfully tapping her nose.

"Hey, is this an engagement ring?" Bailey asked loudly, grabbing Gemma's hand.

Gemma glanced up at Callum and smiled lovingly. "Yes, we're getting married."

Cheers went up in the hospital waiting room. The Westmorelands had a lot to celebrate.

Zane glanced over at Dillon and Pam. "I guess now we're depending on you two to keep us male Westmorelands in the majority."

"Yeah," Derringer agreed.

"You know the two of you could find ladies to marry and start making your own babies," Megan said sweetly to her brothers. Her suggestion did exactly what she'd expected it to do—zip their lips.

Callum pulled Gemma closer into his arms. They shared a look. They didn't care if they had boys or girls—they just wanted babies. There were not going to be any hassles getting a big family out of them.

"Happy?" Callum asked.

"Extremely," she whispered.

Callum looked forward to when they would be alone again and he bent and told her just what he intended to do when they got back to the cabin.

Gemma blushed. Megan shot her sister a look. "You okay, Gem?"

Gemma smiled, glanced up at Callum and then back at her sister. "Yes, I couldn't be better."

Epilogue

There is nothing like a Westmoreland wedding, and this one was extra special because guests came from as far away as Australia and the Middle East. Gemma glanced out at the single ladies, waiting to catch her bouquet. She turned her back to the crowd, closed her eyes and threw it high over her head.

When she heard all the cheering, she turned around and smiled. It had been caught by Lucia Conyers, Chloe's best friend. She glanced across the room and looked at the two new babies. As if Susan's birth had started a trend, Dillon and Pam's son, Denver, came early, too.

"When can we sneak away?"

"You've waited three years. Another three hours won't kill you," she jokingly replied to her husband of two hours.

"Don't be so sure about that," was his quick response.

Their bags were packed and he was going to take her to India, as they'd planned before. Then they would visit Korea and Japan. She wanted to get decorating ideas with a few Asian pieces.

Callum took his wife's hand in his as they moved around the ballroom. He had been introduced to all the Atlanta Westmorelands before when he was invited to the Westmoreland family reunion as a guest. Now he would attend the next one as a bona fide member of the Westmoreland clan.

"How soon do you want to start making a baby?"

Gemma almost choked on her punch. He gave her a few pats on the back and grinned. "Didn't mean for you to gag."

"Can we at least wait until we're alone?"

"To talk about it or to get things started?"

Gemma chuckled as she shook her head. "Why do I get the feeling there will never be a dull moment with you?"

He pulled her closer to him. "Because there won't be. Remember I'm the one who knows what a Westmoreland wants. At least I know what my Westmoreland wants."

Gemma wrapped her arms around his neck. "I'm an Austell now," she said proudly.

"Oh, yes, I know. And trust me—I will never let you forget it."

Callum then pulled her into his arms and in front of all their wedding guests, he kissed her with all the love flowing in his heart. He had in his arms everything he'd ever wanted.

* * * * *

A WIFE FOR
A WESTMORELAND

Chapter 1

Lucia Conyers's heart was beating like crazy as she made a sharp turn around the curve while the wheels of her SUV barely gripped the road. She knew she should slow down, but couldn't. The moment she'd heard that Derringer Westmoreland had been taken to the emergency room due to an injury he sustained after being thrown from a horse, a part of her had nearly died inside.

It didn't matter that most of the time Derringer acted as though he didn't know she existed or that he had a reputation in Denver as a ladies' man—although she doubted the women he messed around with could really be classified as ladies. Derringer was one of Denver's heartthrobs, a hottie if ever there was one.

But what did matter, although she wished otherwise, was that she loved him and would probably always love him. She'd tried falling out of love with him several times and just couldn't do it.

Not even four years of attending a college in Florida had changed her feelings for him. The moment she had returned to Denver and he had walked into her father's paint store to make a purchase, she'd almost passed out from a mixture of lust and love.

Surprisingly, he had remembered her. He'd welcomed her back to town and asked her about school. But he hadn't asked her out, or offered to share a drink somewhere for old times' sake. Instead, he had gathered up the merchandise he'd come to the store to buy and left.

Her obsession with him had started back in high school when she and his sister Megan had worked on a science project together. Lucia would never forget the day that Megan's brother had come to pick them up from the library. She'd almost passed out when she first laid eyes on the handsome Derringer Westmoreland.

She thought she'd died and gone to heaven, and when they were introduced, he smiled at her, showing a pair of dimples that should be outlawed on anyone, especially a man. Her heart had melted then and there and hadn't solidified since. That introduction had taken place a few months after her sixteenth birthday. Now she was twenty-nine and she still got goose bumps whenever she thought about that first meeting.

Ever since her best friend, Chloe, had married Derringer's brother Ramsey, she saw more of Derringer, but nothing had changed. Whenever he saw her he was always nice to her. But she knew he really didn't see her as a woman he would be interested in.

So why wasn't she getting on with her life? Why was she risking it now by taking the roads to his place like a madwoman, needing to see for herself that he was still in one piece? When she'd gotten the news, she'd rushed to the hospital only to receive word from Chloe that he'd been released and was now recuperating at home.

He would probably wonder why she, of all people, was showing up at his place to check on him. She wouldn't be surprised if some woman was already there waiting on him hand and foot. But at the moment it didn't matter. Nothing mattered but to make sure for herself that Derringer was okay. Even the threat of possible thunderstorms this evening hadn't kept her away. She hated thunderstorms, and yet she had left her home to check on a man who barely knew she was alive.

It was a really stupid move, but she continued to speed down the road, deciding she would consider the foolishness of her actions later.

The loud sound of thunder blasting across the sky practically shook the house and awakened Derringer. He immediately felt a sharp pain slice through his body, the first since he'd taken his pain medication, which meant it was time to take more.

Wrenching at the pain, he slowly pulled himself up in bed, reached across the nightstand and grabbed the pills his sister Megan had laid out for him. She'd said not to take more before six, but a quick glance at his clock said that it was only four and he needed the relief now. He was aching all over and his head felt as if it had split in two. He felt sixty-three instead of a mere thirty-three.

He had been on Sugar Foot's back less than three minutes when the mean-spirited animal had sent him flying. More than his ego had gotten bruised, and each and every time he breathed against what felt like broken ribs he was reminded of it.

Derringer eased back down onto the bed and lay flat on his back. He stared at the ceiling, waiting for the pain pills to kick in.

Derringer's Dungeon.

Lucia slowed her truck when she came to the huge wooden marker in the road. Any other time she would have found it amusing that each of the Westmorelands had marked their property with such fanciful names. Already she had passed Jason's Place, Zane's Hideout, Canyon's Bluff, Stern's Stronghold, Riley's Station and Ramsey's Web. She'd heard when each Westmoreland reached the age of twenty-five they inherited a one-hundred-acre tract of land in this part of the state. That was why all the West-morelands lived in proximity to each other.

She nervously gnawed on her bottom lip, finally thinking she might have made a mistake in coming here when she pulled into the yard and saw the huge two-story structure. This was her first time at Derringer's Dungeon and from what she'd heard, most women only came by way of an invite.

So what was she doing here?

She brought her car to a stop and cut off the engine and just sat there a moment as reality set in. She had acted on impulse and of course on love, but the truth of the matter was that she had no business being here. Derringer was probably in bed resting. He might even be on medication. Would he be able to come to the door? If he did, he would probably look at her as if she had two heads for wanting to check on him. In his book they were acquaintances, not even friends.

She was about to back out and leave, when she noticed the rain had started to come down harder and a huge box that had been left on the steps of the porch was getting wet. The least she could do was to move it to an area on the porch where the rain couldn't touch it.

Grabbing her umbrella out of the backseat, she hurriedly got out of the truck and ran toward the porch to move the box closer to the door. She jumped at the sound of thunder and drew in a sharp breath when a bolt of lightning barely missed the top of her head.

Remembering what Chloe had once told her about how the Westmoreland men were notorious for not locking their doors, she tried the doorknob and saw what her best friend had said was true. The door was not locked.

Slowly opening the door, she stuck her head in and called out in a whisper in case he was downstairs sleeping on the sofa instead of upstairs. "Derringer?"

When he didn't answer, she decided she might as well

bring the box inside. The moment she entered the house, she glanced around, admiring his sister Gemma's decorating skills. Derringer's home was beautiful, and the floor-to-ceiling windows took full advantage of the mountain view. She was about to ease back out the door and lock it behind her when she heard a crash followed by a bump and then a loud curse.

Acting on instinct, she took the stairs two at a time and stumbled into several guest bedrooms before entering what had to be the master bedroom. It was decorated in a more masculine theme than all the others. She glanced around and then she saw him lying on the floor as if he'd fallen out of bed.

"Derringer!"

She raced over to him and knelt down beside him, trying to ignore the fact that the only clothing he had on was a pair of black briefs. "Derringer? Are you all right?" she asked, a degree of panic clearly in her voice. "Derringer?"

He slowly opened his eyes and she couldn't stop the fluttering of her heart when she gazed down into the gorgeous dark depths. The first thing she noticed was they were glassy, as if he'd taken one drink too many...or probably one pill too many. She then took a deep breath when a slow smile touched the corners of his lips and those knock-a-girl-off-her-feet dimples appeared in his cheeks.

"Well, now, aren't you a pretty thing," he said in slurred speech. "What's your name?"

"Puddin' Tame," she replied smartly. His actions confirmed he'd evidently taken one pill too many since he was acting as if he'd never seen her in his life.

"That's a real nice name, sweetheart."

She rolled her eyes. "Whatever you say, cowboy. Would you like to explain why you're down here and not up there?" She motioned toward his bed.

"That's easy enough to answer. I went to the bathroom and when I got back, someone moved the bed and I missed it."

She tried keeping the smile from her face. "You sure did miss it. Come on and hold on to me while I help you back into it."

"Someone might move it again."

"I doubt it," she said, grinning, while thinking even when he was under the influence of medication, the deep, husky sound of his voice could do things to her. Make the nipples of her breasts strain against her damp shirt. "Come on, you have to be hurting something awful."

He chuckled. "No, in fact I feel good. Good enough to try riding Sugar Foot again."

She shook her head. "Not tonight you won't. Come on, Derringer, let me help you up and get you back in bed."

"I like it down here."

"Sorry, pal, but you can't stay down here. You either let me help you up or I'll call one of your brothers to help you."

Now it was he who shook his head. "I don't want to see any of them again for a while. All they know how to say is, I told you so."

"Well maybe next time you'll listen to them. Come on."

It took several attempts before she was able to help Derringer to his feet. It wasn't easy to steer him to the bed, and she suddenly lost her balance and found herself tumbling backward onto his bed with him falling on top of her.

"I need you to shift your body a little to get off me, Derringer," she said when she was able to catch her breath.

He flashed those sexy dimples again and spoke in a voice throaty with arousal. "Um, why? I like being on top of you, Puddin'. You feel good."

She blinked and then realized the extent of her situation. She was in bed—Derringer's bed—and he was sprawled on top of her. It didn't take much to feel the bulge of his erection through his briefs that was connecting with the area between her legs. A slow burn began inching from that very spot and spreading all through her, entering her bloodstream and making her skin burn all over. And if that wasn't bad enough, the nipples of her breasts, which were already straining, hardened like pebbles against his bandaged chest.

As if sensing her body's reaction to their position, he lifted his face to stare down at her and the glassy eyes that snagged hers were so drenched with desire that her breath got caught in her throat. Something she'd never felt before, a pooling of heat, settled between her legs, wetting her panties, and she watched his nostrils flare in response to her scent.

The air between them was crackling more than the thunder and lightning outside, and his chest seemed to rise and fall with each and every beat of her heart.

Fearing her own rapid reaction to their predicament, she made an attempt to gently shove him off her, but found she was no match for his solid weight.

"Derringer…"

Instead of answering her, he reached up and cupped her face into his hands as if her mouth was water he needed to sip, and before she could turn her mouth away from his, with perfect aim, he lowered his mouth and began devouring hers.

Derringer figured he had to be dreaming, and if he was, then this was one delusion he didn't care to ever wake up from. Feasting on Puddin' Tame's lips was the epitome of sensual pleasure. Molded perfectly, they were hot and moist. And the way he had plunged his tongue inside her mouth, devouring hers was the sort of fantasy wet dreams were made of.

Somewhere in the back of his lust-induced mind he remembered getting thrown off a horse; in that case, his body should be in pain. However, the only ache he was feeling was the one in his groin that signaled a need so great his body was all but trembling inside.

Who was this woman and where did she come from? Was he supposed to know her? Why was she enticing him to do things he shouldn't do? A part of him felt that he wasn't in his right mind, but then another part didn't give a damn if he was in his wrong mind. The only thing he knew for sure was that he wanted her. He could eat her alive and wouldn't mind testing that theory to see if he really could.

He shifted his body a little and brought her in the center of the bed with him. He lifted his mouth only slightly off hers to whisper huskily against her moist lips, "Damn, Puddin', you feel good."

And then his mouth was back on hers, sucking on her tongue as if he was a man who needed to taste her as much as he needed to breathe, and what was so shocking to him at that moment was that he was convinced that he did.

Lucia knew she had to put a stop to what she and Derringer were doing. He was delirious and didn't even know who she was. But it was hard to stop him when her body was responding to everything he was doing to it. Her mouth had never been kissed like this before. No man had consumed her with so much pleasure for her not to think straight. Never had she known a woman could want a man with such magnitude as she wanted Derringer. She had always loved him, but now she wanted him with a need that had been foreign to her.

Until now.

"I want you, Puddin'..."

She blinked as he slightly leaned up off her and the reality of the moment hit her. Although he was delusional, Lucia realized that the honorable part of Derringer would not force her into doing anything she didn't want to do. Now was her chance to slide from beneath him and leave.

Chances were, he wouldn't even remember anything about tonight.

But something wouldn't let her flee. It kept her rooted in place as she stared up at him, caught in a visual exchange that not only entrapped her sight but also her mind. A part of her knew this would be the one and only time she would have his attention like this. Sadly, it would be the one and only time he would want her. She pushed to the back of her mind that it had taken an overdose of pain medication to get him to this state.

If she didn't love him so much, she probably would have been able to fight this sexual pull, but love combined with lust was a force she couldn't fight, and a part of her truly didn't want to. She would be thirty in ten months and as of yet, she hadn't experienced how it would feel to be with a man. It was about time she did and it might as well be with the one and only man she'd ever loved.

She would take tonight into her soul, cradle it in her heart and keep it safe in the deep recesses of her brain. And when she saw him again she would have a secret he wouldn't know about, although he would have been the main person responsible for making it happen.

Captured by his deep, dark gaze, she knew it was only a matter of minutes before he took her silence as consent. Now that she'd made up her mind about what she wanted to do, she didn't want to wait even that long. And as more liquid heat coiled between her legs, she lifted her arms to wrap around his neck and tilted her mouth to his. The moment she did, pleasure between them exploded and plunged her into a mirage of sensations that she'd never even dreamed about.

He began kissing her senseless and in her lust-induced mind she was barely aware of him pulling her blouse over her head and removing her lace bra from her body. But she knew the exact moment he latched on to a nipple and eased it between heated lips and began sucking on it as though it was just for his enjoyment.

Waves of pleasures shot through every part of her as if she'd been hit with an atomic missile that detonated on impact. She caught his head between her hands to keep his mouth from going anywhere but on her. Several moans she hadn't known she was capable of making eased from her lips and she couldn't help but writhe the lower part of her body against him, needing to feel the hardness of his erection between her thighs.

As if he wanted more, she knew the moment his fingers eased up her skirt and tracked their way to the part of her that was burning more than any other part—her moist, hot center. He slid one hand beneath the edge of her panties and, as if his finger knew exactly what it was after, it slowly and diligently trekked toward her throbbing clitoris.

"Derringer!"

Her entire body began trembling and with all the intent of a man on a mission he began stroking her with fingers that should be outlawed right along with his dimples. Her womanly core was getting more attention than it had ever gotten before, and she could feel sensations building up inside her at such a rapid rate she was feeling dizzy.

"I want you," he said in a low, guttural tone. And then he kissed her again in a deep, drugging exchange that had him sliding his tongue all over her mouth, tasting her as if doing so was his right. Just the thought made her powerless to do anything other than accept his seduction with profound pleasure.

She was so into the kiss that she hadn't realized he had worked his briefs down his legs and had removed her panties, until she felt them flesh to flesh. His skin felt hot against hers and the iron-steel feel of his thighs resting over hers was penetrating through to every pore in her body.

And when he broke the kiss to ease his body over hers,

she was so overcome with desire that she was rendered powerless to stop him.

He lowered his eyes to her breasts and smiled before his eyes slowly returned to her face and snagged her gaze. The look he gave her at that moment was so sexual that she was willing to convince herself that she was the only woman on earth he'd ever given it to. And she was just that far gone to believe it.

Then he leaned down and captured her mouth at the same time he thrust into her body. She couldn't help but cry out from the pain and, as if he sensed what had happened and just what it meant, his body went completely still. He eased his mouth away from hers and glanced down at her while still deeply embedded within her. Not sure just what thoughts were going through his mind about her virginal state and not really wanting to know, she reached up and wrapped her arms around him. And when she began using her tongue to kiss him the way he'd done to her earlier, she felt his body tremble slightly before he began moving inside her. The first time he did so, she thought she would come apart, but as his body began thrusting into hers, smoldering heat from him was being transferred to her, building a fire she could not contain any longer.

He released her mouth long enough for her to call his name. "Derringer!"

He was devouring her in a way she'd never been devoured before and she couldn't help but cry out as his tongue took over. The lower part of him was sending waves of pleasure crashing through her that had her sucking in sharp breaths.

She had heard—mainly from Chloe during one of their infamous girl chats—that making love to a man, especially one you loved, was a totally rewarding and satisfying experience. But no one told her that it could be so mind-consuming and pleasurable. Or that it could literally curl your toes. Maybe Chloe had told her these things and she hadn't believed her. Well, now she believed. And with each hard plunge into her body, Derringer was making all the fantasies she'd ever had of him a reality.

He released her mouth to look down at her while he kept making love to her, riding her the way he rode those horses he tamed. He was good. And he was also greedy. To keep up with him, she kept grinding her hips against his as sensations within her intensified to a degree that she knew she couldn't handle much longer. She cried out again and again as sensations continued to spiral through her.

And then something happened that had never happened to her before and she knew what it was the moment she felt it. He drove deeper and deeper into her, riding her right into a climax of monumental proportions. He lifted his head and met her gaze and the dark orbs gazing at her pushed her even more over the edge.

And when he whispered the name Puddin', thinking it was hers, she accepted it because it had sounded so good coming from him, and it was all she needed to hear to push her into her very first orgasm.

"Derringer!"

He lowered his head again and his tongue slid easily inside her mouth. She continued to grind against him, accepting everything he was giving. Moments later, after breaking off the kiss, he threw his head back and whispered the name again in a deep guttural tone, and he continued to stroke her into sweet oblivion.

Lucia slowly opened her eyes while wondering just how long she'd slept. The last thing she remembered was dropping her head onto the pillow. She'd been weak, spent and totally and thoroughly satisfied after making love to the sexiest man to walk the face of the earth.

He was no longer on top of her, but was asleep beside her. She missed the weight of him pressing down on her.

She missed how his heart felt beating against hers, but most of all she missed the feel of him being inside her.

Remnants of ecstasy were still trickling through her when she thought of what they'd done and all they'd shared. Being gripped in the throes of orgasm after orgasm for several long moments was enough to blow anybody's mind and it had certainly done a job on her. And the way he had looked down at her—during those times he wasn't kissing her—had sent exquisite sensation after exquisite sensation spiraling through her. Even with the bandages covering his chest and parts of his back, she had felt him—the hardness of his shoulders and the way the muscles in his back had flexed beneath her fingertips.

There was no way she could or would forget tonight. It would always be ingrained in her memory despite the fact that she knew he probably would not remember a single thing. That thought bothered her and she fought back the tears that threatened her eyes. They should be tears of joy and not of sorrow, she thought. She had loved him for so long, but at least she had these memories to cherish.

The rain had stopped and all was quiet except the even, restful sound of Derringer's breathing. Day was breaking and she had to leave. The sooner she did so the better. She could just imagine what he would think if he woke and found her there in bed with him. Whatever words he might say would destroy the beautiful memories of the night she intended to keep.

And her guess was that someone—any one of his brothers, sisters or cousins—might show up any minute to check up on him. They, too, would be shocked as heck to find her there.

She slowly eased out of bed, trying not to wake him, and glanced around for her clothes. She found all the items she needed except for her panties. He had taken them off her while she was in bed, so chances were they were somewhere under the covers.

She slowly lifted the covers and saw the pair of pink panties were trapped beneath his leg. It would be easy enough to wake him and ask him to move his leg so she could get them, but there was no way she could do such a thing. She stood there a moment, hoping he would stir just a little so she could pull them free.

Lucia nervously gnawed on her bottom lip, knowing she couldn't just stand there forever, so she quietly began getting dressed. And only when the sun began peeking over the horizon did she accepted that she had to leave quickly... without her panties.

Glancing around the room to make sure that was the only thing she would be leaving behind, she slowly tiptoed out of the room, but not before glancing over her shoulder one last time to look at Derringer. So this was how he looked in the early mornings. With his shadowed face showing an unshaven chin while lying on the pillow, he looked even more handsome than he'd been last night.

He would probably wonder whose panties were left in his bed, but then he might not. He bedded so many women that it wouldn't matter that one had left a pair of their panties behind. To him it might not be any big deal. Probably wouldn't be.

Moments later while driving away, she glanced back in her rearview mirror at Derringer's home, remembering all that had taken place during the night in his bedroom. She was no longer a virgin. She had given him something she had never given another man, and the only sad part was that he would never, ever know it.

Chapter 2

Some woman had been in his bed.

The potent scent of sex brought Derringer awake, and he lifted his lids then closed them when the sunlight coming through his bedroom window nearly blinded him. He shifted his body and then flinched when pain shot up one of his legs at the same time his chest began aching.

He slowly lifted his head from the pillow, thinking he needed to take some more pain pills, and dropped it back down when he remembered he might have taken one too many last night. Megan would clobber him for taking more than he should have, but at least he'd slept through the night.

Or had he?

He sniffed the air and the scent of a woman's perfume and of sex was still prevalent in his nostrils. Why? And why were clips of making love to a woman in this very bed going through his brain? It was the best dream he'd had in years. Usually a dream of making love to a woman couldn't touch the reality, but with the one he'd had last night, he would beg to differ. He could understand dreaming about making love to a woman because it had been a while for him. Getting the horse business off the ground with his brother Zane, his cousin Jason and their newfound relatives, those Westmorelands living in Georgia, Montana and Texas, had taken up a lot of his time lately. But his dream had felt so real. That was one hell of an illusion.

Nevertheless, he thought, stretching his body then wishing he hadn't when he felt another pain, it had been well worth the experience.

He reached down to rub his aching thigh, when his hand came in contact with a lacy piece of material. He brought up his hand and blinked when he saw the pair of lace bikini panties that carried the feminine scent he had awakened to.

Pulling himself up in bed, he studied the underthings he held in his hand. Whose were they? Where had they come from? He sniffed the air. The feminine scent was not only in the panties but all over his bed as well. And the indention on the pillow beside him clearly indicated another head had been there.

Monumental panic set in. Who the hell had he made love to last night? Since now there was no doubt in his mind he'd made love to someone. All that pleasure hadn't been a figment of his imagination, but the real thing. But who had been the woman?

He closed his eyes and tried to come up with a face and couldn't. It had to have been someone he knew; otherwise, who would have come to his house and gotten into his bed? He had messed around with some pretty brazen women in his lifetime, but none would have dared.

Hell, evidently one had.

He opened his eyes and stared at the wall, trying to recall everything he could about yesterday and last night. He remembered the fall off Sugar Foot's back; there was no way he could forget that. He even remembered Zane and Jason rushing him to the emergency room and how he'd gotten bandaged up and then sent home.

He definitely recalled how his brother and cousin kept saying over and over, "We told you so." He remembered that after he'd gotten into bed, Megan had stopped by on her way to the hospital where she worked as an anesthesiologist.

He recalled when she'd given him his pain medicine with instructions of when to take it. The pain had come back sometime after dark and he'd taken some of the pills.

Hell, how much of the stuff had he taken? He distinctly recalled the E.R. physician's warning that the painkillers were pretty potent stuff and had to be taken when instructed. So much for that.

Okay, so he had taken more pain medicine than he was supposed to. But still, what gave some woman the right to enter his home and take advantage of him? He thought of several women who it could have been; anyone who might have heard about his fall and decided to come over and play nursemaid. Only Ashira would have been bold enough to do that. Had he slept with her last night? Hell, he sure hoped not. She might try to pull something and he wasn't in the market of being any baby's daddy any time soon. Besides, what he'd shared with his mystery woman had been different from anything he'd ever shared with Ashira. It had been more profound with one hell of a lasting effect.

He then remembered something vital. The woman he'd slept with had been a virgin—although it was hard to believe he could remember that, he did. And it was pretty far-fetched to think there were still any of them around in this day and time. But there was no way in hell he could have imagined her innocent state even with a mind fuzzy with painkillers. And he knew for certain the woman could not have been Ashira since she didn't have a virginal bone in her body. Besides, he had a steadfast rule to leave innocents alone.

Derringer sighed deeply and wished, for his peace of mind, that he could remember more in-depth details about last night, including the face of the woman whose virginity he had taken. The thought of that made him cringe inside because he knew for certain he hadn't used a condom. Was last night a setup and the result would be a baby just waiting to be born nine months from now?

The thought of any woman taking advantage of him that way—or any way—made his blood boil. And anger began filling him to a degree he hadn't known was possible. If the woman thought she had gotten the best of him she had another thought coming. She had not only trespassed on his private property, but she had invaded his privacy and taken advantage of him when he'd been in a weakened, incoherent state.

If he had to turn over every stone in Denver, he would find out the identity of the woman who'd had the nerve to pull one over on him. And when he found her, he would definitely make her pay for her little stunt.

"Lucia, are you all right?"

It was noon and Lucia was sitting behind the desk of her office at the Denver branch of *Simply Irresistible*, the magazine designed for today's up-and-coming woman.

The magazine, Chloe's brainchild, had started out as a regional publication in the Southeast a few years ago. When Chloe had made the decision to expand to the West and open a Denver office, she had hired Lucia to manage the Denver office.

Lucia loved her job as managing editor. Chloe was editor in chief, but since her baby—a beautiful little girl named Susan—was born six months ago, Chloe spent most of her time at home taking care of her husband and daughter. Lucia had earned a business-management degree in college, but when Chloe had gotten pregnant she had encouraged Lucia to go back to school and get a master's degree in mass communications to further her career at *Simply Irresistible*. Lucia only needed a few more classes to complete that degree.

Lucia figured it would only be a matter of time before Chloe and Ramsey decided they would want another baby, and the running of *Simply Irresistible's* Denver office would eventually fall in her lap.

"Lucia!"

She jumped when Chloe said her name with a little more force, getting her attention. "What? You scared me."

Chloe couldn't help but smile. It had been a long time since she'd seen her best friend so preoccupied. "I was asking you a question."

Lucia scrunched up her face. "You were?"

"Yes."

"Oh, what was your question?"

Chloe shook her head, smiling. "I asked if you were all right. You seem preoccupied about something and I want to know what. Things are looking good here. We doubled our print run for April's issue since the president is on the cover, so that shouldn't cause you any concern. What's going on with you?"

Lucia nibbled on her bottom lip. She needed to tell someone about what happened last night and since Chloe was her best friend, she would be the logical person. However, there was a problem with that. Chloe was married to Ramsey, who was Derringer's oldest brother. There was no doubt in Lucia's mind Chloe would keep her mouth closed about anything if she asked her to, but still…

"Okay, Lucia, I'm only going to ask you one more time. What's wrong with you? You've been acting spaced out since I got here, and I doubt you were listening to anything Barbara was saying during the production meeting. So what's going on with you?"

Lucia breathed in deeply. "It's Derringer."

Frowning, Chloe stared. "What about Derringer? Ramsey called and checked on him this morning and he was doing fine. All he needed was a dose of pain medication and a good night's sleep."

"I'm sure he got the dose of pain medication, but I don't know about the good night's sleep," Lucia said drily, before taking a long sip of cappuccino.

"And why don't you think he got a good night's sleep?"

Lucia shrugged, started to feign total ignorance to Chloe's question and then decided to come clean. She looked up and met her friend's curious gaze.

"Because I spent the night with him and I know for certain we barely slept at all."

She could tell from the look that suddenly appeared on Chloe's face that she had shocked her friend witless. Now that she had confessed her sins, she was hoping they could move on and talk about something else, but she should know better than to think that.

"You and Derringer finally got together?" Chloe asked. The shocked expression had been replaced by a smile.

"Depends on what you mean by got together. I'm no longer a virgin, if that's what you mean," Lucia said evenly. "But he was so over the top on painkillers he probably doesn't remember a thing."

The smile dropped from Chloe's lips. "You think so?"

"I know so. He looked right in my face and asked me for my name."

She took the next ten minutes and told Chloe everything, including the part about the panties she had left behind. "So that's the end of it," Lucia finished her tale by saying.

Chloe shook her head. "I really don't think so for two reasons, Lucia. First, you're in love with Derringer and have been for a very long time. I don't see that coming to an end any time soon. In fact, now that the two of you have been intimate, you're going to see him in a whole new light. Whenever you run into him, your hunger for him will automatically kick in."

Chloe's expression became even more serious when she said, "And you better hope Derringer doesn't find your panties. If he does find them and can't remember the woman he took them off of, he will do everything in his power to track her down."

Lucia preferred not hearing that. She gripped the handle of her cup tightly in her hand. Turning away to look out the window to view downtown Denver, she drew in a deep ragged breath before taking a sip of her coffee. She hoped Chloe was wrong. The last thing she needed was to worry about that happening.

"With his reputation with women it will be like looking for a needle in a haystack."

"Possibly. But what happens if he finds that needle?"

Lucia didn't want to think about that. She had loved Derringer secretly for so long, she wasn't sure she wanted that to change, especially when he didn't love her back.

"Lucia?"

She turned and looked at Chloe. There was a serious expression on her best friend's face. "I don't know what will happen. I don't want to think that far. I want to believe he won't remember and let it go."

A few moments passed. "What I said earlier was true. Whenever you see Derringer, you're going to want him," Chloe said softly.

She shrugged. "I've always wanted him, Clo."

"Now it will be doubly so."

Lucia opened her mouth to deny Chloe's words and decided not to waste her time because she knew Chloe was probably right. She had thought about him all that day, barely getting any work done. She kept playing over and over in her mind just what the two of them had done together. "I will fight it," she finally said.

Chloe bristled at her words. "It won't be that simple."

She could believe that. Nothing regarding Derringer had

ever been simple for her. "Then what do you suggest I do?" Lucia said with resignation in her voice.

"Come out of hiding once and for all and go after him."

She wasn't surprised Chloe would advise her to do something like that. Her best friend was the daring one. She never hesitated in going after anything she wanted and she'd always envied Chloe for being so bold and brave.

Chloe must have seen the wistful look in her eyes and kept pushing. "Go after him, Lucia. Go ahead and take Derringer on. After last night, don't you think it's about time you did?"

A week later, Jason Westmoreland glanced over at his cousin and grinned. "Was that supposed to be a trick question or something?"

Derringer shook his head as he eased back in the chair. He'd done nothing over the past few days but stay on his pain medication and get plenty of sleep. Each time he awoke he would reach under his pillow and pull out the panties he had placed there just to make sure he hadn't dreamed the whole thing. They proved that he hadn't. And the name Puddin' Tame, the alias the woman had given him, kept going through his mind.

This morning he woke feeling a whole lot better and decided to lay off the pills. He hoped clearing his head would trigger something in his memory about what happened a week ago. So far it hadn't.

Jason had dropped by to check on him and the two were sharing early-morning coffee at the kitchen table. "No, it's not a trick question. I figured I'd ask you first before moving on to Riley, Zane, Canyon and Stern. Afterward, I'll compare everybody's answers."

Jason inclined his head with the barest hint of a nod. "Okay, I'll give your question a shot, so go ahead and repeat it to make sure I heard you right."

Derringer rolled his eyes and then leaned closer to the table. His expression was serious. "What can you tell about a woman from the panties she wears, both style and color?"

Jason rubbed his chin a moment. "I would have to say nothing in particular unless they are white, granny-style ones."

"They aren't." He hadn't told Jason why he was asking, and Jason, the easygoing Westmoreland, wouldn't ask... There was no doubt in Derringer's mind that everyone else would.

"Then I really don't know," Jason said, taking a sip of his coffee. "I think some pieces of clothing are supposed to convey messages about people. I picked white because it usually means innocence. But then again, Fannie Nelson had on a pair of low-riding jeans one day that showed her white panties, and she is a long way from being innocent."

"Aren't you curious as to why I want to know?"

"Yes, I'm curious, but not enough to ask. I figure you have your reasons and I don't want to come close to thinking what they might be."

Derringer nodded, understanding why Jason felt that way. His cousin knew his history with women. And what Jason said was true. He had his reasons, all right.

"So what do you plan to do today now that you've returned to the world of the living? I heard the E.R. doc tell you to take it easy for at least a week or so to recuperate, so you're still under restrictions," Jason reminded him.

"Yes, but I'm not restricted from driving. I'm going to hang around here and take it easy for a few more days before venturing out anywhere."

"I'm glad you're following the doc's advice. Although things could have been worse, that was still a nasty fall you took. And as far as your question regarding women's undergarments, I suggest you talk to Zane when he gets back from Boulder." Jason chuckled and then added, "And be prepared to take notes."

Two days later Derringer left home for the first time since his accident and drove to Zane's Hideout. He was glad to see his brother's truck parked in the yard, which meant he was back. Jason was right. He should have been prepared to take notes. Zane, who was only fourteen months older but a heck of a lot wiser where women were concerned, had no qualms about telling him what he wanted to know.

According to Zane, the color and style of a woman's panties said a lot about her. Sexually liberated women wore thongs or barely-there panties, all colors except white, and they rarely wore pastel colors. Most of them preferred black.

Zane further went on to say that women who liked to tease men wore black lace. Women who preferred lace to any other design were women who liked to look and feel pretty. And bikini panties weren't as popular these days as thongs and hipsters, so a woman still wearing bikini panties wasn't as sexually liberated as others.

Derringer smiled when Zane, with a serious look on his face, advised him to steer clear of women who wore granny panties. Zane furthermore claimed that women who wore red panties gave the best blow jobs. Those with yellow panties the majority of the time weren't afraid to try anything and were pretty good with a pair of handcuffs. Blue panties—wearing women were loyal to a fault—although they had a tendency to get possessive sometimes, and those who preferred wearing green were only after your money, so the use of double condoms was in order.

It had taken his brother almost an hour to make it to pink panties and, according to the Laws of Zane, women who wear pink panties were the ones you needed to stay away from because they had the word *marriage* written all over them, blasting like neon lights. They were a cross between innocent and a woman with an inner hunger for getting laid. But in the end she would still want a wedding ring on her finger.

"Okay, now that you've taken up more than an hour of my time, how about telling me why you're so interested in a woman's panties," Zane said, eyeing him curiously.

For a moment Derringer considered not telling his brother anything, but then thought better of it. He, his five brothers and all his cousins were close, but there was a special bond between him, Zane and Jason. Besides, it was evident that Zane knew a lot more about women than he did, so maybe his brother could give him some sound advice about how to handle what had occurred that night, just in case he had been set up.

"Some woman came over to my place the night I was injured and let herself in. I can't remember who she was, but I do remember making love to her."

Zane stared at him intently for a moment. "Are you absolutely sure you made love to her and didn't imagine the whole thing? When we took you home from the hospital— right before I had to take off for the airport—you were pretty high on those pain meds. Megan figured that you would probably sleep through most of the night, although she set out more medicine for you to take later."

Derringer shook his head. "Yeah, I was pretty drugged up, but I remember making love to her, Zane. And to prove I didn't dream the whole thing, I found her panties in bed with me the next morning." What he decided not to say was that as far as he was concerned, it had been the best love-making he'd ever experienced with a woman.

Zane drew in a deep breath and then said on a heavy sigh. "You better hope it wasn't Ashira. Hell, man, if you didn't use a condom she would love to claim you're her new baby's daddy."

Derringer rubbed the ache that had suddenly crept into his temples at the thought. "It wasn't Ashira, trust me. This woman left one hell of an impression. I've never experienced lovemaking like it before. It was off the charts. Besides, Ashira called a few days after hearing about the accident. She left town to go visit her sick grandmother in Dakota the day before the accident and won't be back for a few weeks."

"You do know there's a way for you to find out the identity of your uninvited visitor, don't you?" Zane asked.

Derringer glanced over at him. "How?"

"Did you forget about the video cameras we had installed on your property to protect the horses, the week before your fall? Anyone pulling into your yard would be captured on film if they got as far as your front porch."

Derringer blinked when he remembered the video camera and wondered why he hadn't recalled it sooner. He got up from Zane's table and swiftly strode to the door. "I need to get home and check out that tape," he said without looking back.

"What happens when you find out who she is?" Zane called out.

He slowed to a stop and glanced over his shoulder. "Whoever she is, she will be sorry." He then turned and continued walking.

He meant what he said. Thanks to Zane, the mystery might have been solved. But once Derringer discovered the woman's identity, her nightmare for what she'd done would just be beginning, he thought, getting into his truck and driving away. He had a feeling *his* nightmare would continue until he found her—their night together had been so good, it haunted his dreams.

He made it back to Derringer's Dungeon in record time, and once inside his house he immediately went to his office to log on to his computer. The technician who had installed the video camera had told him he had access to the film from any computer anywhere with his IP address. This would be the first time he had reason to view the footage since the cameras had been installed.

A year ago his Westmoreland cousins from Montana had expanded their very successful horse-breeding and training business and had invited him, Jason and Zane to join as partners. Since all three were fine horsemen—although you couldn't prove how good he was, considering what had happened on Monday—they had jumped at the chance to be included. In anticipation of the horses that would be arriving, they had decided to install cameras on all three of their properties to make sure horse thieves, which were known to pop up every so often in these parts, didn't get any ideas about stealing from a Westmoreland.

Derringer hauled in a deep breath when the computer came to life and he typed in the code to get him to the video-camera channel and almost held his breath as he searched for the date he wanted. He then sat there, with his gaze glued to the computer screen, and waited with bated breath for something to show up.

It seemed it took forever before the lights of a vehicle came into view. The time indicated it wasn't early afternoon, not quite dark, but there had been a thunderstorm brewing. He then recalled it had been raining something awful with thunder and lightning flashing all around. At one point the intensity of it had awakened him.

He squinted at the image, trying to make out the truck that turned into his yard in the torrential rain. It seemed the weather worsened and rain started to pour down on the earth the moment the vehicle pulled into his yard.

It took only a second to recall whose SUV was in focus and he could only lean back in his chair, not believing what he was seeing. The woman who got out of her truck, battling the weather before tackling the huge box on his porch by dragging it inside his place was none other than Lucia Conyers.

He shook his head trying to make heads or tails of what he was seeing. Okay, he had it now. He figured, for whatever reason, Lucia had come by—probably as a favor to Chloe—to check on him and had been kind enough to bring the box inside the house, out of the rain.

He sat there watching the computer screen, expecting her to come back out at any minute and then get in her truck and pull off. He figured once she left, another vehicle would drive up, and the occupant of that car would be the woman he'd slept with. But as he sat there for another twenty minutes or so viewing the screen, Lucia never came back out.

Lucia Conyers was his Puddin' Tame?

Derringer shook his head, thinking that there was no way. He then decided to fast-forward the tape to five o'clock the next morning. His eyes narrowed suspiciously when a few minutes later he watched his front door open and Lucia ease out of it as if she was sneaking away from the scene of some crime. And she was wearing the same clothes she had on when she'd first arrived the night before. It was obvious she had dressed hurriedly and was moving rather quickly toward her SUV.

Damn. He couldn't believe it. He wouldn't believe it if he wasn't seeing it for himself. She was the one woman he would never have suspected, not in a million years. But from the evidence he'd gotten off his video camera, Lucia was the woman he had slept with. Lucia, his sister-in-law's best friend. Lucia was innocent—at least his assumption of that had been right. His mystery lover had been Lucia, the woman who would shy away from him and act skittish whenever he came around her.

Last month he recalled hearing Chloe and his sisters tease her about this being the last year of her twenties and challenge her to write a list of everything she wanted to do before hitting the big three-oh. He couldn't help wondering if she had added something outlandish like getting pregnant before her biological clock stopped ticking or ridding herself of her virginity.

Anger filled him, seeped through every pore in his body. Lucia Conyers had a hell of a lot of explaining to do. She better have a good reason for getting into bed with him that night two weeks ago.

He pulled his cell phone out of his pocket and punched in the number to his sister-in-law's magazine.

"*Simply Irresistible,* may I help you?"

"Yes, I'd like to speak to Lucia Conyers, please," he said, trying to control his anger.

"Sorry, but Ms. Conyers just stepped out for lunch."

"Did she say where she was going?" he asked.

The receptionist paused and then asked. "Who may I ask is calling?"

"This is Mr. Westmoreland."

"Oh, Mr. Westmoreland, how are you? Your wife and baby were here a couple of days ago, and your daughter looks just like you."

Derringer shook his head. Evidently the woman thought he was Ramsey, which was okay with him if he could get the information he wanted out of her.

"I take that as a compliment. Did Lucia say where she was going for lunch?"

"Yes, sir. She's dining at McKay's today."

"Thanks."

"You're welcome, sir."

Derringer hung up the phone and leaned back in his chair as an idea formed in his mind. He wouldn't let her know he had found out the truth about her visit. He would let her assume that she had gotten away with it and that he didn't have a clue that she was the woman who'd taken advantage of him that night.

And then when she least expected it, he would play his hand.

Chapter 3

Something, Lucia wasn't sure exactly what, made her glance over her menu and look straight into the eyes of Derringer Westmoreland. She went completely still as he moved in fluid precision toward her, with an unreadable expression on his face.

Staring at him, taking him all in, all six-three of him, while broad shoulders flexed beneath a blue Western shirt, and a pair of jeans clung to him like a second layer of skin and showed the iron muscles in his thighs. And then there was his face, too handsome for words, with his medium-brown skin tone, dark coffee-colored eyes and firm and luscious-looking lips.

For the moment she couldn't move; she was transfixed. A part of her wanted to get up quickly and run in another direction, but she felt glued to the chair. But that didn't stop liquid heat from pooling between her thighs when her gaze locked onto his face and she looked at the same features she had seen almost two weeks ago in his bed.

Why was he here and approaching her table? Had he found her panties and figured out she was the woman who had left them behind? She swallowed, thinking there was no way he could have discovered her identity, but then she asked herself why else would he seek her out?

He finally came to a stop at her table and she nervously moistened her lips with the tip of her tongue. She could swear his gaze was following her every movement. She swallowed again, thinking she had to be imagining things, and opened her mouth to speak. "Derringer? What are you doing here? Chloe mentioned you had taken a nasty fall a couple of weeks ago."

"Yes, but a man has to eat sometime. I was told McKay's serves the best potpie on Thursdays for lunch and there's always a huge crowd. I saw you sitting over here alone and thought the least we can do is help the place out," he said.

She was trying hard to follow him and not focus on the way his Adam's apple moved with every word he said, as if it was on some sensuous beat. She lifted a brow. "Help the place out in what way?"

He gave her a smooth smile. "Freeing up a table by us sharing one."

Lucia was trying really hard not to show any emotion—especially utter astonishment and disbelief—as well as not to let the menu she was holding fall to the floor. Had he just suggested that they share a table during lunch? Breathe the same air?

She was tempted to pick up the glass filled with ice water and drink the whole thing in one gulp. Instead, she drew in a deep breath to stop her heart from pounding so hard in her chest. How could spending only one night in his bed cause her to want to let go of her sensibilities and play out these newfound urges at the sight of him?

Of course, there was no way she would do something like that. In fact, a part of her was shaking inside at the thought he wanted to join her for lunch. She quickly wondered how Chloe would handle the situation if she was in her place. The answer came easy, but then she wasn't Chloe. However, she had to keep her cool and respond with the confidence Chloe possessed. The confidence that she lacked.

Lucia forced a smile to her lips. "I think that's a good idea, Derringer."

His lips eased into a smile right before her eyes. "Glad you agree," he said, taking the chair across from her.

She forced herself to breathe and belatedly realized just what she'd done. She had agreed to let him sit at her table. What on earth would they have to talk about? What if she let something slip and said something really stupid like, *"Oh, by the way, when can I drop by and get the panties I left behind the other night?"*

She sighed heavily. For all she knew, he might have figured things out already. Seriously, why else would he give a royal flip whether or not McKay's was crowded for lunch? That in itself was suspect because he'd never sought out her attention before.

She glanced over at him and he smiled at her, flashing those same dimples that he'd flashed that night she almost melted in her chair. He looked the same, only thing was that his eyes no longer had a hungover look. Today his gaze was as clear as glass.

The waitress saved them from talking when she walked up to take both their lunch orders. When she left, Lucia wished she had a mirror to see how she looked. She would die if she didn't at least look halfway decent. Absently, she ran a finger through her hair and pressed her lips together. She was grateful to feel her lipstick still in place, although she was tempted to get the tube of lipstick from her purse and apply a fresh coat.

"I understand you're back in school."

She was watching his mouth and his lips moved. She realized he'd said something. "Excuse me?"

He smiled again. "I said I heard you were back in school."

"Yes, I am. How did you know?"

"Chloe mentioned it."

"Oh." She wondered why Chloe would mention such a thing unless he'd asked about her. Had he? She shook her head, finding the idea unlikely. Her name must have popped up for conversational purposes and nothing more than that. If there had been anything more, Chloe definitely would have told her.

"Yes, I'm back at school taking night classes to get my master's degree in mass communications." Then, without missing a beat, she said, "You seem to be doing well from your fall." No sooner had the words left her mouth than she wished she could take them back. Why on earth would she bring up anything relating to that day?

"Yes, but I'm doing better now. I've been taking it easy for the past week or so and sleeping most of the time. It helped. I feel in pretty good shape now."

She didn't know how to tell him that as far as she was concerned, he'd been in pretty good shape that night as well. His movements hadn't been hindered in any way. The thought of all he'd done to her sent heat soaring all through her body.

"So, what else have you been up to lately?"

Lucia felt her heart give a loud thump in her chest and wondered if he'd heard it. Dragging her gaze from her silverware, she thought that she could remember in vivid detail just what she'd been up to lately with him. Sitting across from her was the man who'd taken her virginity. The man who'd introduced her to the kind of pleasure she'd only read about in romance novels, and the man whom she'd loved forever. And knowing he probably had no idea of any of those things was the epitome of insane. But somehow she would fake it and come off looking like the most poised person that ever existed.

"Not a whole lot," she heard herself saying. "School and the magazine keep me pretty busy, but because I enjoy doing both I won't complain. What about you?" His gaze seemed to linger on her lips.

He chuckled. "Other than making a fool of myself with Sugar Foot, I haven't been up to a whole lot either."

She inclined her head. "What on earth would entice you to ride that horse? I think everyone has heard how mean he is."

He chuckled and the sound was a low, sexy rumble that made goose bumps form on her arms. "Ego. I figured if Casey could do it then so could I."

She knew his cousin Casey and her husband, along with his cousin Durango and his wife, Savannah, had come visiting a few weekends ago. She'd heard everyone had been amazed at the ease with which Casey had gotten on Sugar Foot's back and held on even when the horse had been determined to get her off.

"I'm a pretty good horseman," Derringer said, breaking into her thoughts. "Although I'd be the first to admit I wasn't personally trained by the renowned and legendary Sid Roberts like Casey and her brothers while growing up."

Lucia nodded. His cousins Casey, Cole and Clint were triplets, and she had heard that they had lived with Roberts, their maternal uncle, while growing up. "We can all learn from the mistakes we make," she said, taking a sip of her water to cool off.

"Yes, we sure can."

Deciding she needed to escape, if only for a short moment, Lucia stood. "Would you excuse me for a moment? I need to go to the ladies' room."

"Sure, no problem," he said, standing.

Lucia drew in a deep breath, wishing she was walking out the restaurant door with no intention of returning and not just escaping to the ladies' room. And as she continued walking, she could actually feel Derringer staring at her back.

Derringer watched Lucia leave, thinking she looked downright sexy in her below-the-knee skirt and light blue pullover sweater. And then he couldn't help but admire her small waistline and the flare of her hips in the skirt as she walked. Standing about five-seven, she had a pair of nice-looking black leather boots on her feet, but he could recall just what a nice pair of legs she had and remembered how those legs had felt wrapped around him the night they'd made love.

He would be the first to admit that he'd always thought Lucia was pretty, with her smooth brown skin and lustrous shoulder-length black hair that she usually wore pulled back in a ponytail. Then there were her hazel eyes, high cheekbones, cute chin and slim nose. And he couldn't forget her luscious-looking mouth, one that could probably do a lot of wicked things to a man.

He leaned back in his chair remembering how years ago when she'd been about eighteen—about to leave home for college—and he had been in the process of moving back home from university, she had caught his eye. In memory of his parents and his aunt and uncle, who'd died together in a plane crash while he was in high school, the Westmorelands held a charity ball every year to raise money for the Westmoreland Foundation, which had been founded to aid various community causes. Lucia had attended the ball that year with her parents.

He had been standing by the punch bowl when she had arrived, and the sight of her in the dress she'd been wearing that night had rendered him breathless. He hadn't been able to take his eyes off her all evening. Evidently others had noticed his interest, and one of those had been her father, Dusty Conyers.

Later that same night the older man had pulled him aside and warned him away from his daughter. He let Derringer know in no uncertain terms that he would not tolerate a Westmoreland sniffing behind his daughter, creating the kind of trouble that Carl Newsome was having with Derringer's cousin Bane.

Bane had had the hots for Crystal Newsome since junior high school, and since Bane had a penchant for getting into trouble, Newsome hadn't wanted him anywhere near his daughter. Unfortunately, Crystal had other ideas and had been just as hot for Bane as he'd been for her, and Crystal and Bane managed to get into all kinds of naughty trouble together. Once, they'd even tried their hand at eloping before Carl Newsome had found his daughter and shipped her off to heaven knows where. A brokenhearted Bane had decided to take charge of his life by going into the Navy.

Derringer knew that although he didn't have Bane's badass reputation, he was still a Westmoreland, and a lot of mamas and daddies were dead set on protecting their daughters from what they thought was a Westmoreland heartbreak just waiting to happen. A part of him couldn't fault Dusty Conyers for being one of them; especially since Derringer had made it known far and wide that he had no plans to settle down with any one woman. A wife was the last thing on his mind then as well as now. Making a success of the horse-training business he'd just started was his top priority.

"I'm back."

He glanced up and stood for her to sit and thought that Lucia was even more beautiful up close. She had a nervous habit of licking her lips with her tongue. He would do just about anything to replace her tongue with his the next time she did it. And he also liked the sound of her voice. She spoke in a quiet yet sexy tone that did things to his insides, and he decided to keep her talking every chance he got.

"Tell me about the classes you're taking at the university and why you decided to go back and get your master's degree."

She lifted a brow and then her lips curved into one of her smiles again. Evidently, he'd hit on a subject she liked talking about. "Although Chloe hasn't made any announcements about anything, I can see her spending less and less time with *Simply Irresistible.* Whenever she does come into the office she has the baby with her, and it's obvious that she prefers being home with Susan and Ramsey."

He nodded, thinking he'd had that same impression as well. Whenever he paid Ramsey and Chloe a visit, they appeared to be a content and very happy couple who thoroughly enjoyed being parents. He'd heard from his other brothers that already Ramsey and Chloe were thinking about having another child.

"And I want to be prepared if she decides to take a leave of absence for a while," Lucia continued. "She and I talked about it, and because my bachelor's degree was in business, we thought it would be a good idea for me to get a degree in communications as well."

The waitress chose that moment to return with their food, and once the plates had been placed in front of them, she left.

"I understand Gemma is adjusting to life in Australia."

He couldn't help but smile. Although he missed his sister, it seemed from all the phone calls they got that she *was* adjusting to life in Australia. He'd known Callum, the man who used to be the manager of Ramsey's sheep farm, had loved Gemma for a while, even if his sister had been clueless. He'd always known Callum's feelings for Gemma had been the real thing and not for the sole purpose of getting her into bed. He'd wholeheartedly approved of Gemma and Callum's relationship.

"Yes, I talked to her a few days ago. She and Callum are planning to come home for the Westmoreland Charity Ball at the end of the month." He wondered if she planned to go and if so, if she already had a date.

"Are you dating anyone seriously?" he decided to ask and set his plan into motion.

She looked over at him after popping a strawberry into her luscious mouth, chewed on it a moment, and then she swallowed it before replying. "The only dates I have these days are with my schoolbooks."

"Um, what a pity, that doesn't sound like a lot of fun. How about a movie this weekend?"

She cocked a surprised eyebrow. "A movie?"

He could tell his suggestion had surprised her. "Yes, a movie. Evidently, you're not spending enough time having fun, and everyone needs to let loose now and then. There's a new Tyler Perry movie coming out this weekend that I want to see. Would you like to go with me?"

Lucia's heart began pounding in her chest as she quickly reached the conclusion that Derringer had to have figured out that she was the woman who'd brazenly shared his bed. What other reason could he have for asking her out? Why the sudden interest in her when he'd never shown any before?

Their eyes held for what seemed like several electrifying moments before she finally broke eye contact with him. But what if he *didn't* know, and asking her out was merely a coincidence? There was only one way to find out. She glanced back over at him and saw he was still staring at her with that unreadable expression of his. "Why do you want to take me out, Derringer?"

He gave her a smooth smile. "I told you. You're spending too much time studying and working and need to have a little fun."

She still wasn't buying it. "We've known each other for years. Yet you've never asked me out before. In fact, you've never shown any interest."

He chuckled. "It wasn't that I didn't want to show an interest, Lucia, but I love my life and all my body parts."

She raised a brow and paused with the fork halfway to her mouth. "What do you mean?"

He took a sip of his iced tea and then his mouth curved ruefully. "I was warned away from you early on and took the warning seriously."

She nearly dropped the fork from her hand and had to tighten her grip to place it back down. "What do you mean you were warned away from me?" That was impossible. She'd never had a boyfriend jealous enough to do such a thing.

A grin flashed across his face. "Your dad knows how to scare a man off, trust me."

Her head began spinning at the same time her heart slammed hard against her rib cage. "My dad warned you away from me?"

He smiled. "Yes, and I took him seriously. It was the summer you were about to leave for college. You were eighteen and I was twenty-two and returning home from university. You attended the Westmoreland Charity Ball with your parents before you left. He saw me checking you out, probably thought my interest wasn't honorable, and pulled me aside and told me to keep my eyes to myself or else…"

Lucia swallowed. She knew her dad. His bark was worse than his bite, but most people didn't know that. "Or else what?"

"Or else my eyes, along with another body part I'd rather not mention, would get pulled from their sockets. The last thing he would put up with was a Westmoreland dating his daughter."

Lucia didn't know whether to laugh or cry. She could see her father making a threat like that because he was overprotective of her. But she doubted Derringer knew how much his words thrilled her. He had been checking her out when she was eighteen?

She nervously moistened her lips with the tip of her tongue and couldn't help noticing the movement of his gaze to her mouth. Her skin began burning at the thought that he had been attracted to her even when she hadn't had a clue. But still…

"Aw, come on, Derringer, that was more than ten years ago," she said in a teasing tone.

"Yes, but you probably don't recall a few years ago I dropped by the paint store to make a purchase and you were working behind the counter and waited on me."

Oh, she definitely remembered that day, and three years later hadn't been able to forget it. But of course she couldn't tell him that. "That was a long time ago, but I think I remember that day. You needed a can of paint thinner." She could probably tell him what brand it was and exactly how much he'd paid for it.

"Yes, well, I had planned to ask you out then, but Mr. Conyers gave me a look that reminded me of the conversation we'd had years before and that his opinion of me pursuing you hadn't changed."

She couldn't help but laugh and it felt good. He had actually wanted to talk to her then, too. "I can't believe you were afraid of Dad."

"Believe it, sweetheart. He can give you a look that lets you know he means business. And it didn't help that he and Bane had had a run-in a few years before when Bane swiped a can of paint on display in front of the store and used it to paint some not-so-nice graffiti all over the front of Mr. Milner's feed store and signed off by saying it was a present from your father."

Lucia wiped tears of laughter from her eyes. "I was away at college, but I heard about that. Mom wrote and told me all the details. You're right, Dad was upset and so was Mr. Milner. Your cousin Bane had a reputation for getting into all kinds of trouble. How are things going with him and the Navy?"

"He's doing fine at the Naval Academy. It's hard to believe he's been gone for almost two years already, but he has."

"And he hasn't been back since he left?"

Derringer shook his head sadly. "No, not even once. He refuses to come back knowing Crystal isn't here, and he's still angry that he doesn't know where she is. The Newsomes made sure of that before they moved away. We are hoping he'll eventually forget her and move on, but so far he hasn't."

In a way, she knew how Bane felt. She hadn't looked forward to returning to Denver either, knowing she was still harboring feelings for Derringer. It was hard running into him while he was dating other girls and wishing they were her. And now to find out they could have been her. Her father had no idea what he'd done and the sad thing was that she couldn't get mad at him. Bane hadn't been the only Westmoreland with a reputation that had made it hard on the other family members. Derringer's younger brothers—the twins, Adrian and Aidan—as well as his baby sister Bailey had been Bane's sidekicks and had gotten into just as much trouble.

Needless to say, it had gotten to the point everyone in town would get up in arms when they saw any Westmoreland headed their way. But she had heard her father say more than once lately that considering everything, he thought Dillon and Ramsey had done a pretty good job in raising their siblings and in keeping the family together, and that he actually admired them for it. She knew that several people in town did. All the Westmorelands were college-educated and in some sort of business for themselves or holding prestigious jobs. And together they were the wealthiest family in the county and the largest landowners. People no longer feared them, they highly respected them.

"Just look how things turned out, Derringer," she heard herself say. "The twins are at Harvard. Bailey will be finishing up her studies at the university here in a year, and Bane is in the hands of Uncle Sam. Ramsey mentioned that Bane wants to become a Navy SEAL. In that case, he has to learn discipline, among other things."

Derringer chuckled. "For Bane, even with Uncle Sam, that won't be easy to do." He picked up his glass to take a sip of his iced tea. "So do we have a date for Saturday night or what?"

A date with Derringer Westmoreland…

She couldn't stop herself from feeling all giddy inside. She almost trembled at the thought. But at the same time she knew she had to be realistic. He would take her out on Saturday night and probably some other girl on Sunday. He'd asked her out to the movies, not a trip to Vegas to get married.

She would take the date for what it was and not put too much stock in it. She hadn't been born yesterday and she knew Derringer's reputation around town. He dated a lot, but let it be known that he didn't like women who clung or got too possessive.

Still, she couldn't help but smile at the thought that he was attracted to her and had been since she was eighteen. Didn't that account for something? She decided that it did.

"Yes, I'd love to go to the movies with you Saturday night, Derringer."

Chapter 4

Derringer frowned the moment he pulled into his yard and saw his sister Bailey's car parked there. The last thing he needed was for her to drop by to play nursemaid again. Megan was bad enough, but his baby sister Bailey was worse. She had only been seven when their parents had gotten killed. Now at twenty-two, she attended college full-time, and when she didn't have her nose stuck in some book it was stuck in her five brothers' personal affairs. She liked making it her business to know anything and everything about their comings and goings. Now that Ramsey was married, she'd given him some slack, but she hadn't let up with him, Zane and the twins.

He wondered how long she'd been there waiting on him and figured she probably wouldn't like the fact that he hadn't been home and had driven into town. Since she wasn't out on the porch, that meant she had let herself inside, which wouldn't be a hard thing to do since he never locked his doors. His sister flung open the door the moment his foot touched the step. The look on her face let him know he was in trouble. She was there when the doctor restricted him from doing almost anything, other than breathing and eating, for two weeks.

"Just where have you been, Derringer Westmoreland, in your condition?"

He walked past her to put his hat on the rack. "And what condition is that, Bailey?"

"You're injured."

"Yes, but I'm not dead."

He regretted the words the moment they left his mouth when he saw the expression that suddenly appeared on her face. He and his brothers knew the real reason Bailey was so overprotective of them was that she was afraid of losing them the way she'd lost their parents.

But he could admit to having the same fears, and if he were to analyze things further, he would probably conclude that Zane had them as well. All of them had been close to their parents, aunt and uncle. Everyone had taken their deaths hard. The way Derringer had managed to move on, and not look back, was by not getting too attached to anyone. He had his cousins and his siblings. He loved them, and they were all he needed. If he were to fall in love, give his heart to a woman, and then something were to happen to her—there was no telling how he'd handle it, or even if he could. He liked things just the way they were. And, for that reason, he doubted he would ever marry.

He crossed the room and placed a hand on her shoulder when he saw her trembling. "Hey, come on, Bail, it wasn't that bad. You were there at the hospital and heard what Dr. Epps said. It's been almost two weeks now and I'm fine."

"But I also heard him say that it could have been worse, Derringer."

"But it wasn't. Look, unless you came to cook for me or do my laundry, you can visit some other time. I'm going to take a nap."

He saw the sad look on her face turn mutinous and knew his ploy had worked. She didn't like it when he bossed her around or came across as if she was at his beck and call. "Cook your own damn meals and do your own laundry, or get one of those silly girls who fawn all over you to do it."

"Whatever. And watch your mouth, Bailey, or I'll think

you're slipping back to your old ways and I'll have to wash your mouth out with soap."

She grabbed the remote off the table, dropped down on the sofa and began watching television, ignoring him. He glanced at his watch and fought to hide his smile. "So, how long are you staying?" he asked. Because she hadn't yet inherited her one hundred acres, she had a tendency to spend time at any of their places. Most of the time she stayed with Megan, which suited all her brothers just fine because Bailey had a tendency to drop in unannounced at the most inconvenient times.

Like now.

She didn't even look over at him when she finally answered his question. "I'm staying until I'm ready to leave. You have a problem with it?"

"No."

"Good," she said, using the remote to flip to another channel. "Now go take your nap and I hope when you wake up you're in a lot better mood."

He chuckled as he leaned down and planted a brotherly kiss on her forehead. "Thanks for worrying about me so much, kid," he said softly.

"If me, Megan and Gemma don't do it, who will? All those silly girls you mess around with are only after your money."

He lifted a brow in mock surprise. "You think so?"

She glanced up at him and rolled her eyes. "If you don't know the truth about them then you're in real trouble, Derringer."

Derringer chuckled again thinking yes, he knew the truth about them…especially one in particular. Lucia Conyers. He didn't think of her as one of those "silly girls" and knew Bailey wouldn't either. He would be taking Lucia to the movies Saturday night. He intended to return her panties to her then. He looked forward to the moment her mouth fell open and she realized he knew what she'd done and had known all this time. He couldn't wait to see what excuse she would come up with for what she had done.

Before heading up the stairs, he decided to feel his sister out about something. "I ran into Lucia Conyers a few moments ago at McKay's."

Bailey didn't take her gaze off the television and for a moment he thought that possibly she hadn't heard him, but then she responded. "And?"

He smiled. "And we shared a table since McKay's was crowded." He paused a moment. "She's pretty. I never realized just how pretty she is." The latter he knew wasn't true, because he'd always known how pretty she was.

He watched as Bailey slowly turned toward him with a frown on her face. "I hope you're not thinking what I think you're thinking."

He smiled. "Oh, I don't know. What do you think I'm thinking?"

"That you plan to hit on Lucia."

He grinned. "If by 'hit on her' you mean ask her out, I've already done so. We have a date to go to the movies this Saturday night."

Bailey's eyes widened. "Are you crazy? That's Chloe's best friend."

Now it was his turn. "And?"

"And everybody around these parts knows how most of the single male Westmorelands operate. You're used to those silly girls and wouldn't know how to appreciate a woman with sense like Lucia."

"You don't think so?"

"I know so and if you end up doing something stupid like hurting her, Chloe would never forgive you for it."

He shrugged at the thought. Chances were, Chloe had no idea what her best friend had pulled that night. And as far as what Bailey said about Lucia's having sense, he didn't doubt that, which made him uneasy about just what she would gain from tumbling into bed with him.

"Lucia is an adult. She can handle me," he said. He wouldn't break it down and tell her that Lucia *had* handled him and had done a real good job doing so. He got a hard-on every time he thought about that night.

"I'm still warning you, Derringer. And besides being Chloe's best friend, Megan, Gemma and I like her as well."

He cocked an amused brow. "I guess that means a lot. The three of you never like any of the girls I date. I'll have to keep that in mind."

Without giving his kid sister time to say anything else, he quickly moved up the stairs for his nap.

Lucia couldn't wait to get back to her office to give Chloe a call and tell her about her date on Saturday night with Derringer.

"I'm happy for you," Chloe said with a smile in her voice that Lucia heard. "Falling off that horse must have knocked some sense into him. At least you know why he never approached you before. I can see your dad warning him off. I heard the Westmorelands had quite a reputation back in the day."

Lucia nodded. "And you think I did the right thing in agreeing to go out with him?"

"Come on, Lucia, don't you dare ask me that. You've loved the guy forever. You've even gone so far as to sleep with him."

She drew in a deep, ragged breath. "But he doesn't know that. At least I don't think he does."

"You honestly think he doesn't know?"

"I assumed he did and that was the only reason he wanted to share my table."

She heard Chloe bristle at that assumption. "Why do you continue to think you're no match for Derringer when you're classier than all those other women he messes around with?"

"But that's just it, Chloe. I'm not the kind of woman he

prefers, the kind he has a history of dating. I can't hold a candle to someone like Ashira Lattimore. And everyone knows she has been vying for his attention for years."

"I've met her and she's spoiled, self-centered, possessive and clingy. Definitely not wife material."

"Wife material?" Lucia laughed. "A wife is the furthest thing from Derringer's mind. You know that as well as I do."

"Yes, but I'm sure a lot of people said the same thing about Ramsey before I arrived on the scene. So that means a man's mind can change with the right woman. All you have to do is convince Derringer you're the right woman."

Lucia cringed at the thought of trying to do that. She wouldn't even know where to begin. "That's easy for you to say and do, Chloe. You've always been sure of yourself in everything you did."

"In that case, maybe you ought to try it for yourself. Just think, Lucia. Evidently Derringer is on your hook and now you have the chance to reel him right on in. You know how I feel about missed opportunities. How would things have turned out had I accepted Ramsey's refusal to be on the cover of my magazine? I saw what I wanted and decided to go after it. I think you should use that same approach."

"I don't know," Lucia said on a heavy sigh. This wasn't the first time Chloe had made that suggestion. A part of her knew her friend was right, but what she was suggesting was easier said than done. At least for her it was.

"Think about it. Saturday is only two days away and if I were you, when Derringer arrived at my place to pick me up I'd make sure he would take one look at me and know he would enjoy every minute of his time in my presence. Now's your chance, Lucia. Don't let it go by without taking advantage of it."

A few moments later, after hanging up the phone with Chloe, indecisiveness weighed heavy in her chest. More than anything she would love to pique Derringer's interest, but what if she failed in her efforts to do so? What if she couldn't get the one man she loved to want to love her back? Was there a possibility that she was wrong about the type of women Derringer actually preferred?

One thing Chloe had said was true. No one would have figured that Ramsey Westmoreland would have fallen for any woman. The man had been set in his ways for years and the last woman he'd attempted to marry had announced she was pregnant from another man in the middle of the wedding. Yet, he had fallen in love with Chloe, whether he had wanted to or not. So maybe there was hope for all those other single Westmorelands; but especially for Derringer.

"I've heard you're interested in women's undergarments these days, Derringer. Is there a reason why?"

Derringer slowly turned away from the pool table with a cue stick in his hand to gaze at each man in the dimly lit room inside his basement. Now that he knew who his late-night visitor had been, he wouldn't tell anyone, not even Zane, her identity.

"No reason," he answered his cousin Canyon who was four years younger.

Canyon smiled. "Well, you never got around to asking me anything, but just so you know, the women I date don't wear underwear."

Derringer shook his head and chuckled. He didn't find that hard to believe. He studied the other men who had gone back to sipping their beers while waiting their turn at shooting pool—his brother Zane and his cousins Jason, Riley, Canyon and Stern. They were as close as brothers. Zane knew more than the others about the situation with him and the underwear, but Derringer was confident his brother wouldn't say anything.

"So, what's this I hear about you going on a date with Lucia? I thought old man Conyers pretty much scared you off her years ago," Jason said, chuckling.

Derringer couldn't help but smile. "He did, but like you said, it was years ago. Lucia isn't a kid anymore. She's an adult and old enough to make her own decisions about who she wants to date."

"True, but she's not your type and you know it," Riley piped in.

Derringer lifted a brow. That was the same thing Bailey had alluded to earlier that day. "And what, supposedly, is my type?"

"Women who wear black panties," Canyon said, chuckling.

"Or no panties at all," Riley added, laughing.

"Hmm, for all you all know, my taste in women might have changed," he said, turning back to the pool table.

Zane snorted. "Since when? Since you got thrown off Sugar Foot's back and hit your head?"

Derringer frowned as he turned back around. "I didn't hit my head."

"Makes us wonder," Riley said. "First you're going around asking about women's underwear and now you're taking Lucia Conyers out on a date. You better treat her right or Chloe will come gunning for you."

"Hell, we'll all come gunning for you," Zane said, taking a sip of his beer. "We like her."

Derringer turned back to the pool table and proceeded to chalk his stick. At the moment, he didn't give a royal flip how his family felt about Lucia. He still planned to deal with her in his own way and if they didn't like the outcome that was too bad.

Chapter 5

By the time seven o'clock came around on Saturday night, Lucia was almost a nervous wreck. She had pulled her father aside that week to verify what Derringer had told her. With a sheepish grin on his face, Dusty Conyers hadn't denied a thing, and had laughingly agreed he had intentionally put the fear of God in Derringer. He didn't regret doing so and was glad it had worked.

He did agree that now she was old enough to handle her own business and wouldn't butt in again. She had ended up giving him a kiss on his bald head after telling him how much she loved him, and that he was the best dad in the whole wide world.

His confirmation meant that what Derringer had said the other day was true. He had shown interest in her years ago, but her father had discouraged him. Although she knew she would always wonder how things might have gone if her father hadn't intervened, she was a firm believer that things happened for a reason. Besides, at eighteen she doubted she would have been able to handle the likes of Derringer Westmoreland and was even doubtful she could have at twenty-two. She wasn't even confident she had the ability to handle him now, but was determined to try. She was convinced there was a reason she had shared his bed that night.

She just wished she had a clue what that reason was.

She was grateful that one didn't have anything to do with the other. The reason he had asked her out had nothing to do with them sleeping together and she felt good about that. She had played the details of their night together over and over in her mind so many times that she knew practically every single movement by heart.

All week she had found herself going to bed but unable to sleep until she replayed in her mind every sensation she'd felt that night. It didn't take much to remember how it felt to grip his iron-steel shoulders beneath her fingers while he thrust in and out of her. The thought of making love with a man like Derringer sent sensuous chills up her spine.

She knew the exact moment Derringer pulled into her driveway. From the smooth hum of the engine she could tell he was driving his two-seater sports car instead of his truck. That meant the car's interior would be that much cozier. The thought of being in such proximity to Derringer stirred all kinds of feelings inside.

She had spoken to Chloe earlier and her best friend had said the Westmorelands were torn as to whether or not her dating Derringer was a good idea, considering his history with women. Bottom line was that no one wanted to see her get hurt. But what they didn't know was that she had loved Derringer so long that to her tonight was really a dream come true. And if he never asked her out again that would be fine because she would always have memories of tonight to add to those she had of that Monday night. Not that she expected things would get as heated tonight as they had in his bedroom, mind you. But she couldn't wait to see what was in store for her tonight. Just knowing she was Derringer's date made her feel good inside, and knowing he had no ulterior motive in taking her out made it that much more special.

* * *

Derringer smiled when he pulled into Lucia's driveway, thinking her house was the brightest on the block with floodlights in every corner, the porch light on and a light pole shining in the front of the yard. He thought it was a real nice neighborhood with beautiful trees on both sides of the street and the silhouette of mountains in the background. But he felt crowded. One of the pitfalls of being a Westmoreland was that because each of them owned a hundred acres of land, living anywhere else would seem restrictive and too confining.

As he walked up to the porch, he felt as if he was under the bright lights and wouldn't be surprised if some of her neighbors were watching him. In fact, he was certain he saw the front curtain move in the house across the street. He chuckled, thinking if she could deal with her nosy neighbors then he certainly could.

Besides, he had enough on his plate dealing with his own nosy relatives. Maybe it had been a bad idea to mention his date to Bailey. She hadn't wasted time spreading the word. He'd gotten a number of calls warning him he had best behave tonight—whatever that meant. And yet, the one call he'd expected, the one from Chloe, had never come. That made him wonder if she knew a lot more than he thought she did.

He glanced at his watch before ringing Lucia's doorbell. It was seven-thirty exactly. He'd made good time and since he'd already reserved tickets online, they wouldn't have to stand in line at the theater. He had thought of everything, including when would be the best time to drop the bomb on her about that night. He had decided that they would enjoy the movie first before dealing with any unpleasantness.

He heard the lock turn on her door and then seconds later she was standing there, illuminated in the doorway. He blinked in surprise when he gazed down at her. She looked different. She'd always been a pretty girl, but tonight she looked absolutely stunning.

Gone was the ponytail. Instead, her hair was curled and fell in feathered waves to her shoulders. And she had done something with her eyes that made them look more striking and the entire look somehow showcased her dazzling sophistication.

And then there was the outfit she was wearing. Not too daring, but enough to keep him on the edge all evening. Her sweater dress was a plum color and she had black suede boots on her feet. She wasn't overly dressed for the movie and he thought her attire was perfect…and it fit her just that way, emphasizing her small waist, and falling above the knees, it definitely showed off a beautiful pair of thighs encased in tights.

A second passed and then several before he was able to open his mouth to speak, and from the smile that touched her lips she was well aware of the effect she was having on him. He couldn't help but smile back. She had definitely pulled one over on him. Gone was just the "pretty" Lucia and in her place stood a creature so gorgeous that she took his breath away.

"Derringer."

He exhaled an even breath. At least he tried to. "Lucia."

"I just need to get my jacket. Would you like to come in for a second?" she asked.

He felt another smile pull at his lips. She was inviting him in. "Sure."

When he brushed by her, he almost buckled to his knees when he took a whiff of her perfume. It was the same scent he had awakened to that Tuesday morning. The same scent that was all in his head. She was the one woman who had him sleeping each night with her panties under his pillow. He took in a deep breath to pull more of the fragrance into his nostrils. There was just something potent about the scent of a woman.

"Would you like a drink before we leave?"

"No, but thanks for the offer," he said, glancing around her living room.

"It won't take but a minute to grab my jacket."

"Take your time," he said, watching as she walked away, appreciating her movements in the dress, especially how it fit her from behind. He forced his gaze away from her when she entered her bedroom and continued his study of her house, thinking it was small but just the right size for her. And it was tidy, not a single thing out of place, even the magazines on the table seemed to lie in a perfect position. He liked her fireplace and could imagine how it would look with a fire blazing in it. He could imagine her on the floor, stretched out in front of it on one of those days that was cold, snowy and dreary outside.

On the drive over, he did notice that this particular subdivision was centrally located to just about everything; shopping, fast-food places, grocery stores and a dry cleaner. That had to be pretty advantageous to her. He rolled his eyes wondering why the heck he cared if it was or not.

"I'm ready now, Derringer."

He turned and glanced back at her. She was standing beside a floor lamp and the lighting totally captured her beauty. For a moment he just stood there and stared, unable to tear his gaze away from her. What the hell was wrong with him? He knew the answer when he felt blood rush straight to his groin. It would be so easy for him to suggest that they forget about the movie and hang here instead. But he knew he couldn't do that.

However, there was something he could do, something he definitely felt compelled to do at that moment. He slowly moved toward her with his heart pounding hard in his chest with every step he took. And when he stood directly in front of her, he said the only words he could say at that moment. Words he knew were totally true. "You look simply beautiful tonight, Lucia."

Lucia didn't know what to say. His compliment caused soothing warmth to spread all through her. In the back of her mind something warned her that the man was smooth, sophisticated and experienced. Like most men, he would say just about anything to score. But at that moment she didn't care. The compliment had come from Derringer Westmoreland and to her that meant everything.

"Thank you, Derringer."

He lowered his head a little, bent low to murmur in her ear, "You're so very welcome."

He kept his head lowered to that angle and she knew without a shadow of a doubt that he intended to kiss her. And that knowledge caused several heated anticipatory sensations to flow from the toes of her feet to the crown of her head.

"Lucia?"

The throaty tone of his voice seemed to stroke everything within her and was doing so effortlessly.

"Yes?"

He lifted his hand to cradle her chin and tilt her face up to his. Her pulse rate increased when a slow smile touched his lips the moment their eyes connected. "I need to kiss you." And before she could draw her next breath, he lowered his mouth to hers.

He had kissed her that night numerous times in the throes of passion, but she immediately thought this kiss was different. The passion was still there, but unlike before it wasn't flaming out of control. What he was doing was slowly and deliberately robbing her senses of any and all control.

His tongue eased between her lips on a breathless moan

and he seemed in no hurry to do anything but stand there, feed on every angle of her mouth, every nook and cranny. His kiss burned her in its wake, sharing its heat. He tasted like the peppermint candy he'd obviously been sucking on earlier.

But now he was sucking on her—her tongue at least; and he wasn't letting up as he probed deeply, gently but thoroughly, plunging her into an oasis of sensations as his tongue continued to sweep over her mouth.

She felt something roll around in her belly at the same time he moved his body closer, and automatically the cradle of her thighs nestled the hard erection pressing against her, causing an ache that was so engaging she couldn't do anything but moan.

This was the sort of kiss most men left a girl with after a date and not before the start of their evening. But evidently no one told that to Derringer and he was showing her there was no particular order in the way he did things. He made his own rules, set his own parameters. Now she knew why he was so high in demand with women, and why fathers warned him not to pursue their daughters. And why heat could resonate off his body like nobody's business.

But tonight he was making it her *business.*

He shifted the intensity of the kiss without warning and the hands that were already wrapped around her waist tightened in a possessive grip. The probing of his tongue deepened and she could only stand there and continue to moan while her pulse throbbed erratically in her throat. Her hips moved instinctively against his and the heat that spread lower all through her belly didn't slow down any.

There was no telling how long they would have stood there, going at each other's mouths, if she hadn't pulled back for air. She closed her eyes and took a deep breath, licking her lips and and tasting him on her tongue. The pleasure she felt just being kissed by him was almost unbearable. She slowly opened her eyes to calm the turbulent emotions inside her.

For the second time that night, his hand lifted to capture her chin, lifting her face to meet his gaze. The look in his eyes was dark, intense, sexually hungry. At that moment, he looked as rugged as the landscape in which he lived. Westmoreland country. She never realized until now just how much that had defined him. She continued to hold his gaze. Mesmerized. Falling deeper and deeper in love.

"You, Lucia Conyers, are more than I bargained for," he said in a deep, husky tone that sounded intimate and overwhelming at the same time.

She chuckled unevenly while wondering if this was how a kiss could easily get out of hand. Was this how a couple could take a kiss to another level without realizing they'd done so until it was too late to do anything about it?

"Is being more than you bargained for a good thing or a bad thing, Derringer?" she asked him.

He laughed softly at her question and released her chin, but not before lowering his head and brushing his lips across hers. "I'll let you decide that later," he whispered hotly against her lips. "Come on. Let's get out of here while we can."

Tonight was not going the way he'd planned, Derringer thought. Even the smell of popcorn couldn't get rid of her scent. His nostrils were inflamed with it. This was their first date and he had fully intended for it to be their last. But...

And there was a *but* in there someplace. For him there were probably several and each of them were messing with his mind. Making him not want to end their evening together. Or to spoil just how good things were going between them.

After the movie he suggested they go to Torie's for coffee. She was everything a man could appreciate in a date, while at the same time not fully what a man expected—but in a positive way. She had the ability to ease into a conversation that wasn't just about her. And as he maneuvered his sports car through downtown Denver, he quickly reached the conclusion that he liked the sound of her voice and in the close confines of the car, her scent continued to overtake his senses.

Derringer couldn't help but wonder if there was something with this "scent of a woman" theory that men often talked about behind closed doors and in dimly lit, whiskey-laden poolrooms. Over his lifetime he had encountered a lot of women who smelled good, but the one sitting next to him right now, whose eyes were closed as she took in the sound of John Legend on his CD player, not only smelled good but was good to smell. And he decided then and there that there was a difference. He chuckled and shook his head at his conclusion.

"Um, what's so funny?" she asked, opening her eyes and turning her head to glance over at him.

"I was just thinking about the movie," he lied, knowing there was no way he would tell her what really had amused him.

She laughed lazily. "It was good, wasn't it?"

When the car slowed in traffic, he gave her a sidelong glance. "Yes, it was. Are you comfortable?"

"Yes. And thanks. This car is nice."

"Glad you like it." He was certain his smile flashed in the dimly lit interior. He appreciated any woman who liked his car. A number of his former dates had complained that although his car was sleek and fast, it was not roomy enough.

"Can you believe they are expecting snow next weekend?"

He chuckled. "Hey, this is Denver. Snowstorms are always expected." They passed a moment in silence. "Did you enjoy living in Florida those four years?"

She nodded. "Immensely."

"Then why did you return to Denver?"

She didn't answer right away. "Because I couldn't imagine living anywhere else," she said finally.

He nodded, understanding completely. Although he had enjoyed living in Phoenix while attending college, he never could wait to return home...to see her again. He hadn't been back a week when Ramsey had sent him into town to pick up a can of paint thinner and he'd seen her again.

At first he'd been taken aback, nearly not recognizing her. She had gone from the gangly young girl to a twenty-something-year-old woman who had grown into a beauty that he had noticed right away. It was a good thing her father had been on guard and had intervened again, because there was no telling where his lustful mind would have led him that day. She had gotten spared from being added to the list as one of Derringer's Pleasers. When he'd returned home it seemed women had come out of the woodwork vying for his attention.

They soon arrived at Torie's, an upscale coffee shop that was known for its signature award-winning coffee and desserts. He helped her out of his sports car, very much aware of the looks they were getting. But now, unlike the other times, he wasn't so sure the focus was on his specially-designed Danish car and not on the woman he was helping out of it. For the first time since he could remember, he relinquished the car to the valet without giving the young man a warning look and strict instructions to be careful on how his prize was handled.

"Mr. Westmoreland, it's nice to see you," the maître d' greeted when they entered the coffee shop.

"Thanks, Pierre. And I'd like a private table in the back."

"Most certainly."

He cupped Lucia's arm as they were led to a table that overlooked the mountains and a lake. The fire that was blazing in the fireplace added the finishing touch. A romantic setting that for even someone like him—a man who probably didn't have a romantic bone in his body until it suited him—was clearly defined. "We can have just coffee if you like, but their strawberry cheesecake is good," he said, smiling when they were seated.

Lucia chuckled. "I'm going to take your word for it and try some."

The waiter came to take their drink order. She ordered a glass of wine and when he ordered only a club soda she glanced over at him curiously. "I'm driving, remember? And I'm still on medication," he said by way of explanation. "And the doctor was adamant about me not consuming alcohol while I'm taking them."

She nodded. "Are you still in pain?"

A rueful smile touched his lips. "Not unless I move too fast. Otherwise, I'm doing fine."

"I guess you won't be getting on Sugar Foot's back again any time soon."

"What makes you say that? In fact, I plan to try him again tomorrow."

Her look of horror and disbelief was priceless, he thought, and he chuckled as he reached across the table to engulf her hand in his. "Hey, I was just kidding."

She frowned over at him. "I hope so, Derringer, and I certainly hope you've learned your lesson about taking unnecessary risks."

He laughed. "Trust me, I have," he said, although he knew she was a risk and he had a feeling spending too much time with her wasn't a good thing. It was then that he realized he was still holding her hand, and with supreme effort he released it.

He should know better than to get too attached to a

woman like Lucia. She was the kind of woman a man could become attached to before he knew it. His attraction to her seemed too natural, but way too binding. She was a woman who seemed to be created just for the purpose of making a man want her in ways he had never wanted a woman before. And that wasn't good.

After their initial drinks, they ordered coffee and then shared a slice of strawberry cheesecake, and while they sat there she had his undivided attention. They conversed about a number of topics. More than once he caught his gaze roaming across her face, studying her features and appreciating her beauty. Whether she knew it or not, her facial bone structure was superb and any man would definitely find her attractive. But he knew there was more to her than just her outside beauty. She was beautiful on the inside as well. Derringer listened as she told him about a number of charities and worthwhile events she supported, and he was impressed.

A couple of hours later while driving her back home, he couldn't help but reflect on how the evening had gone. Certainly not the way he had planned. When the car came to a traffic light, he glanced over at her. Not surprisingly, she had fallen asleep. He thought about all the things he wanted to do to her when he got her back to her place, and knew the only thing he should do was walk her to her door and then leave. Something was going on with him that he didn't understand and he was smart enough to know when to back off.

That thought was still on his mind when he walked her to the door later. For some reason, he was being pulled in another direction and frankly he didn't like it. Her kiss alone had shot his brain cells to hell and back and knocked his carefully constructed plans to teach her a lesson to the wind. Even now the taste from her kiss was lingering in his mouth.

"Thanks again for such a wonderful evening, Derringer. I had a great time."

He'd had a great time, too. "You're welcome." He forced his lips closed to stop from asking her out again. He simply refused to do that. "Well, I guess I'll be going now," he said, trying to get his feet to step back and trying to figure out why they wouldn't budge.

"Would you like to come inside for more coffee?"

He shook his head. "Thanks, but I don't think my stomach can hold much more. Besides, my restrictions are over and I can return to work soon. I'll be helping Zane and Jason with the horses in the morning. I need to get home and get to bed."

"All right."

He made a move to leave but couldn't. Instead, his gaze settled on the face staring at him and he felt something pull at his gut. "Good night, Lucia," he whispered, just seconds before leaning down and brushing a kiss across her lips.

"Good night, Derringer."

He straightened and watched as she let herself inside the house. When the door clicked locked behind her, he turned to move down the walkway toward his car. He opened the door and slid inside. He needed to go home and think about things, regroup and revamp. And he had to figure out what there was about Lucia Conyers that got to him on a level he wasn't used to.

Chapter 6

Zane stopped saddling his horse long enough to glance over at his brother. "What's going on with you, Derringer? Last week you were inquiring about women's panties and now this week you want to know about a woman's scent. Didn't you get that mystery solved by viewing the tape on that video camera?"

Derringer rubbed his hand down his face. He should have known better than to come to Zane, but the bottom line was his brother knew more about women than *he* did and right now he needed answers. After he got them he'd be able to figure out what was going on with him when it came to Lucia. It had been almost a week after their date to the movies and he still didn't have a clue. And he had yet to confront her about being his late-night visitor.

He glanced over at Zane across the horse's back. "There's nothing going on with me. Just answer the damn question."

Zane chuckled. "Getting kind of testy, aren't you? And how did your date go with Lucia Saturday night? I haven't heard you say."

"And I'm not going to say either, other than we had a nice time."

"For your sake I think that's all you better say or Chloe, Megan and Bailey will be coming down on you pretty hard.

You might get a reprieve from Gemma since she's out of the country, but I wouldn't count on it if I were you, because she's coming home later this month for the charity ball."

Derringer grunted. The women in his family ought to stay out of his business and he would tell them so if the topic of Lucia ever came up with any of them again. So far, he'd been lying low this week, and when he had dropped by to see Ramsey, Chloe and baby Susan, the topic of Lucia hadn't come up. He could inwardly admit the reason he'd made himself scarce was his fear of running into her at Ramsey's. It was unheard of for Derringer Westmoreland to avoid any woman.

"So, will you answer my question?"

Zane crossed his arms over his chest. "Only after you answer mine. Did you or did you not watch that video footage?"

He glared over at his brother. "Yes, I watched it."

"And?"

"And I'd rather not discuss it."

A smirk appeared on Zane's face. "I bet you'll be glad to discuss it if you get hit with a paternity suit nine months from now."

Zane's words hit Derringer below the belt with a reminder that Lucia could be pregnant with his child. They'd had unprotected sex that night. She had to know that as well. Was she not worried about that possibility? He met his brother's intense gaze. "I'll handle it if that were to happen, now answer the question."

Zane smiled. "You're going to have to repeat it. My attention span isn't what it used to be these days."

Like hell it's not, Derringer thought. He knew Zane was trying to get a rise out of him and he didn't like it, but since he needed answers he would overlook his brother's bad attitude for now. "I want to know about the scent of a woman."

Zane smiled as he leaned back against the corral post.

"Um, that's an easy one. Every woman has her own unique scent and if a man is attentive enough he's able to tell them apart by it. Some men will know their woman's location in a room before setting eyes on her just from her scent alone."

Derringer pulled in a deep breath. He knew all that already. He tilted his Stetson back off his head. "What I want to know is the effect that scent can have on a man."

Zane chuckled. "Well, I know for a fact that a woman's natural scent is a total turn-on for most men. It's all in the pheromones. Remember that doctor I dated last year?"

Derringer nodded. "Yes, what about her?"

"Man, her scent used to drive me crazy, and she damn well knew it. But it didn't bother me one bit when she took that job in Atlanta and moved away," Zane said.

Derringer decided not to remind Zane of the bad mood he'd been in for months after the woman left. "Every woman has her unique scent, but many douse it with cologne," Zane continued. "Then every woman that wears that cologne practically smells the same. But when you make love to a woman, her natural scent will override everything."

Zane paused a minute and then said, "And the effect it can have on a man depends on what degree of an attractant her scent can be. A woman's scent alone can render him powerless."

Derringer lifted his brow. "Powerless?"

"Yes, the scent of a woman is highly potent and sexually stimulating. And some men have discovered their own male senses can detect the woman who was meant to be their mate just from her scent. Animals rely on scent for that purpose all the time, and although some people might differ with that theory, there are some who believes it's true for humans as well. So if the scent of some woman is getting to you, that might be your cue she's your mate."

Derringer studied his brother's gaze, not sure if Zane

was handing him a bunch of bull or not. The thought of his future being shared with a woman because of her scent didn't make much sense, but he'd watched enough shows on *Animal Kingdom* to know that was basically true with animals. Was man different from other animals?

"Some woman's scent has gotten to you," Zane taunted.

He didn't answer. Instead, he looked away for a second, wondering about that same thing. When he looked back at Zane moments later, his brother was grinning.

"What the hell do you find amusing?"

"Trust me, you don't want to know."

Derringer frowned. Zane was right; he didn't want to know.

"And you haven't heard from Derringer since your date Saturday night?"

A lump formed in Lucia's throat with Chloe's question. It was Friday night, late afternoon, and she sat curled on her sofa. Although she really hadn't expected Derringer to seek her out again, the notion that he didn't still bothered her, especially because she thought they'd had such a good time. At least she knew for a fact *she* had, and he'd seemed to enjoy himself as well. But she figured when you were Derringer Westmoreland, you could have a different girl every day.

When he had brought her home Saturday night, she had expected him to accept her invitation to come inside for coffee, although she would be the first to admit they had drunk plenty of the stuff at Torie's. He had declined her offer and given her a chaste kiss on the lips then left.

"No, I haven't heard anything, but that's okay. I was able to write in my diary that I had a date with him and that's good."

"One date isn't good when there can be others, Lu. You

do know that women don't have to wait for the man to call for a date, we have that right as well."

Yes, but Lucia knew she couldn't be that forward with a man. "I know, but—"

There was a knock at her door. "Someone's at the door, Chloe. It's probably Mrs. Noel from across the street. She bakes on Fridays and uses me as her guinea pig, but I have no complaints. I'll call you back later."

When the knock sounded again, she called out after hanging up the phone. "I'm coming."

She eased off the sofa and headed to the door, thinking she would chow down on Mrs. Noel's sweets and get her romance groove on by watching a romantic movie on Lifetime. If you couldn't have the real thing in your life then she figured a movie was second best.

She nearly choked when she glanced out her peephole. Her caller wasn't her neighbor. It was Derringer. She suddenly felt hot when she realized he was staring at the peephole in the door as if he knew she was watching him. She closed her eyes trying to slow down the beating of her heart. He was the last person she expected to see tonight. In fact, she'd figured he wouldn't appear on her doorstep any time soon, or ever again. She assumed they would get back into the routine of running into each other whenever she visited Chloe, Ramsey and the baby.

Forcing her brain cells to stop scrambling, she turned the doorknob to open the door and there he stood in a pair of jeans, a sweater, a leather jacket and boots. He looked good, but then he always did. He was leaning against a post on her porch with his hands in his pockets.

She cleared her throat. "Derringer, what are you doing here?"

He held her gaze. "I know I should have called first."

She stopped herself from saying that he could appear on her doorstep anytime. The last thing a woman should do is let a man assume she was pining for him…even if she was. "Yes, you should have called first. Is anything wrong?"

"No, I just needed to see you."

She tried to ignore how low his voice had dropped and how he was looking at her. Instead, she tried to focus on what he'd said. *He just needed to see her.*

Yeah, right. She thought he could really do better than that, especially since he hadn't done so much as picked up a phone to call her since their date on Saturday night. Was she to believe needing to see her had brought him to her door? She wondered if his date tonight had canceled and she had been his backup plan. Curious about that possibility, she decided to ask him.

Crossing her arms over her chest, she said. "Um, let me guess, your date stood you up and I was next on the list." After saying the words, she realized her mistake. First, she doubted very seriously that any woman stood him up and she really thought a lot of herself to even assume she was on any list he had.

He tilted his head as if he needed to see her more clearly. "Is that what you think?"

She shook her head. "To be honest with you, Derringer, I really don't know what to think."

He made a slow move and inched closer to her face. He then leaned over and whispered against her ear. "Invite me in and I promise you won't be thinking at all."

And that was what she was afraid of.

She drew in a deep breath, thinking she would be able to handle him. She opened the door and stepped back, hoping at that moment that she could.

What the hell am I doing here? Derringer wondered as he brushed by her. He had caught a whiff of her scent the moment she had opened the door, and as always it was playing hard on his senses.

He turned when he heard her close the door behind him and his gaze studied her. For some reason he didn't have the strength or inclination to tear his eyes away from her. What was wrong with him? When had he ever let a woman affect him this way? She was standing there leaning back against the door in her bare feet and a pair of leggings and a T-shirt. Her hair was back in that signature ponytail. She looked comfortable. She looked sexy. Damn, she looked good enough to eat.

He cleared his throat. "What are your plans for tonight?"

She shrugged. "I didn't have any. I was just going to watch a movie on Lifetime."

He was familiar with that channel, the one that was supposed to be for women that showed romance movies 24/7. His sisters used to be glued to their television sets, and in Bailey's case, sometimes to his.

"How would you like to go roller skating?"

The glow from a table lamp captured the expression of surprise on her face. "You want us to go out again?"

He noted that there was a degree of shock in her voice. There was a note of wariness as well.

"Yes, I know I should have called first, and I am sorry about that. And just to set the record straight, when I left home I didn't have a date. I didn't have any plans for tonight. I got in my car and I ended up here. What I said earlier was true. I needed to see you."

Serious doubt was etched in her features. "Why, Derringer? Why did you need to see me?"

It should be so easy to use this moment and come clean and say because I know who you are. I know you are the woman to whom I made love in what should have been a weak and crazy moment, but it ended up being the one time I slept with a woman that I remember the most. That no matter what I do or where I go, your scent is right there with me. You are responsible for the lust that rages through my body every time I think of you, whenever I see you. Even now there is a throbbing in my groin that you're causing and I want more than anything to make love to you again.

"Derringer?"

He realized at that moment that he hadn't answered her. Instead, he had been standing there and staring at her like a lust-crazed maniac. He slowly crossed the floor, pinning her in when he braced his hands on both sides of her head, and leaned in close to her mouth.

"I really don't know why I needed to see you tonight," he whispered huskily against her lips. "I can't explain it. I just needed to see you, be with you and spend time with you. I enjoyed Saturday night and—"

"Could have fooled me."

He noticed her voice had barely been audible, but he'd heard that, and he'd heard the hurt in her tone. He hadn't called her. He should have. He had wanted to. But he had fought the temptation. If only she knew to what degree he had fought it. A part of him knew being here with her now wasn't good; especially when he was thinking of all the things he wanted to do to her right now—against the door, on the floor, on her bed, the table, the sofa, every damn place in her house. But even more important was that he knew more about the situation than she did. He had yet to tell her that he knew about her visit to his home that night.

He had spent the last few days going over the video time and time again. It was evident from viewing the footage and seeing how she had merely stuck her head in the door that initially she'd had no intention of staying. Then she had glanced back at the box and decided to put it inside. She must have heard him fall once she was inside, because this week he remembered that part—missing the bed when he'd gotten up to use the bathroom and falling flat on his behind when he was returning to bed. He remembered someone, his Puddin' Tame, helping him back into bed, and the only thing he remembered after that was making love to a woman.

And the woman he had made love to had been her.

Things were still kind of fuzzy, but he remembered that much now. "I apologize for not calling you this week. I should have," he murmured.

She shook her head. "You didn't have to. I'm the one who should be apologizing. I should not have given you the impression that you should have called, just now."

His heart beat hard in his chest. That statement alone showed how different she was from the other women he messed around with. And that difference, among other things, he was convinced, was what had him here with her now.

"I don't want any apologies from you," he said, leaning in closer, drawing one of her earlobes between his lips. "This is what I want." He then brushed his tongue across her lips and when she gave a sharp intake of breath, he did it again. And again.

"Why, Derringer…why me?" she whispered moments before she began trembling against the door.

"Why not you?" he breathed huskily against her lips before bending close to taste them again. Her flavor as well as her scent was getting to him on a level that made him want to push forward instead of drawing back.

Then deciding they had done enough talking for now, he sidled up closer to her and pressed his mouth to hers.

By rights she should send him away, Lucia's mind screamed over and over again. But it was hard to listen to what her mind was saying when Derringer was causing so much havoc with her body. This was the kind of kiss that could knock the sense out of a woman. It was long, deep and downright greedy. He was eating at her mouth as if it were his last meal, and there was no doubt in her mind this kiss was definitely X-rated.

And if that wasn't bad enough, his erection was pressing into her right at the juncture of her thighs, cradled against her womanly mound as if it had specifically sought out that part of her. And then there were the nipples of her breasts that were piercing his chest through the material of her T-shirt. She couldn't help but remember how it felt when they had been flesh to flesh, skin to skin. If he was seducing her then he was certainly going at it the right way.

He suddenly pulled back. Puzzled as to why, she nervously chewed on her bottom lip—a lip he'd just released from devouring—and stared up at him. He was staring back. "I think we need to take time and think through a few things," he said huskily.

She arched a bemused brow. He evidently was speaking for himself. As far as she was concerned there was nothing to think through. She knew what she wanted and had a feeling that he did, too. So what was the problem? She knew the score. Nothing was forever with Derringer Westmoreland and she was okay with that. Although she was hopelessly in love with the man, she knew her limitations. She had accepted them long ago. She had made more strides within the last twelve days than she'd expected in her entire lifetime. They had made love, for heaven's sake, and he had kissed her senseless a week ago tomorrow.

But still…she was no longer a teenager with fantasies of him marrying her and living happily ever after with each other. She totally understood that was not the way the ball would bounce. She was not entering into anything with him blindly; she had both eyes wide open. Bottom line was that she didn't have to safeguard her heart. Although she wished otherwise, the man had her heart, lock, stock and barrel, and it was too late to do anything about it but gladly take whatever she could and live the rest of her life on memories.

"I think I need to give you time to get dressed so we can get to the skating rink."

She couldn't help but smile softly. "Do you really want to do that?"

He shook his head. "No, but if you knew what I really want to do you would probably kick me out."

"Try me."

He threw his head back and laughed. "No, I think I'll pass. I'll wait out here until you change clothes."

She moved around him to head down the hall and stopped right before crossing the threshold into her room. "You know it would probably be more fun if we stayed here, don't you?"

He smiled then said in a firm voice, "Go get dressed, Lucia."

Laughing, she entered the bedroom and closed the door behind her. While removing her clothes, Lucia made a decision about something.

For the first time ever she intended to try her luck at seducing a man.

Chapter 7

Derringer glanced over at Lucia, who was across the room standing in line to check out their roller skates. He had two words to describe the jeans she was wearing—snug and tight. And then the first two words that would describe her overall appearance tonight were hot and sexy.

Deciding he needed to stop staring at her every chance he got, he glanced around. He had expected the place to be crowded since it was a Friday night, but why were there more kids than adults? Granted, it had been years since he'd gone skating, but still, he would think it was past these kids' bedtime.

He laughed recalling how some smart-mouthed preteen had come up to him a few minutes ago and said he hoped he and Lucia were fast enough on the skates to keep up and not get in anyone's way. Hell, he and Lucia weren't *that* old.

"What's so funny?"

He glanced down to see Lucia had returned with their skates. He then told her about the smart-mouthed kid and she smiled. "Doesn't this city still have a curfew?" he asked her.

She shook her head. "Not anymore."

He lifted a brow. "When did they do away with it?" He

figured she would know because her dad had been a member of Denver's city council for years.

She smiled sweetly up at him. "They did away with it when Bane turned eighteen."

He stared at her for a second, saw she was serious and threw his head back and laughed so hard they couldn't help but get attention. "You're making a scene, Derringer Westmoreland," she whispered.

He shook his head and pulled her closer to him. "Is there anywhere Bane didn't leave his mark?"

"According to my father, the answer to that question is a resounding no. Now, come on, *old man,* or that kid will return and ask us to step aside."

He took her teasing of his age in stride, but still he reached out and grabbed her around the waist. "I'll show you who's old and who's not," he said, and then he took off, pulling her with him.

It was past three in the morning when Derringer returned Lucia home, and he smiled as he escorted her inside her home. It had taken a while, but he'd eventually shown that smart-mouthed kid why he once had earned the reputation of being hell on wheels with roller skates. And then when the kid had found out he was a Westmoreland—a cousin to the infamous Bane Westmoreland—he had to all but sign autographs.

"Can you believe those kids actually think Bane is some kind of hero?" he said, dropping onto Lucia's love seat.

She chuckled as she sat down on the sofa across from him. "Yes, I can believe that. Bane was bold enough to do some of the horrific things they would probably love to try but know that they can't get away with doing. Tell me, who in their right mind would take off in the sheriff's car while he's giving someone a ticket other than Bane? He became something of a legend if you were to read some of the stuff the girls wrote all over the walls in the bathroom at the local high school. He and the twins."

He glanced over at her. "How do you know about those walls? That was after your time."

She smiled as she settled back against the cushions, wrapping her arms across the back. "I have a young cousin who used to have a crush on Aidan and he's all she used to talk about then, in addition to all the trouble Aidan, Adrian and Bane would get into."

Derringer shook his head and chuckled, remembering those times. "And let's not forget Bailey—she was just as bad. At one time we considered sending all four of them to military school, but that would be like giving up on our own, and we knew we couldn't do that."

A serious expression touched his features before he said, "I don't tell Ramsey and Dillon enough how much I appreciate them keeping our family together. Losing my parents and my aunt and uncle at the same time was hard on everyone, but they helped us get through it." Derringer inwardly struggled with what he'd just told her, realizing he had never shared those emotions and feelings with anyone, certainly not any of his women.

"I'm sure they know you appreciate what they did, Derringer. The proof is in the successful, law-abiding men and women you all became. That's a testimony in itself. The Westmorelands are getting something now the townspeople figured they wouldn't ever get after your parents and aunt and uncle passed away."

He lifted a brow. "And what's that?"

"Respect." A smile touched her lips when she added, "And admiration. I wish you would have noticed the look on that kid's face tonight when he realized you were a Westmoreland."

Derringer snorted. "Yes, but he was admiring me for all the wrong reasons."

"It doesn't matter."

He knew deep down that Lucia was right—it didn't matter, because in the end what Dillon and Ramsey had done was indeed a success story in his book. He stretched his legs out in front of him thinking how throughout the evening he had enjoyed the time he was spending with Lucia. It had been the first time he'd spent with a woman when he'd had honest-to-goodness fun. She had been herself and hadn't gone out of her way to impress him and draw all the attention on her.

Even on the drive to and from the skating arena he had enjoyed their conversation, and although it was hard to believe, they had a lot in common and shared the same interests. They both enjoyed watching Westerns, they enjoyed a good comedy every once in a while and were huge fans of the Wayans brothers, Bill Cosby and Sandra Bullock. She also rode horses and enjoyed going hunting.

But more than anything, he had enjoyed being with her, sharing her space and breathing the same air that she did. And he smiled, thinking she wasn't too bad on roller skates either. He had enjoyed going around the rink with her, often hearing her throaty laugh, looking over at her and seeing the huge smile on her face; and he especially liked wrapping his arms around her waist when they skated together.

"I had a wonderful time tonight, Derringer. I really enjoyed myself."

He glanced over at her. At some point, she had removed her boots and shifted position on the sofa to tuck her jeans-clad legs beneath her. But still, it didn't take much to remember how her long, curvy legs looked in a pair of shorts, a skirt or a dress. But most of all, he could recall those same legs wrapped around his waist while they had made love. The more time he spent with her, the more things were coming back to him that he had forgotten about their night together.

"I enjoyed myself as well," he responded.

"You were pretty good on those skates."

"You weren't so bad yourself." He wondered why he was sitting here making small talk with her when what he really wanted to do was to cross the room and join her on that sofa. His attention was trained directly on her and he could tell by the way she was moving her fingers on her knee he was making her nervous.

"Lucia, does my being here bother you?"

"What makes you think that?"

"Because you're over there and I'm here," he didn't hesitate to say. He watched as she nervously licked her bottom lip, and immediately the lower part of his body—directly behind his zipper—responded in a hard-up way.

"There's nothing keeping you over there, Derringer," she said softly.

He couldn't help but smile at her deduction. She was right. There was nothing keeping him on this love seat when more than anything he wanted to be on that sofa with her. Knowing what he should do was stand up, thank her again for a good time and head toward the door and leave, never to return again, he remained seated for a minute. But he knew, just as much as he knew that tomorrow would bring another day, he wasn't going to do that.

And he also knew that she didn't know, she didn't have a clue just what she did to him, what being here with her was doing to him. He figured his intense attraction to her had everything to do with the night they had made love. But that wouldn't make sense since he'd made love to a number of women before and none had left the kind of lasting impression that she had. So why had the time with her been different, and why was he so quick to accept that it was?

The answer nearly made him tremble inside. It made his chest clench and made blood rush through his veins. She was deeply embedded in his system and he knew only one way to get her out of there. When they'd made love before, he hadn't been completely coherent and maybe that was the problem. Now he needed to make love to her in his right mind, if for no other reason than to purge her from his thoughts, mind and body. Then he could get on with his life and she could get on with hers. But before it was all over, he intended to let her know he was well aware that she had been his visitor that night.

Deciding he was doing too much thinking and not delivering enough action, he eased off the love seat.

Nowhere to run and nowhere to hide.

Deep down, Lucia knew she didn't want to do either as she watched Derringer slowly move toward her. Why was she getting all tense and nervous? Hadn't she made up her mind to seduce him tonight? But it seemed as if he had beat her to the punch and he was about to take things into his own hands. Literally.

His visit had been a surprise. She hadn't expected him tonight. He was the most unlikely person to show up at her place tonight or any other time. Not only had he shown up, but he'd taken her out again. Skating. It was their second date and he claimed the reason he was here was because he had needed to see her.

She knew needing to see her had only been a line and men like Derringer were good at saying such things. They said whatever they thought a woman wanted to hear. But that hadn't stopped her from allowing herself to be taken in, relish the moments spent with him and be greedy enough to want more. She would take whatever part of Derringer she could get. Tomorrow she would wake up and hate herself for being such a weakling where he was concerned, but she would also wake wearing the blush of a satisfied woman all over her face.

There was no doubt in her mind that he intended to make

love to her. He'd done it before, and from the dark, intense look in his eyes, he planned to do so again. And tonight he wouldn't get any resistance, because she loved him just that much and was secretly grateful for this time with him.

He slid down beside her on the sofa. "There is just something tantalizingly sweet about your scent, Lucia."

Another line, she was sure of it. "Is there?"

"Yes. It makes my body burn for you," he said, wrapping his arms around her shoulders.

She drew in a deep breath, thinking she would love to believe what he was saying, but knew better. However, tonight it was all about make-believe. Besides, it was hard not to melt under the intense look he was giving her and the way his arm felt around her shoulders. And he was sitting so close, every time he spoke his warm breath blew across her lips.

He then pulled back slightly and gazed at her thoughtfully. "You don't believe a word I've said, do you?"

She began nibbling on her bottom lip. She could easily lie and assure him that she did, but deep down she knew she didn't believe him. She tilted her chin upward. "Does it matter whether or not I believe you, Derringer?"

He continued to stare at her for a moment with an unreadable expression on his face, and for a split second she thought he was going to say something but he didn't. Instead, he reached out and cupped her chin with his fingertips before slowly lowering his mouth to hers.

Sensations ripped through her the moment their lips touched. She closed her eyes when his tongue eased into her mouth and he began kissing her with a hunger that had her groaning deep in her throat.

Her heart thundered when he captured her tongue with his and began doing all kinds of erotic things to it, sucking on it as if there was a time limit to get his fill, mating their tongues as if all they had was the here and now. This was the kind of kissing that made a woman forget that she was supposed to be a lady.

She wanted this. She wanted every mind-blowing moment because she knew there *was* a time limit on this fantasy. Everyone around town knew of Derringer's reputation for getting tired of his women quickly. There was only a chosen one or two who were determined to hang in for the long haul no matter what—by their choice and not his. She refused to be one of those women. She would take this and be satisfied.

When he broke off the kiss to shift their positions to press her back against the sofa cushions, she moved willingly with him. She gazed up at him when his body eased on top of hers. She could feel his hard erection between her thighs.

He lowered his head and began nibbling around her throat, taking the tip of his tongue and licking around her chin. "Too many clothes." She heard him utter the word moments before he leaned up and, without warning, pulled the sweater over her head. He tossed it to the floor. He then proceeded to tug her jeans down her legs.

He looked down at her and smiled at her matching red lace bra and panties. She wondered what was going through his mind and why he was so captivated by her lingerie. He then glanced back up at her. "I like a woman who wears lace," he whispered huskily before leaning down and taking her mouth once more.

His lips seemed incredibly hot and he had no problem sliding his tongue where he pleased while kissing her with slow, deep strokes. And when she felt his fingers move toward her breasts, ease under her bra to stroke a nipple, she nearly shot off the sofa when sensations speared through her.

"Derringer…" she whispered in a strained voice.

This was getting to be too much and she began quivering almost uncontrollably, knowing what she'd heard for years was true. Derringer Westmoreland was almost too much for any woman to handle.

She was wrong. It did matter to him that she believed what he said.

That thought raged through Derringer's mind as he continued to kiss her with a hunger he could not understand. What was there about her that made him want to taste her all over, make her groan mercilessly and torture her over and over again before exploding inside her? The mere thought of doing the latter made his groin throb.

He pulled back slightly, wanting her to watch exactly what he was doing. What he was about to do. When he released the front fastener of her bra, his breath quickened when her breasts came tumbling out. They were full, firm and ripe and the nipples were dark and tightened even more into hard nubs before his eyes. And when he swooped his mouth down and captured a peak between his lips, she moaned and closed her eyes. "Keep them open, Lucia. Watch me. I want you to see what I'm doing to you."

He saw her heavy-lidded eyes watch as he tugged a nipple into his mouth and begin sucking on it, and the more he heard her moan the more pressure he exerted with his mouth.

But that wasn't enough. Her scent was getting to him and he needed to touch her, to taste her, to bury himself in a feminine fragrance that was exclusively hers. He left one breast and went to another as he lowered a hand underneath the waistband of her lace bikini panties. And when his fingers ran over the wetness of her feminine folds, she writhed against his hand and let out a deep moan and whispered his name.

He lifted his head to stare down at eyes that were dazed with passion. "Yes, baby? You want something?"

Instead of answering, she began trembling as his fingers slipped inside her and he began stroking her while watching the display of emotions and expressions appear on her face. The breathless wonder drenched with pleasure that he saw in her gaze, in response to his touch, was a sight to behold and the sweetest thing he'd ever seen.

Lust thundered through him with the force of a hurricane and he knew he had to make love to her in the most primitive way. Leaning back, he eased to his feet and continued to hold her gaze while he tugged off his boots, pulled off his socks and unzipped his jeans. He took the time to remove a condom from the back pocket and held it between his teeth while he yanked down his jeans, careful of his engorged erection.

"Derringer…"

If she said his name like that, with that barely-there voice, one more time, he would lose it. The sound was sending splendorous shivers up his spine and there was a chance he would come the minute he got inside her, without making a single thrust. And he didn't want that. He wanted to savor the moment, make it last for as long as he could.

When he was totally naked, he stood before her and watched her gaze roam over him, seeing some parts of him that she probably hadn't seen their other night together. There was no shame in his game, but he knew deep down this wasn't a game with him. He was serious about what was taking place between them.

Thinking he had wasted more than enough time, he bent over her to remove the last item of clothing covering her body. Her panties. He touched the center of her and she sucked in a deep breath. He tossed aside the condom packet he'd been holding between his teeth. "You're drenched, baby," he said in a low, rough voice. "I know you don't believe me, but there is something about you that drives me crazy."

When he began tugging her panties down her legs, he whispered throatily, "Lift your hips and bend your legs for me."

She did, and when he removed her panties, instead of tossing them aside, he rubbed the lacy material over his face before he bent to the floor and tucked them into the back pocket of his jeans. He knew she was watching his every move and was probably wondering what on earth possessed him to do such a thing.

Instead of mounting her now, as he wanted to do, there was something he wanted to do even more. Taste her. He wanted to taste all that sweetness that triggered the feminine aroma he enjoyed inhaling. It was a scent he was convinced he had become addicted to.

He lowered his body to his knees and before she could pull in her next breath, he pressed an open mouth to the wet, hot feminine lips of her sex. She groaned so deep in her throat that her body began trembling. But he kept focused on the pleasure awaiting him as he leisurely stroked her with his tongue, feasting on her with a hunger he knew she could not understand, but that he intended her to enjoy.

Because he was definitely enjoying it.

He'd been of the mind that no other woman had her scent. Now he was just as convinced that no other woman had her taste as well. It was unique. It was hers. And at the moment, as crazy as it sounded, he was also of the mind that it was also *his,* in a possessive way he'd never encountered before with any woman. The mere thought should have scared the hell out of him, but he was too far gone to give a damn.

When heat and lust combined and resonated off his mind he knew he had to be inside her or risk exploding then and there. He tore his mouth from her and threw his head back and released a deep savage groan. He then stared down at her while licking her juices from his lips. He felt as if he was taking part in a scorching-hot, exciting and erotic dream, and it was a dream he was dying to turn into a reality. And there was only one way he knew to do that.

He would take her and now.

Without saying a word, he leaned over and spread her thighs and placed a kiss on each before moving off his knees to shift his body over hers. Instinctively she arched her back and wrapped her arms around his neck. Their gazes held as he eased his body down, the thick head of his shaft finding what it wanted and working its way inside her wet tightness. He paused when he'd made it halfway, glorying in the feel of her muscles clamping down on him, convulsing around him.

He wanted to take things slow, but the feel of her gripping him had him groaning deep in his throat, and when in a naughty, unexpected move she flicked out her tongue and licked his budded nipple before easing it into her mouth with a hungry suck, he took in a sharp breath at the same time he thrust hard into her.

When he heard her cry out, he apologized in a soothing whispered voice. "I'm sorry. I didn't mean to hurt you. Just lie still for a moment."

He used that time to lick around her mouth, nibble at the corners, and when she parted her mouth on a sweet sigh, he eased his tongue inside and sank right into a hungry kiss filled with more urgency and desire than he'd ever known or had ever cared knowing. Until now.

And then he felt the lower part of her body shift beneath the weight of his. He pulled back from the kiss. "That's it, baby," he crooned close to her ear. "Take it. All that you want."

His body remained still as she moved her body, grinding against him, dipping her hips into the sofa cushions before lifting them up again, arching her back in the process. Then she began rotating her hips, pushing up and lowering back down.

Derringer's body froze when he remembered the condom he'd tossed aside and he knew he needed to pull out now. But heaven help him, he couldn't do so. Being inside of her like this felt so darn right. He kept his body immobile until he couldn't stay still any longer and then he joined her, driving his erection deeper into her. He thrust in and out with precise and concentrated strokes that he felt all the way to the soles of his feet.

He had thought their first time together had been off the charts, but nothing, he decided, could compare to this. Nothing could compete with the incredible feeling of being inside her this way. Nothing. Desperate to reach the highest peak with her, he took total possession of her, kissing her with urgency while their bodies mated in the most primitive pleasure known to humankind.

He whispered erotic things in her ear before reaching down and cupping her face in his hands to stare down at her while his body continued to drive heatedly into hers. Their gazes locked and something happened between them at that moment that nearly threw him off balance. Somewhere in the back of his mind a voice was taunting that this had nothing to do with possessing but everything to do with claiming.

Denial froze hard in his throat and he wanted to scream that it wasn't possible. He claimed no woman. Instead, he grunted savagely as his body exploded, and then he heard her scream as she cried out in ecstasy. He kept thrusting into her, pushing them further and further into sweet oblivion and surging them beyond the stars.

Chapter 8

Lucia moved her head slowly, opened her eyes and then came fully awake when a flash of sunlight through her bedroom window hit her right in the face. It was then that she felt the male body pressed tightly against her back and the heated feel of Derringer's breathing on her neck.

She then remembered.

They had made love on the sofa before moving into her bedroom where they had made love again before drifting off to sleep. Sometime during the wee hours of early morning they had made love again. The entire thing seemed unreal, but Derringer's presence in her bed assured her that it had been real.

Her body felt sore, tender in a number of places, but mostly between her legs, and she wouldn't be surprised if her lips were swollen from all the kissing they had done. Her cheeks flooded with heat thinking about a number of other things they'd gotten into as well. She had proven to him in a very sexual way that she definitely knew how to ride a stallion. He had taunted her to prove it and she'd done so.

Her eyes fluttered closed as she thought how she would handle things from here on out. She knew last night meant more to her than it had to him, and she could handle that.

But what she wouldn't be able to handle was letting things go beyond what they'd shared these past few hours. She loved him and for him to ever make love to her again would turn things sexual, into a casual relationship that would tarnish her memories rather than enhance them. She was smart enough to know when to let go and move on. Now was the time.

Tears flooded her eyes. Derringer would always have her heart, but the reality was that she would never have his. And being the type of person that she was, she could never allow herself to become just one in a long line of women vying for his attention. She preferred letting things go back to the way they were between them before they'd become intimate.

The way she saw things, if she never had him then there was no way she could lose him. She couldn't risk a broken heart because of Derringer and she knew her place in his life. She didn't have one. If she began thinking of developing something serious with him knowing the kind of man he was, she was setting herself up for pain from which she might never be able to heal.

She would continue to love him like this—secretly. She had gotten used to doing things that way and, no matter what, she couldn't let their sexual encounters—no matter how intense they'd been—fill her head and mind with false illusions.

She swallowed when she felt Derringer's penis swell against her backside and tried to convince herself it wouldn't be a good idea to make love to him one last time. But she knew the moment he pulled her closer to his hard, masculine body that she would. This would be saying goodbye to the intimacy between them. She knew it even if he didn't.

"You're awake?" He turned her in his arms to face him. Desire rippled through her the moment she looked into his face. Propped with his head on her pillow, his eyes had the same desire-glazed look they'd had that first night they'd made love. It was a sexy, drowsy look, complete with a darkened shadow on his chin. No man had a right to look this good in the morning. He looked so untamed, wild and raw. His rumpled look was calling out to her, arousing her and making her want him all over again.

"Sort of," she said, yawning, and couldn't help the anticipation she heard in her voice. And when he gave her a dimpled cowboy smile, sensations shot through her entire body, but especially in the area between her thighs.

"Then let me wake you up the Derringer Westmoreland way." He then captured her mouth at the same time he tossed his leg over hers, adjusting their positions to ease inside her body.

"Oh," she whispered, and when he locked his leg on her and began slowly moving in and out of her and capturing her lips with his, she figured there was nothing wrong with one for the road…even though she knew she would end up in heaven.

Derringer's smile faded as he buttoned up his shirt and stared at Lucia. "What do you mean we can't ever make love again?"

He saw the flash of regret that came into her eyes before she stopped brushing her teeth long enough to rinse out her mouth. "Just what I said, Derringer. Last night was special and I want to remember it that way."

He was confused. "And you don't think you can if we make love again?"

"No. I know about the women you usually sleep with and, personally, I don't want to be one of them."

He frowned, crossing his arms over his chest, not sure he liked what she'd said. "Then why did you sleep with me last night?"

"I had my reasons."

His frown deepened. He couldn't help but wonder if those reasons were the same ones he had initially suspected her of having. And it didn't help matters to know that every time he had made love to her they had been unprotected. The first time had been a slip-up, and then after that, he'd deliberately chosen not to think about it. Why he'd done such a thing, he didn't know. He usually made it a point to always use protection. Even now, Lucia might be pregnant with his child.

"And just what are those reasons, Lucia?"

"I'd rather not say."

Anger ignited inside him. That response wasn't good enough.

"Oh!" she cried out in surprise when he reached out, snatched her off her feet and tossed her over his shoulders like a sack of potatoes and strode out of the bathroom.

"Derringer! What in the world is wrong with you? Put me down."

He did. Tossing her on the bed and glaring down at her. "I want to hear these reasons."

She glared back. "You don't need to know them. All you need to know is that I won't be sharing a bed with you again."

"Why? Because you think you're pregnant now and that's what this is about?"

Shock leaped into her face. "Pregnant? What are you talking about?"

"Are you on the pill or something?"

He could tell his question had surprised her. "No."

His frown deepened. "There's only one reason I can think of for a woman to let a man come inside her. Are you going to deny that sleeping with me this time around…as well as the last time…has nothing to do with you wanting a Westmoreland baby?"

He saw her throat tighten. "The last?"

"Yes," he said between clenched teeth. "I know all about your little visit that night when I was drugged up on pain medication."

She blinked. "You know?"

"Yes, and I couldn't figure out why you, a virgin, would get into my bed and take advantage of me. And, yes, I do remember you were a virgin even if I couldn't recall your identity."

She angrily reared up on her haunches. "I did not take advantage of you! I was helping you back into bed after you fell. If anything, you're the one who took advantage of me."

"So you say." He could see fury consume her body. and smoke was all but coming out her ears, but he didn't care.

She rolled off the bed and stood in front of him, almost nose to nose. "Are you insinuating I slept with you that night to deliberately get pregnant? And that I only slept with you last night and this morning for the same reason?"

"What am I supposed to think?"

She threw her hair over her shoulders. "That maybe I am different from all those other women you spend your time with, and that I would not have an ulterior motive like that," she all but screamed at him.

"You said you had your reasons."

"Yes, I have my reasons and they have nothing to do with getting pregnant by you, but everything to do with being in love with you. Do you have any idea how it is to fall in love with a man knowing full damn well he won't ever love you back?"

"In love with me," he said in a shocked stupor. "Since when?"

"Since I was sixteen."

"Sixteen!" He shook his head. "Hell, I didn't know."

She placed her hands on her hips and her eyes sparked with fire. "And you weren't *supposed* to know. It was a secret I had planned to take to my grave. Then like a fool I rushed over to your place when I heard you'd gotten hurt. And when you fell, I rushed up the stairs to help you back into bed and you wouldn't get off me."

He lifted a brow. His head was still reeling from her admission of love. "Are you saying I forced myself on you?"

"No, but I would not have gotten into bed with you if you hadn't fallen on top of me. And then, when you began kissing me, I—"

"Didn't want me to stop," he finished for her. Her cheeks darkened and he knew he'd embarrassed her. "Look, Lucia, I—"

"No, *you* look, Derringer. You're right. The thought of pushing you off me only entered my mind for a quick second, but I didn't set out to get pregnant by you that night or any other night."

"But you let me make love to you without any protection." He remembered all too well that he hadn't used a condom this time either.

"Then I can accuse you of the same thing. Trying to *get* me pregnant," she all but snarled.

"And why would I do something like that?"

"I don't know, but if you're willing to think the worst of me, then I can certainly do the same thing with you. You had taken the condom out of your wallet last night, why didn't you put it on?"

Derringer tensed. To say he'd been too carried away with making love to her would be to admit a weakness for her that he didn't want to own up to. "I think this conversation has gotten out of hand."

"You're right. I want you to leave."

He arched his brow. "Leave?"

"Yes. And my front door is that way," she said as she pointed to the door.

He narrowed his eyes. "I know where your door is located and we haven't finished our conversation."

"There's nothing else left to say, Derringer. I've already told you more than I should have and I'm ashamed of doing it. Now that you know how I feel, I won't let you take advantage of those feelings. For me it's even more important to protect my heart more than ever. Nothing has changed from the way you've always looked at me. Most of the time you acted like I didn't exist."

"That's not true. I told you I was attracted to you a few years back."

"Yes, and I honestly thought it meant something and that you were seeking me out after all that time. Now I know you only did so because you knew I was the one who slept with you that night."

She didn't say anything for a moment and then asked, "How did you know? I figured you wouldn't remember anything."

He jammed his hands into his jeans. "Oh, I remembered just fine, and you left a little something behind that definitely jogged my memory. Something pink and lacy. I just couldn't remember who they belonged to. My security system gave me the answers I needed. I had video cameras installed outside my place last month. You were the woman I saw entering my house that evening and the same one I saw sneaking out the next morning with a made-love-all-night-long look all over you."

Lucia tightened her bathrobe around her. "Like I said, that wasn't the purpose of my visit. I just wanted to make sure you were okay."

"It had been storming that night. You hate storms. Yet you came to check on me," he said.

That realization touched something within him. The reason he knew about her aversion to storms was because of something Chloe had once teased her about from their college days in Florida that involved a torrential thunder-storm and her reaction to it.

"Doesn't matter now."

"And what if I say it matters to me?" he all but snarled.

"Then I would suggest you get over it," she snapped back.

"I can't. I want to be with you again."

She narrowed her gaze. "And I told you that we won't be together that way ever again. So get it through that thick head of yours that I won't become just another woman you sleep with. You have enough of those."

Emotions he had never felt before stirred in Derringer's stomach. He should leave and not come back and not care if he ever saw her again, but for some reason she had got-ten in his blood and making love to her again hadn't got-ten her out. Instead the complete opposite had happened; she was more in his blood than ever before.

"I'll give you time to think about what I said, Lucia." He turned to leave the room knowing she was right on his heels as he moved toward the living room.

"There's nothing to think about," she snapped behind him.

He turned back around after snagging his Stetson off the rack. "Sure there is. We will be making love again."

"No, we won't!"

"Yes, we will," he said, moving toward the door. "You're in my blood now."

"I'm sure so are a number of other women in this town."

There was no point in saying that although he'd had a lot of women in the past, none had managed to get into his blood before. When he got to the door, he put on his hat before turning back to her. "Get some rest. You're going to need it when we make love again."

"I told you that we—"

He leaned forward and swiped whatever words she was

about to say from her lips with a kiss, effectively silencing her. He then straightened and smiled at the infuriated face staring back at him and tipped the brim of his hat. "We'll talk later, sweetheart."

He opened the door and stepped outside and it didn't bother him one bit when she slammed the door behind him with enough force to wake up the whole neighborhood.

Chloe leaned forward and kissed Lucia on the cheek. "Hey, cheer up. It might not be so bad."

Lucia covered her face with both hands. "How can you say that, Clo? Now that Derringer knows how I feel, he's going to do everything in his power to find a weakness to get me back in his bed. I should never have told him."

"But you did tell him, so what's next?"

She lowered her hands and narrowed her eyes. "Nothing is next. I know what he's after and it's not happening. And just to think he knew I was the one who slept with him that night, when silly me thought he didn't have a clue. And now he wants to add me to his list."

Chloe raised a brow. "Did he actually say that?"

"He didn't have to. His arrogance was showing and that was enough." She doubted she could forget his exit and his statement about their talking later. She was so angry with him. The only good part about his leaving was the mesmerizing view of his backside before she slammed the door shut on him.

"I've known Derringer a lot longer than you, Chloe, and he doesn't know the meaning of committing to one woman," she decided to add.

Chloe shrugged. "Maybe he's ready to change his ways."

Lucia rolled her eyes. "Fat chance."

"I don't know," Chloe said, tapping her finger against her chin. "Of the three die-hard-bachelor Westmoreland men who hang tight most of the time—Jason, Zane and

Derringer—I think Jason will get married first...then Derringer...and last, Zane." She chuckled. "I can see Zane kicking, screaming and throwing out accusations all the way to the altar."

Lucia couldn't help but smile because she could envision that as well. Zane was more of a womanizer than Derringer. Jason didn't have the reputation the other two had, but he was still considered a ladies' man around town because he didn't tie himself down to any one woman.

"Derringer is so confident he's getting me back into his bed again, but I'm going to show him just how wrong he is."

Chloe took a long sip of her iced tea. She had been out shopping and had decided to drop by Lucia's. Unfortunately, she had found her best friend in a bad mood and it didn't take long for her to get Lucia to spill her guts about everything.

"Now, tell me once more your reason for not wanting to sleep with Derringer again."

Lucia rolled her eyes as she sat back on the sofa. "I know how those Westmoreland brothers and cousins operate with women. I don't want to become one of those females, pining away and sitting by the phone hoping I'm next on the list to call."

"But you've been pining away for Derringer for years anyway."

"I haven't been pining. Yes, I've loved him, but I knew he didn't love me back and I accepted that. I was fine with it. I had a life. I didn't expect him to phone or show up on my doorstep making booty calls."

Chloe laughed. "He didn't make a booty call exactly. He did take you out on a date."

"But that's beside the point."

Chloe leaned forward, grinning. "And what is your point exactly? I warned you that once you had a piece of a Westmoreland you'd become addicted. Now you've had Derringer more than once, so watch out. Staying away from him is going to be easier said than done, Lucia."

Lucia shook her head. "You just don't understand, Chloe."

Chloe smiled sadly. "You're right, I don't. I don't understand how a woman who loves a man won't go after him using whatever means it takes to get him. What are you afraid of?"

Lucia glanced over at Chloe. "Failing. Which will lead to heartbreak." She drew in a deep breath. "I had a cousin who had a nervous breakdown over a man. She was twenty and her parents sent her all the way from Nashville to live with us for a while. She was simply pathetic. She would go to bed crying and wake up doing the same thing. It was so depressing. I hate to say this, but I couldn't wait until she pulled herself together enough to leave."

"How sad for her."

"No, that's the reality of things when you're dealing with a man like Derringer."

Chloe quirked a brow. "I still think you might be wrong about him."

Lucia figured she couldn't change the way her best friend thought; however, she intended to take all the precautions where Derringer was concerned. Now he saw her as a challenge because she was the woman not willing to give him the time of day anymore.

Some men didn't take rejection well and she had a feeling that Derringer Westmoreland was one of them.

Chapter 9

Jason snapped his fingers in front of Derringer's face. "Hey, man, have you been listening to anything I've said?"

Derringer blinked, too ashamed to admit that he really hadn't. The last thing he recalled hearing was something about old man Bostwick's will being read that day. "Sort of," he said, frowning. "You were talking about old man Bostwick's will."

Herman Bostwick owned the land that was adjacent to Jason's. For years, Bostwick had promised Jason if he ever got the mind to sell, he would let Jason make him the first offer. The man died in his sleep and had been laid to rest a couple of days ago. It didn't take much to detect from the look in Jason's eyes that he wanted the land and Hercules, Bostwick's prize stallion. A colt from Hercules would be a dream come true for any horse breeder.

"So who did he leave the land to?" Derringer asked. "I hope it didn't go to his brother. Kenneth Bostwick is one mean son of a gun and will take us to the cleaners if we have to buy the land and Hercules from him."

Jason shook his head and took a sip of his beer. "The old man left everything to his granddaughter. Got Kenneth kind of pissed off about it."

Derringer lifted a brow. "His granddaughter? I didn't know he had one."

"It seems not too many people did. I understand that he and his son had a falling-out years ago, and when he left for college the son never returned to these parts. He married and settled down in the South. He had one child, a girl."

Derringer nodded and took a sip of his own beer. "So this granddaughter got the land and Hercules?"

"Yes. The only good thing is that I heard she's a prissy miss from Savannah who probably won't be moving here permanently. More than likely she'll be open to selling everything, and I want to be ready to buy when she does."

Jason then slid down to sit on the steps across from him, and Derringer looked out across his land. It was late afternoon and he still couldn't get out of his mind what had happened earlier that day with Lucia. If she thought he was done with her then she should think again.

He glanced over at his cousin. "Have you ever met a woman that got in your blood, real good?"

Jason just stared at him for a long moment. It didn't take much to see that Derringer's question had caught his cousin off guard. But he knew Jason; he liked mulling things over—sometimes too damn long.

"No. I'm not sure that can happen. At least not with me. Any woman who gets in my blood will end up being the one I marry. I don't have a problem with settling down and getting married one day, mind you. One day, when I'm ready, I want to start a family. I want to will everything I've built up to my wife and kids. You know what they say, 'You can't take it with you.'"

Jason then studied Derringer. "Why do you ask? Have you met a woman that's gotten deep in your blood?"

Derringer glanced away for a moment and then returned his gaze to Jason. "Yes...Lucia."

"Lucia Conyers?"

"Yeah."

Jason stood, almost knocking over his beer bottle.

"Damn, man, how do you figure that? You only had one date with her."

Derringer smiled. "I've had two. We went skating last night." He didn't say anything and wanted to see what Jason had to say. Jason sat back down without opening his mouth.

"She's different," Derringer added after a moment.

Jason glanced over at him. "Of course she's different. You're not talking about one of your usual airheads or Derringer's Pleasers. We're discussing Lucia Conyers, for heaven's sake. She used to be one of the smartest girls at her school. Remember when Dillon and Ramsey paid her to tutor Bailey that time so she wouldn't be left back? Lucia was only seventeen then."

Derringer smiled. He had almost forgotten about that time. And if he wanted to believe what she'd told him earlier, she had been in love with him even then. "Yes, I remember."

"And remember the time Megan got her first A on a science project because she was smart enough to team up with Lucia?"

Derringer chuckled, recalling that time as well. "Yeah, I recall that time as well." At least he did now.

"And you actually think someone that smart is destined to be your soul mate?"

"Soul mate?"

"Yes, if a woman is in your blood that much then it means she's destined to be your soul mate. Someone you want to be with all the time. Think about it, Derringer. Like I said, Lucia is not some airhead, she's pretty smart."

He didn't say anything for a moment as he studied his boots, grinning, thinking Jason's question had to be a joke. Then he lifted his gaze to find a serious-looking Jason staring at him, still waiting for a response. So he gave him the only one he knew. "Yes, I'm not exactly a dumb ass, Jason, so what does her being so smart have to do with anything? And as far as being my soul mate if that means sharing a bed with her whenever I want, then I intend to do everything in my power to convince her that she is the one."

Jason rolled his eyes and then rubbed his chin thoughtfully as he stared at Derringer. "So are you saying you've fallen in love with Lucia?"

Derringer looked taken aback. "Fallen in love with her? Are you crazy? I wouldn't go *that* far."

Jason appeared confused. "You have no problem wanting to claim her as your soul mate and sleep with her, but you aren't in love with her?"

"Yes. That's pretty much the shape and size of it."

Jason shook his head, grinning. "I hate to tell you this, but I'm not sure that's how it works."

Derringer finished off his beer and said, "Too bad. That's the way it's going to work for me."

On Monday morning, Lucia stood in the middle of her office refusing to let the huge arrangement of flowers get to her. They were simply gorgeous and she would be the first to admit Derringer had good taste. But she knew just what the flowers represented. He wanted her back in his bed and would try just about anything to get her there. She wished things could go back to how they used to be when he hadn't had a clue about her feelings. But it was too late for that.

Six hours later, Lucia glanced over at the flowers and smiled. They were just as beautiful as they had been when they'd been delivered that morning. She glanced at her watch. She would leave in a couple of hours to go straight to class. Mondays were always her busiest days with meetings and satellite conference calls with the other *Simply Irresistible* offices around the country during the day and class at night.

She kicked off her shoes, leaned back in her chair and closed her eyes. The office would be closing in less than twenty minutes and since she would be there long after that, she figured there was no reason she couldn't grab a quick nap.

With her eyes shut, it didn't surprise her when an image of Derringer came into view. Boy, he was gorgeous. And arrogant. She frowned, thinking he was as arrogant as he was gorgeous. Still…

She wasn't sure how long she slept. But she remembered she was dreaming of Derringer, and wherever they were, she had whispered for him to kiss her and he had. She heard herself moan as the taste of him registered on her brain, and she couldn't help thinking how real her dream was. And was that really the feel of his fingertips on her chin as he devoured her mouth with plenty of tongue play. She could actually inhale his scent. Hot, robust and masculine.

They continued kissing in her dream and she simply melted while he leisurely explored the depths of her mouth. Nobody could kiss like him, she thought as he probed his tongue deeper. She had dreamed of him kissing her many times before, but for some reason this was different. This was like the real deal.

Her eyes flew open and she squealed when she realized it wasn't a dream! It was the real deal! She jerked forward and pushed him away from her. "Derringer! How dare you come into my office and take advantage of me."

He stood back, licked his lips and smiled. "The way I assume you took advantage of me that night? Just for the record, Lucia, you asked me to kiss you. When I entered your office, you were whispering my name. And I distinctively heard you ask me to kiss you."

"I was dreaming!"

He gave her an arrogant smirk. "Nice to know I'm in your dreams, sweetheart."

She eased out of her chair and crossed her arms over her chest. When she saw where his gaze went—directly to where her blouse dipped to reveal more cleavage than she wanted—she dropped her arms, scowling. "What are you doing here and who let you into my office?"

He jammed his hands into the pockets of his jeans. "I came to see you and I arrived when your administrative assistant was leaving. She remembered me from Chloe and Ramsey's wedding and let me in."

His smile widened. "She figured I was safe. I did knock on the door a few times before I entered, and would not have come in if I hadn't heard you call out my name."

Lucia swallowed. Had she really called out his name? She ignored that possibility. "Why are you here?"

"To make sure you liked your flowers."

She dragged her gaze from him to the huge floral arrangement she had been admiring all day. In fact, everyone in the office had admired it, and she knew they were wondering who'd sent the flowers. She glanced back at Derringer. Okay, maybe she should have called and thanked him; she hadn't wanted to give him any ideas, but it seemed he'd gotten plenty without her help.

"Yes, they're beautiful. Thank you. Now you can leave."

He shook his head. "I figured while I'm here I might as well drop you off at school. You do have class tonight, right?"

"Yes, but why would I want you to drop me off at school when I can drive myself? I do have a car."

"Yes, but I wouldn't want you to get a ticket. You told me all about your Monday-night professor and how he hates it when anyone is late. You also mentioned that tonight is your final. You're going to be late."

Lucia glanced down at her watch and went still. She wasn't aware she had slept that long. She needed to be in class in twenty minutes and it would take her longer than that to get through town. Professor Turner had already warned the class that he would close his door exactly at seven, and Derringer was right, tonight she was to take her final.

She slipped into her shoes and quickly moved around the desk to grab her purse out of the desk drawer. "And just how are you supposed to get me there any sooner than I can drive myself?" she asked, hurrying out the office door. He was right behind her.

"I have my ways." He then pulled his cell phone out of his back pocket. "Pete? This is Derringer. I need a favor."

She glanced over her shoulder as she was locking the door. He was calling Pete Higgins, one of the sheriff's deputies and also one of his good friends.

"I need escort service from *Simply Irresistible* to the U, and we need to be there in less than fifteen minutes." Derringer smiled. "Okay, we're on our way down."

He glanced over at her when he put his phone in his back pocket. "We'll leave your car here and come back for it after class."

She frowned over at him as they stepped into the elevator. "Why can't I drive my own car and your friend Pete can just give me escort service?"

He shook his head. "It doesn't work that way. He knows I'm trying to impress my girl."

"I am not your girl, Derringer."

"Sure you are. Why else would you moan my name in your sleep?"

Lucia turned her head away from him, deciding that question didn't need an answer. Besides, what response could she give him?

Once they reached the bottom floor, things moved quickly. He took her laptop bag off her shoulder and put it in the backseat of his truck. By the time he escorted her to the passenger side, Pete pulled up in the patrol car with his lights flashing and a huge grin on his face. He nodded at her before giving Derringer a thumbs-up.

Luckily, she got to school in one piece and was able to make it to class on time. An hour or so later, after she'd finished her exam and placed her pencil aside, instead of glancing back over her exam to make sure she didn't need to do any last-minute changes, her mind drifted to Derringer.

Lucia shook her head. What some men wouldn't do for a piece of tail, she thought. Regardless of what Chloe assumed, she knew that was probably all she was to him. Of course he was trying to impress her just to prove a point, and just the thought that he had caught her dreaming about him, and that in her sleep she had asked him to kiss her, was enough for her to wear a brown bag over her head for the rest of the year.

And what was even worse was that he would be picking her up when class was over. She had no choice if she wanted to get home without taking the bus. A part of her steamed at the thought of how things had worked out nicely for him in that regard. He would be driving her to get her car and nothing more. If he thought there would be more, he had another think coming.

The moment she stepped out of the Mass Communications Building, she glanced around. Derringer's truck was parked in a space in a lighted area and he was leaning against it as if he was expecting her, which was odd since he hadn't known when her class would let out. Had he been here the entire time?

She quickly crossed to where he stood. "How did you know I was about to walk out?"

He glanced over at her as he opened the truck door for her. "I didn't. I figured that you would catch a cab to get your car if I wasn't here, so I thought the best thing to do was to be here when you came out."

She frowned at him before stepping up into the truck. "You've been here the whole time?"

"Yep."

"Don't you have anything better to do?" she asked coolly.

"Nope." He then closed the door and moved around the front of the truck to get into the driver's side.

He closed the door, buckled his seat belt and turned the key in the ignition.

"Don't you think you're getting carried away with all this, Derringer?"

He chuckled. "No."

She rolled her eyes. "Seriously. I couldn't have been that great in bed."

His mouth tilted in a slow, ultrasatisfied smile. "Trust me, Lucia. You were."

She crossed her arms over her chest as he pulled out of the parking lot. "So you admit this is only about sex."

"I didn't say that, so I won't be admitting anything. I told you what I wanted."

She glanced over at him. "To sleep with me again."

"Yes, but not just a couple more times. I'm talking about the rest of my life. You're my soul mate." Derringer smiled thinking that sounded pretty darn good and had to thank Jason for putting the idea into his head.

Her mouth dropped. "Soul mate?"

"Yes."

"That's insane," she threw out

"That's reality. Get used to it," he threw back.

She turned around in her seat as much as her seat belt would allow. "It's not reality and I won't get used to it, because it doesn't make sense. If this has anything to do with you thinking I got pregnant from our previous encounters you don't have that to worry about. My monthly visitor arrived this morning."

"That wasn't it, although that would have definitely been important to me if you had gotten pregnant. But like I told you before, you're in my blood now. You were a virgin and I'd never been with a virgin before."

"Whoop-de-do," she said sarcastically. "No big deal."

"For me it is."

She just stared at him, deciding not to argue with him anymore. Doing so would give her a friggin' headache.

She shifted positions to sit straight in her seat and closed her eyes, but she wouldn't go to sleep for fear of waking up with her lips locked to his again.

Each time she felt herself being lulled to sleep by the smooth jazz sounds coming from the CD player, she would open her eyes to gaze out the window and study all the buildings they passed. She thought Denver was a beautiful city and there was no other place quite like it.

Due to the lack of traffic, they returned to her office building sooner than she had anticipated. And, she tried convincing herself, not as quickly as she would have liked. But she knew that was a lie. She liked the fact that she was the woman riding in the truck with him tonight. She had been the one he had waited for outside her classroom building. And she was the one for whom he had ordered a special escort service to get her to school on time. Then there were the flowers. A girl could really succumb to him if she wasn't careful.

"How do you think you did on your test tonight?"

His question surprised her and she glanced over at him when he parked his truck behind her car. She couldn't help but smile. "I think I aced it. I'm almost sure of it. There were a lot of multiple-choice questions, but there was one essay question to test our writing skills."

"I'm happy for you then."

"Thanks."

She watched as he opened his door and then walked around the back of the truck to open the door for her. Once he helped her out, they stood there facing each other. "I appreciate all you did tonight, Derringer. Because of you I got to school on time."

"No problem, baby."

The term of endearment sent sensations rippling through her. "Don't call me that, Derringer."

"What?"

"Baby."

He leaned against his truck. "Why?"

"Because I'm sure I'm not the only woman you've called that."

"No, you're not, but you're the only one I've called that when it meant something."

She shook her head as she walked slowly to her car with him strolling beside her. The April air was cold and everyone was talking about a snowstorm headed their way this weekend. "You just won't give up, will you?"

"No."

"I wish you would."

They came to a stop next to her car. The smile he gave her was slow and sexy. "And I wish you would let me make love to you again, Lucia."

She was certain that irritation showed on her face. "Yet you want me to believe it's not just about sex?"

She shook her head sadly, thinking he just didn't get it. She loved him and now that he knew how she felt, she refused to settle for anything less than being loved in return. She knew for him to fall in love with her was something that wouldn't happen—not in her wildest dreams—so all she wanted to do was get on with her life without him being a part of it. "Good night, Derringer."

He moved out of the way when she got into her car and quickly drove away.

Later that night, Derringer tossed and turned in his bed. Finally, he pulled himself up and reached out to turn on the light. Brightness flooded the room and he rubbed his hands down his face.

Tomorrow would be a busy day for Denver's branch of D&M Horse-Breeding and Training Company. In fact, the rest of the week would be hectic. His cousin Cole would be delivering more than one hundred horses from Texas at the end of the week and they needed to make sure everything was ready. It didn't help matters that a snowstorm was expected this weekend. That made things even more complicated as well as challenging.

He reached behind him and lifted his pillow and smiled when his hand touched the lacy items. He had two pairs of Lucia panties. Added to the pink pair were the red ones he'd taken off her last weekend. He wondered if she'd missed them yet and figured she probably hadn't; otherwise, she would have mentioned it.

And she wasn't pregnant. He'd actually been disappointed when she'd made that announcement. He had gotten used to the idea that perhaps she could be pregnant with his child. He knew that kind of thinking didn't make much sense, but he had.

He settled back down in bed thinking she just wouldn't let up with this "only sex" thing. He had all but told her she was his soul mate so what else did she want?

He knew the answer without thinking much about it. She wanted him to love her, but that wouldn't and couldn't happen. What if she got real sick or something and he couldn't get her to the hospital in time? What if she was in a car accident and didn't survive? What if she got stampeded by a herd of horses? What if…he lost her like he had his parents? His aunt and uncle? They were here one day and had been gone the next. He rubbed his hand down his face, not liking how his thoughts were going. He was freaking out for no reason; especially when he didn't intend to get attached to her like that.

He liked things just the way they were and didn't intend for any woman, not even Lucia, to start messing with his mind…and definitely not with his heart. But he wanted her.

There had to be a middle ground for them, something they could both agree on. It would have to be something that would satisfy them both.

He would come up with a plan. Because, no matter what, he had no intention of giving up on her.

Chapter 10

Lucia closed the lid to her washing machine and leaned back against it thinking that Derringer had not given her back the panties he'd taken off her the other night. The red pair. Now he had two. What was he doing with them? Collecting them as souvenirs?

She strolled to the window and glanced out. It looked totally yucky outside. The forecasters' predictions had been correct. She had awakened to see huge snowflakes falling outside. That's the only thing she missed about the time she lived in Florida. This was the middle of April, spring break in most states and it was hard to believe that in some other place the sun was shining brightly. A week spent on Daytona Beach sounded pretty darn good about now. At least the snow had waited for the weekend and most people didn't have a reason to venture outside.

Her parents had gotten smart and decided to fly to Tennessee for a few weeks to visit her mother's sister. Chloe had called this morning to chat and to tell her how she, Ramsey and the baby were snuggled inside in front of the roaring fireplace and planned to stay that way. Lucia sighed deeply, thinking this was the only time she regretted being an only child. Things could get lonely at times.

She moved away from the window to go into the kitchen to make herself a cup of hot chocolate and watch that movie she had planned to watch last week, and she remembered why she hadn't.

Derringer had dropped by.

She hadn't heard from him since the night he had taken her to school. Maybe he had finally admitted to himself that he only wanted one thing from her and had moved on to some other willing female. The thought of him making love to someone else had her hurting inside, but she could deal with it the way she'd always done. It wasn't the first time she'd known the man she loved was sleeping with others and it wouldn't be the last. But it hurt knowing someone else was the recipient of his smile, his look and his touch. More than anything, a part of her wished she hadn't experienced any of it for herself. But then a part of her was glad that she had and would not trade in a single moment.

Moments later, with a cup of hot chocolate in her hand, she moved toward the living room to watch her movie. She had a fire blazing in the fireplace and it added soothing warmth to the entire room. Why she wanted to watch a romantic movie when she lacked romance in her own life was beyond her. But then, women had their dreams and fantasies, didn't they?

Lucia had settled back against her sofa with a cup in one hand and a remote in the other when the doorbell rang. She frowned, wondering what on earth could get Mrs. Noel to come across the street in this weather, unless her heating unit was on the blink again. Standing, she placed the cup and the remote on the table and headed for the door. She looked out the peephole and caught her breath.

Derringer!

Denying the rush of heat she immediately felt between her thighs, seeing him standing there and looking sexier than any man had a right to look—this time of day and in this horrid weather—she drew in a deep breath and fought the anger escalating in her chest. She would not hear from him for a week or so and then he would show up at her place unannounced. It didn't matter that she had told him to leave her alone. That was beside the point. The only point she could concentrate on was that he evidently thought he could add her to his booty-call list. Well, she had news for him.

She snatched the door open and was about to ask what he was doing there, but wasn't given the chance to do so.

Derringer didn't give Lucia the chance to ask any questions, but leaned in and covered her mouth with his. He not only wanted to silence her, he also wanted the heat from his kiss to inflame her as they stood just inside with a frigid snowstorm raging outside. There was no doubt in his mind the kiss had enough spark, power and electricity to light the entire city of Denver. And he felt it all rush through his body.

She didn't resist him, and at the moment that was a good thing. He didn't need her resistance, what he needed was this—the taste of her all over his tongue.

He had tried not thinking about her all week. Hell, with the delivery of those horses he'd had enough to keep his mind and time occupied. But things hadn't happened quite that way. She'd still managed to creep into his thoughts most of the time, and he had awakened that morning with a need to see her so intense that he just couldn't understand it. And nothing, not elephant snowflakes nor below-zero-degree temperature would keep him from her. From this.

He finally pulled back from the kiss. Somehow they had made it inside her house and closed the door behind them and that was a good thing. Having an X-rated kiss on her doorstep would definitely have given her neighbors something to talk about for years.

She gazed up at him and he thought at that moment she was the most beautiful person he had ever seen. No other women he'd messed around with before could claim that. He inwardly flinched when he thought of what he'd just done. He had compared her with all the other women in his womanizing life and in essence none could compare to her. In fact, her biggest beef about having an affair with him were those other women in his life. But he knew at that moment he would give them all up for her.

The reality of him willingly doing that hit him below the belt and he nearly tumbled over. Derringer Westmoreland would give up his lifestyle for a woman? Make a commitment to be only with her? He drew in a sharp breath. He'd never made such an allegiance with any female. Had never intended to be dedicated or devoted to one. There were too many out there and he enjoyed being footloose and fancy-free. Was she worth all of that? He knew in that instant that she was.

"What are you doing here, Derringer?"

He could tell she had regained control of the senses they'd both lost when she had opened her door. He had initiated the kiss, but she had reciprocated, which told him that although she wished otherwise, she had enjoyed it as much as he had.

"I needed to see you," he said simply.

She rolled her eyes. "That's what you said the last time."

"And I'm saying it again."

She drew in a deep breath and then turned and walked toward the sofa. He followed, thinking at least she hadn't asked him to leave…yet. She sat down on the couch and he dropped down on the love seat.

"If you had to venture out in this blasted weather, why not go visit Ashira Lattimore? I'm sure she has a bed warming for you."

The last thing he needed to do was to admit there was a strong possibility the woman did. As far as he knew, Ashira had gotten it into her head that she would eventually become Mrs. Derringer Westmoreland. He wouldn't marry Ashira if she was the last woman on earth. She was too possessive and clingy. On the other hand, the woman sitting across from him wasn't possessive and clingy enough.

Yet she claimed to love him, when he knew all Ashira wanted was the Westmoreland name and all his worldly possessions.

"She isn't the woman I want warming a bed for me," he said quietly, glancing over at her intently. Not only did she look good as usual, she smelled good, too. He was so familiar with her scent that he could probably pick her out of any room even if he was blindfolded.

"Do most men care what woman warms their bed?"

He'd never cared until now.

"Don't answer, Derringer, you might incriminate yourself," she said bitterly.

That should have gotten him off the hook, but he felt a need to respond anyway. "Those who find the woman they want care. Then they are willing to give up all the others."

She lifted a brow and he knew the moment she thought she had boxed him into the perfect corner, one she figured he wouldn't be able to get out of because there was no way he would give up his other women for her. It amazed him that he could discern just how his woman thought.

His woman?

He smiled thinking that yes, she was definitely *his* woman.

"And you want me to believe you're willing to give up all other women for me," she said, chuckling with a look on her face that said the whole idea of him doing such a thing was simply ridiculous.

"Yes, I'd give up all other women for you," he said, meeting her gaze with a look that told her he was dead serious. She almost dropped the cup she was holding in her hand.

She shook her head. "Don't be silly."

"I'm not," he responded. "I'm as serious as a Bugatti Veyron on an open road."

"No, you're not."

"Oh, yes, sweetheart, I am."

She simply stared at him for a moment and then asked in a cautious and quiet tone, "Why?"

"Because you are the only woman I want," he said.

"But love has nothing to do with it?"

He knew he had to be completely honest with her. He didn't want to give her false hope or misguided illusions. "No. Love has nothing to do with it. But we'll have something just as important."

"What?"

"Respect for each other and a sense of caring. I do care for you, Lucia, or I wouldn't be here." There. He'd painted her the picture he intended for her to see. She loved him and had admitted to doing so and he had no reason not to believe her. But he knew a woman's love went deep and things could get rather messy if she expected or anticipated those feelings in return. She wouldn't get them.

"Are you willing to accept being the only woman in my life in a long-term exclusive affair, Lucia?"

She stared at him, not saying anything and then as if to be certain she'd heard him correctly and clearly understood the parameters of what he'd proposed, she asked, "And during that time you won't be involved with any woman but me?"

"Yes, I give you my word on it. Something I've never given any woman I've been involved with in the past. You are the first woman." It was on the tip of his lips to add, *Just like I was your first man.*

Lucia sat there, staring at Derringer and searching his face for any signs that he was being anything but aboveboard. Was he giving her a line? She drew in a deep breath. He had given her his word, and most people knew that the Westmorelands' word meant everything to them. But could it withstand temptation? What if he got tired of her and was tempted to test the waters elsewhere with someone else?

"And if you change your mind about this exclusivity

thing, you will let me know? I wouldn't find out from others?"

He shook his head. "No, you wouldn't find out from others. I wouldn't do you that way, Lucia. If and when I get ready to end things between us, you will be the first to know."

He paused for a moment and then inclined his head. "So, if you fully accept those terms, please come over here for a second," he murmured in seductive invitation.

She hesitated, still uncertain. She knew there was sexual chemistry between them, she could feel the snap, crackle and pop even now with the distance separating them. On what was probably the coldest day in Denver this year, he was sitting over there looking hotter than any man had a right to look, and he got finer and finer each time she saw him. His dark eyes were pulling her in, mesmerizing her down to her panties. And that luscious mouth of his seemed to be calling out to her, tempting her in ways she really didn't need to be tempted; especially when she went to bed each night dreaming of him.

She would be the first to say that his offer of an exclusive affair surprised her because she knew that's not how he operated. In fact, that was not how any of the single Westmorelands handled their business with women. So why was he treading off the beaten track?

One thing was for certain; his blatant honesty about the kind of relationship he wanted with her had caught her off guard. He wasn't promising love, although he was well aware of how she felt about him. Instead of offering her love in return, he was offering her an exclusive affair.

Suddenly something happened that she hoped she didn't live to regret. At that moment, she began listening to her heart and not her mind. Her heart was telling her that she loved him too much not to take him up on the offer he'd laid out to her. She would be entering the affair with both eyes open and no expectations except one. He would give her advance notice when he was ready to end things between them.

That meant that while things lasted she would spend all the time with him she desired. She would be the only woman sharing his bed. The one and only woman claiming Derringer Westmoreland's full attention. She glanced down at her hand and accepted the fact that the only drawback was that he would never put a ring on her finger.

She glanced back up and her gaze returned to the deep, dark eyes that were staring at her. And waiting. And as she returned his stare, she was getting wet just thinking about all the things they would probably spend their time doing together as an exclusive couple.

She moistened her lips with the tip of her tongue and watched his gaze take in her every movement as she slowly stood. And then he stood and at that moment she realized what he was doing. Something she hadn't expected. He was meeting her halfway.

He began walking toward her the moment she began walking toward him and they met in the center. "I wasn't sure you were going to take those steps," he whispered throatily when they stood face-to-face, his mesmerizing dark gaze locked on hers.

"I wasn't sure either."

He then cupped her face in his hands and took possession of her mouth in the way she'd gotten used to him doing.

When Lucia began responding to his kiss that had liquid heat flaming inside him, he knew what they both wanted and needed. And this was the perfect day for it. He broke off the kiss and swept her off her feet and into his arms and purposefully moved toward her bedroom. Wanting her this much was the epitome of insanity, but he might as well get used to it.

He placed her on the bed and stepped back to quickly

remove his clothes, sending them flying all over the place. And then for the first time since they'd made love, he took the time to use a condom.

When he returned to the bed, he captured her hand and drew her toward him to remove her clothes, slowly stripping her bare. Today she was wearing a pair of white panties, but they weren't of the granny style. They were bikinis. But the style or color of her undergarments didn't matter to him.

"Nice panties," he said, picking up his jeans and placing the panties in the back pocket.

"Why are you doing that? You have two pairs of mine already. Is there something I should know?" she asked when he tossed his jeans back to the floor and eased down onto the bed to join her.

"Yes," he said, pulling her into his arms. "I go to sleep every night with them under my pillow."

Her mouth dropped. "You're kidding, right?"

He smiled. "No, I'm not kidding, and before you ask, the answer is no. I've never collected the underwear of other women, Lucia. Just yours."

He saw the confused look on her face and thought she could dwell on what he'd confessed at another time. He needed her full concentration for what he intended to do to her right now.

Now that she was his, he wanted to get to know each and every inch of her body. Reaching out, he cradled her chin in his hand, forcing her to meet his gaze again. He could tell she was still trying to understand what he'd said earlier about her panties.

He smiled, thinking this was where he needed to shift her focus.

Lucia saw the sexy-curvy smile that touched Derringer's lips and knew she was in trouble in the most sensual way. For some reason, she knew this lovemaking session would be different, but she didn't know in what way.

"We're staying in all weekend," he whispered in a voice so low and hot that a burning sensation began at the tips of her toes and moved upward through her body.

She was trying to understand what he'd said about staying in all weekend. Was he letting her know that he intended to keep her here, in this bed, the majority of the time? Before she could think further about it, he lifted his hand and went straight to her breasts and his fingers began toying with a darkened nipple.

"I like your breasts. I especially like how well defined they are and how easy they can slip into my mouth. Like this."

He lowered his head and his stiffened tongue laved the nipple, licking all around it a few times before easing the firm pebble between his lips, and began sucking.

Her eyes fluttered closed as a multitude of sensations pulled at the juncture of her thighs in response to the pulling motion to her breasts. His mouth was like a vacuum, drawing her nipple more and more into his mouth as his hot tongue did all kinds of wicked things to it. He switched breasts, to take on nipple number two, and she watched through hooded eyes as he continued to devour her this way.

Moments later, he drew away to lean back on his haunches to look down at her with a satisfied smile on his lips. It was then that she sensed a need in him, and the thought of him wanting her that much sent a rush of excitement through her bloodstream.

"Now for your pillows," he said, reaching behind her and grabbing both to place under her hips. She didn't have to ask what he was about to do and groaned softly at the vision that flowed through her mind. When he'd gotten her in the position he wanted, with the lower part of her elevated to his liking, he just continued to gaze at that part of her.

"You're beautiful," he whispered. "All over. But especially here," he said, reaching out and gently tracing a hand inside her inner thigh, slowly letting his fingers work their way toward the feminine folds that she knew were wet and ready for his touch.

She couldn't help but respond, and moaned as his fingers continued to lightly skim over her most intimate parts, causing sensuous shivers to flow through her. By the time he inserted two fingers inside her, she let out a deep groan and threw her head back, unable to help the way her hips rolled against the pillows cushioning them. And when he lowered his head, her fingers sank into the blades of his shoulders.

"Scent is closely linked to taste," he whispered, his breath hot against her womanly folds. "You're so wet here," he said softly, and proceeded to blow air through his lips onto her. "Since I can't blow you dry, that means I'm going to have to lap you up."

His words turned every cell in her body into a wild, unrestrained state. Instinctively, she bucked wildly against his mouth and he retaliated by grabbing her hips and diving his tongue between her womanly folds.

"Derringer!"

Her hands left his shoulders to grab hold of his head. Not to push him away, but to keep him there. Right there at that perfect angle, that most sensuous position as his mouth devoured her as if she were the tastiest meal he'd ever consumed.

She continued to cry out his name over and over, but there was no stopping him. He used his mouth to brand the woman he wanted. And the mere thought that that woman was her made her become more and more deeply entranced with every stroke of his tongue.

And when she couldn't take any more and her body began shuddering violently in the wake of one gigantic orgasm, he wouldn't let up, but continued to make love to her this way until the last jolt passed through her body. It was then that he quickly removed the pillows from beneath her body before mounting her.

"Lucia."

* * *

Her name was a whispered hunger from Derringer's lips. Hunger that had only slightly been appeased. And when she opened glazed eyes to look up at him the exact moment he slid into her, his nostrils flared and he felt his shaft thicken even more inside her. He knew she felt it the moment that it did.

"Take me, baby, hold me, clench me. Get everything out of me that you want," he prodded in a deep, guttural voice.

And from the way her inner muscles began clenching him, clamping down tight, compressing him, he could only throw his head back, knowing he was about to enjoy the ride of his life. This was one mating he would never forget.

He began moving, thrusting in and out of her, and when she began moving in rhythm with him, the sound of flesh smacking against flesh, he let out a ragged groan. And when she locked her legs around him and rubbed her breasts against his chest, he leaned close to her mouth and captured her lips with his.

There was nothing like kissing a woman while you made love to her, he thought. Knowing your body was planted deep in hers, knowing sensual aches were being satisfied and an earth-shattering climax was on the horizon. And when she moaned deep within his mouth, he pulled back, looked down at her, wanting to see the exact moment an orgasm ripped through her.

He watched in breathless fascination as the pleasure he was giving her contorted her features, made her tremble, almost took her breath away. It was then that he felt his own body explode, and he thrust into her deeper than he'd ever gone before.

"Lucia!"

No woman had ever done this to him; reduce him to a ball of fiery sensations that had him bucking wildly all over the place. He gripped her hips as sensations continued to tear into him, enthrall him, and each desperate thrust only called for another.

And when she came again, he was right there with her and together their bodies quaked violently as unrestrained pleasure took them over the edge.

"How are we going to explain things to your family, Derringer?"

His eyes popped open and he shifted his gaze to look over at Lucia. They had taken a nap after their last love-making session and she was leaning down over him, still naked and with strands of her hair hanging in arousing disarray around her shoulders. He glanced beyond her to the window to look outside. Was it getting dark already? He hadn't eaten breakfast or lunch yet.

"Derringer?"

His gaze returned to her and he saw the anxiety in her eyes and the way she was nervously biting her lower lip. "We don't owe them any explanations, Lucia. We're adults."

"I know that, but…"

When she didn't complete what she was going to say, he decided to finish it off for her. "But they're going to think you've lost your mind for getting involved with me."

He knew it was true and really didn't like the way it sounded. His family knew of his reputation more than anyone, and for him to have talked Lucia into an affair wouldn't sit too well with them. But as he'd told her, he and Lucia were adults.

"They're going to think you'll eventually hurt me," she said quietly.

"Then I guess it will be on me to prove otherwise, because I'm not letting what they think cause a rift between us. Besides, they know we've been out a couple of times, and once they see how taken I am with you, they'll start minding their own business."

And he *was* taken with her, he'd admit that much. He

was taken with her in a way no other woman could claim. He couldn't help but smile when he then said, "But I'm not the one they need to be concerned about. Zane's and Canyon's womanizing ways are probably right up there with Raphel's."

"Your great-grandfather? The one who was married to all those women?" she asked.

"Well, we're still trying to figure out what's fact and what's fiction. So far, the women we thought were his first two wives actually weren't. Dillon gave all the records he'd accumulated to Megan. She's determined to find out the truth as to whether Raphel actually lived all those lives," he said, pulling her down to him before he would be tempted to take one of her nipples into his mouth. As much as he loved tasting her, he figured they needed to eat something more nourishing now.

"I think I'll shower and then go into your kitchen to see what I can throw together for us," he said.

She looked surprised. "You're going to feed me?"

He couldn't help but smile, thinking that wasn't all he intended to do to her. "Yes, but trust me, I have a reason for doing so. I meant what I said earlier about keeping you inside all weekend, sweetheart."

And then he leaned down and locked his mouth with hers. This was one snowstorm that he would never forget.

Chapter 11

"So how are things going with you and Derringer?"

Sensations of excitement rippled in Lucia's stomach at the mention of Derringer's name. She and Chloe had decided to do lunch at McKay's, and as soon as the waitress had taken their orders and moved away, Chloe had begun asking Lucia a number of questions.

The weather had started clearing up a little on Sunday night, and Derringer had talked her into going to his ranch and leaving for work on Monday morning from there. He had even helped her pack an overnight bag. What she hadn't expected was his siblings and cousins showing up early Monday morning to check on him because no one had seen or heard from him all weekend. She hadn't missed the look of surprise on their faces when she'd come down the stairs dressed for work, giving everyone a clear idea of how he'd spent those snowed-in hours and with whom.

That had been a couple of weeks ago. "So far, so good. I enjoy spending time with him."

And truly she did. He'd taken her to the movies several times and picked her up from work on several occasions, and had spent the night over at her place a number of times as well.

Chloe beamed. "I'm glad. Ramsey is too. Already he's seen a change in Derringer."

Lucia raised a brow as she took a sip of her iced tea. "What kind of change?"

"Peace. Calm. He seems more focused. Less untamed and wild. Not only Ramsey but the other Westmorelands think you're good for him."

Lucia nervously nibbled at her lower lip. "I hope they aren't getting any ideas. I told you what's between me and Derringer is only temporary. He made sure I understood that, Chloe."

Chloe waved her words away. "All men think nothing is forever at first, only a few have love on their minds initially. Callum was an exception. He knew he loved Gemma before she had a clue."

"But Derringer doesn't love me. He's said as much. I'm in this relationship with both eyes open."

Later, back in her office, she recalled her words to Chloe as she sat staring at the huge arrangement of flowers that was sitting on her desk that had been delivered while she was at lunch. The card had simply said, *I'm thinking of you.*

Just the thought that he was thinking of her made everything inside her rock with anticipation to see him again. It was Friday and they were going skating again tonight and she couldn't wait.

The intercom on her desk went off, almost startling her. "Yes?"

"Someone is here to see you, Ms. Conyers."

Excitement flowed in her stomach. The last time she'd received flowers from Derringer, he had shown up at her office later. Was he here to see her now? "Who is it, Wanda?"

"Ashira Lattimore."

Lucia's throat tightened. Why would Ashira Lattimore be visiting her? There was only one way to find out. "Thanks, Wanda, ask her to come in."

Lucia clicked off her intercom and glanced at the flowers on her desk. Something about them gave her inner strength to deal with what was about to take place. She wasn't exactly sure what would happen, but she figured it had something to do with Derringer.

It wasn't long before the woman knocked on her door. "Come in."

Ashira walked in and just like all the other times Lucia had seen her she looked beautiful. But Lucia knew that beauty was merely on the outside. She had heard a number of stories about the spoiled and reckless woman who had long ago stamped ownership on Derringer. In a way she was surprised Ashira hadn't confronted her before now.

"Ashira, this is a surprise. What can *Simply Irresistible* do for you?" Lucia plastered a smile on her lips.

The woman didn't bother returning her fabricated smile. "I've been gone, Lucia, visiting a sick relative in Dakota, and thought I'd let you know I'm back."

Lucia placed her arms across her chest. "And that's supposed to mean something to me?"

The woman glanced at the flowers on Lucia's desk, paused a minute and then said, "I think it would where Derringer is concerned. Not sure if he told you, but the two of us have an understanding."

"Do you?"

"Yes. No matter who he dallies with, I'm the one he'll always come back to. I'm sure you've known him long enough to know our history."

"Unfortunately, I don't, and for you to pay me a visit to stake a claim you think you have speaks volumes. It makes me think you're not as confident as you want to claim," she said with more bravado than she actually felt.

"Think whatever you want. Just remember, when he's done with you he'll come back to me. He and I have plans to marry one day."

Lucia's heart dropped at the woman's announcement. "Congratulations on your and Derringer's future plans. Now, if you've said everything you've come here to say, I think you should leave."

It was then that Ashira smiled, but the smile didn't quite reach her eyes. It didn't come close. "Fine, just remember my warning. I'm trying to spare you any heartbreak." The woman then walked out of her office.

Derringer's gaze flickered over Lucia's face. "You okay? You've been quiet most of the evening."

They had gone skating with what he was now beginning to think of as the regular crowd. Most of the kids and teens had gotten used to him and Lucia invading their turf. And now they were back at her place, but she hadn't said a whole lot since he'd picked her up that evening.

She smiled over at him. "Yes, I'm fine. This has been a busy week at work and I'm just glad it's the weekend. I need it."

He pulled her into his arms. "And I need it as well. More horses are arriving this week and then all our relatives start arriving the week after that for the Westmoreland Charity Ball. You are going to the ball with me, aren't you?"

He watched her features and she seemed surprised he'd asked. Her next question proved him right. "You really want to take me?"

"Of course I do."

"Thanks."

He stared down at her for a moment. "Why are you thanking me?"

"Um, no reason. I just wasn't sure what your plans would be."

It was on the tip of his tongue to say that whatever his plans were they would always include her, but he didn't. Lately, he was encountering feelings and emotions when it came to Lucia that he didn't quite understand and didn't want to dwell on.

"I hear Gemma is coming home in a few days," she said, cutting into his thoughts.

A smile touched his lips. "Yeah, and I miss her. I'd gotten used to Gemma being underfoot and wasn't sure how I'd handle her up and moving to Australia. But Callum loves her and we know he's taking good care of her. Besides, homecomings are good."

"Yes, he does love her."

There was something about her tone of voice that sounded contemplative and reflective, as if she was wondering, considering just how that would be for a man to love her that way. For a moment he didn't know what to say, so he decided not to say anything.

Instead, he did something he always enjoyed doing to her. He touched her chin, making rotary motions with his thumb on her soft skin before tilting her head back to lower his mouth to kiss her.

The sound of her sensual purr fueled his desire, making him so aroused his erection thickened painfully against the zipper of his jeans. And when she wrapped her arms around his neck as he deepened the kiss, he went crazy with lust for her.

Not able to hold back any longer, he swept her off her feet into his arms and carried her upstairs to the bedroom.

"Why haven't you mentioned Ashira's visit to Derringer, Lucia?"

Lucia glanced over at Chloe. They had just finished a business meeting and she'd known something had been on her best friend's mind all morning. "And how do you know I haven't?"

"Trust me, had you told him, all hell would have broken loose. He's never appreciated Ashira's possessiveness."

Lucia shrugged. "For all I know they could have an understanding just like she claims."

"I can't believe you would think that."

"In all honesty I'm trying not to think about anything regarding Derringer and Ashira. I'm just taking one day at a time."

Chloe frowned. "She would never have come into *my* office with that haughty I'm-Derringer's-real-woman foolishness, trust me."

"Because you know Ramsey loves you, I can't say that for Derringer and me. I know he doesn't love me," she said softly.

Later that night she lay in Derringer's arms with her naked body spooned intimately to his. His arm was thrown over her and he slept with his hand cupping her breast. His warm body and the scent of his musky masculinity surrounded her and she became aroused by it. That was something she couldn't help.

Since becoming sexually involved with Derringer, she had become more aware of herself as a woman, particularly her needs and wants, mainly because he made her feel as if she was the most enticing and alluring woman he'd ever met. And coming from a man like Derringer, that meant a lot.

She then thought about her conversation with Chloe earlier that day. Maybe she should have mentioned Ashira's visit to her office to Derringer. And yet a part of her didn't want to draw him into any women-over-man drama. Besides, time would tell if what the woman said was true.

She knew the moment he'd awakened by the change in his breathing. The other telltale sign was the feel of his erection beginning to swell against her naked backside. And then he began touching her. With the hand that wasn't cupping her breast he started at the dip in her thigh and let his fingers do a little walking, tracing a line toward her waist. It then followed the curve toward the juncture at her inner thighs.

"Shift open your legs for me, baby," he leaned over to whisper in her ear. "I need to touch you there."

She did what he asked and moments later she was moaning at his exploratory touch. And then when the hand cupping her breasts began doing its own thing by torturing her nipples, she clenched her lips to keep from crying out his name.

"You're so passionate," he murmured close to her ear. "You are the most sensuous woman I know."

She wanted so much to believe him. She wanted to believe it was her that he wanted and not Ashira. And when she couldn't take his torture any longer, she cried out for him to make love to her.

"My pleasure."

He then eased her onto her back and straddled her, and before she could draw her next breath, he entered her, melding their bodies as one. And each time he stroked into her and retreated, she ground her body against him ready for his reentry.

Over and over, back and forth, performing the mating dance the two of them had created as he thrust in and out of her and all she could do was continue to groan out her cries of pleasure. And when a guttural moan flowed from Derringer's lips, she knew they had been tossed into the turbulent waves of pure ecstasy.

Incredible.

Derringer pulled in a deep breath. That's how he always thought of making love with Lucia. Each and every time was simply incredible. And she was incredible. He glanced over at her and saw she had fallen asleep with her body spooned against his.

The room was quiet as images flickered in his mind of

all the things they'd done together over the past few weeks, and not all of them had been in the bedroom. He enjoyed taking her places, being seen with her and spending time with her. Exclusivity was working, but he knew it was only because the woman was Lucia.

No other woman crossed his mind. He didn't want any other woman but her. And his inner fear of something happening to her lessened more and more each day. When he considered all the possibilities, weighed all his options and thought of what could happen, none of it was more significant than spending time with her, being with her. For the rest of his life. He loved her.

Derringer drew in a sharp breath because at that moment he couldn't imagine being without her.... He wanted to live each day to the fullest with her, loving her completely. She was the only woman he wanted. For his soul mate and then one day for his wife.

His wife.

A smile touched his lips. No other woman deserved that title. And he was determined that Lucia—only Lucia—would wear it. He knew he couldn't rush her. He had to take things slow and believe that one day she would realize she was the only woman who could be a wife for this Westmoreland.

The following days passed quickly and everyone was excited when Gemma returned home and confirmed the rumor that she and Callum would become parents in seven months. It was decided that a cookout was in order to welcome the couple home and to celebrate their good news. Another Westmoreland baby was on the way.

Derringer, his brothers and cousins were playing a friendly game of horseshoes when someone rang the bell letting them know it was time to eat. The men went into Dillon's kitchen to wash up, when Zane leaned over and whispered, "Lucia looks just like she belongs with the Westmorelands, Derringer."

His gaze moved across the yard to where she was helping Chloe and Megan set the table. Zane was right. She did look as if she belonged, mainly because she did belong. In a way, he'd always known that. And now he was waiting patiently for her to realize it as well.

They had been spending a lot of time together lately. It had become his regular routine to go home and shower after working with the horses and then head on over to her place each day. School was out, so she was home most evenings now. They cooked dinner together, on occasion they would go out to take in a movie or shoot pool—something he had shown her how to do. Then on Friday nights they went roller skating. But he also enjoyed those times they would stay inside to cuddle on the sofa and watch videos.

As if she felt him looking at her, she glanced over at him and an intimate connection, as well as sexual chemistry, flowed between them the way it always did. A slow, flirty smile touched his lips and he tipped his hat to her. She returned his smile and nodded before returning to what she was doing.

"I think you like her," Zane said, reminding Derringer he was there.

Derringer smiled at his brother, refusing to let Zane bait him. "Of course I like her. We all do."

"Hey, don't be an ass, Derringer. You're in love with the woman. Admit it."

Derringer only smiled and glanced back to where Lucia was sitting. The women were crowded together on the porch listening to Gemma share stories about her Australian adventure and how she was settling into her role as Mrs. Callum Austell.

He couldn't help it, but he kept looking at Lucia. Each and every time he saw her, spent time with her, he fell more and more in love with her. Now he understood how Dillon could have left home to investigate all the rumors they'd heard about Raphel and return less than a month later an engaged man. At first he thought his cousin had needed to have his head examined, but once he met Pam and had seen how Dillon would light up around her, he sort of understood. But he'd figured nothing like that would ever happen to him.

He had been proven wrong.

He loved everything about Lucia, including her interaction with his family. But mainly he loved the way she made him feel whenever they were together.

His thoughts were pulled back to the present when Jason took a minute to provide an update on old man Bostwick's granddaughter from Savannah. Folks were saying the woman was supposed to arrive in town to claim her inheritance in a couple of weeks. Jason was anxious about that and he was hoping his offer for the land and Hercules was the one the woman would accept.

"Looks like we have a visitor," Canyon whispered. "At least, she's *your* visitor, Derringer."

Derringer frowned when he saw the sports car driven by Ashira Lattimore pull up in the yard. He couldn't help wondering what she wanted since he knew she hadn't been invited. Also, Ashira and his sisters didn't get along. But that had never stopped Ashira from thinking her lack of an invite was merely an oversight on someone's part. She was her parents' only child and was spoiled rotten. In contrast, he thought, Lucia was her parents' only child, yet she was sweet as wine. The difference in the two women was like night and day.

"Hello, everyone," she called out, waving, while glancing around as if she had every right to show up at a family function uninvited. Her face lit up in a huge smile when she saw Derringer, and she immediately headed toward him.

"Derringer, sweetheart, I've missed you." She leaned over, wrapped her arms around his neck and placed a kiss on his lips in full view of everyone.

He took her arms from around his neck and stared down at her. "What are you doing here, Ashira?"

She gave him a pouty look. "I came to see you."

"This is not where I live," he said in an annoyed voice.

"I know, but you weren't home and we need to talk."

"About what?"

She leaned up on tiptoe and whispered close to his ear, "About that horse you're trying to sell Daddy. Since he's buying it for me, I think we need to discuss it, don't you?"

"I'm busy right now, Ashira."

"But you want to make that sale, don't you? Daddy is ready. He wants to see you now, at the ranch."

Derringer knew he needed to put Ashira in her place once and for all, but here was not the place to do it. "Okay, let's go," he said, gripping her hand and pulling her with him toward her car. "I'll be back later," he called over his shoulder to everyone. "I've got some business to take care of."

He was angry. He didn't care about the horse sale as much as Ashira assumed that he did. If she thought it was a carrot she could dangle in front of him to make him do what she wanted then she had another thought coming. What ticked him off more than anything was her underhanded behavior. He should have put her in her place regarding him years ago.

He was so intent on taking her off somewhere to give her a piece of his mind, that he didn't notice the haughty look of victory the woman shot over her shoulder at Lucia.

Chloe drew in a deep breath. "I don't think you should leave, Lucia."

Lucia wiped the tears from her eyes. "There's no reason

for me to stay," she said, gathering up her things. "You saw it for yourself. Ashira shows up and he leaves. She wanted to prove what she told me that day was true and she did."

Chloe shook her head. "But I don't think that's the way it was. According to Zane and Jason, Derringer said it was about business and probably had to talk to her about that horse he's trying to sell her father."

"And it couldn't wait? Please don't make excuses for what I saw with my own eyes, Chloe. She snaps her fingers and he takes off. He was leading her over to the car and not the other way around. And I truly don't want to be here when they come back."

She reached out and hugged Chloe and whispered in a broken voice, "I'll call you later."

Lucia knew it would be hard telling the others goodbye. They would see the hurt in her eyes and they would pity her. Or it might be one of those you-should-have-known-better-than-to-fall-in-love-with-Derringer looks. In her book, one was just as bad as the other.

Somehow she made it through, but nearly broke when Zane pulled her into his arms and asked her to stay a while longer. She forced a smile up at him and told him she couldn't, before rushing to her car, getting inside and driving away.

Derringer returned over an hour later. He hadn't meant to be gone that long, but when he'd arrived at the Lattimores' place he had encountered more drama. Ashira had given her father the impression things were serious between them and he had to first break the news to Phillip Lattimore that they weren't. And then he had to let Ashira know that he didn't consider her a candidate as a wife, at least not for him since there was no way in hell he would ever get shackled with someone as spoiled and selfish as she was. Those words hadn't been too well received, and Derringer had found himself stranded on the Lattimore land. He'd had to call Pete to give him a lift back here.

The moment he got out of Pete's patrol car he knew something was wrong. He could understand everyone staring at him, probably wondering why Pete, instead of Ashira, had brought him back. But they weren't just staring at him. They were openly glaring.

"Looks like your family is pissed off at you for some reason," Pete said.

"Yes, looks that way," he responded. "Thanks for bringing me here."

Once the patrol car had driven off, Derringer's gaze roamed over the group that were outside in the yard cleaning up from today's activities. He looked for one person in particular, but he didn't see her. "Where's Lucia?"

It was Canyon who answered in a belligerent tone, "Oh, so now you remember that she does exist?"

Derringer frowned. "What are you talking about?"

Dillon folded his arms over his chest. "You invited Lucia here, yet you took off with another woman without giving her a backward glance. I expected better of you, Derringer."

Derringer's frown deepened. "That's not the way it was."

It was Ramsey who spoke up. "That's the way we saw it."

"And that's the way Lucia saw it," Bailey snapped, losing her cool. "I can't believe you would leave here with one of those 'silly' girls—in fact, the silliest of them all—deserting Lucia and then showing back up an hour later expecting her to still be here waiting on you. You are so full of yourself."

"Like I said, that's not the way it was," he said, glancing around at all his family circling around him.

"You're going to have a hard time convincing Lucia of that," Chloe said, not with the same snappish tone Bailey had used, but there was no doubt in everyone's mind that if given the chance she would clobber this particular brother-in-law right about now.

"Especially when just a couple of weeks ago Ashira paid Lucia a visit at *Simply Irresistible* and warned her that she could get you back anytime she wanted, and that the two of you have an understanding and that she would be the one who would eventually become your wife," Chloe added in disgust.

"Like hell," Derringer snarled.

"Doesn't matter. Ashira came here today to prove a point and in Lucia's eyes, she did."

"But like I said, it wasn't that way," Derringer implored. He then outlined everything that had happened once he'd left with Ashira and the reason that he'd left with her in the first place. "And I won't let that sort of misunderstanding come between me and Lucia," he said, moving toward his truck. "I need to go see her."

She wasn't home when Derringer got there, but according to her neighbor, Mrs. Noel, she had been there, rushing in and then leaving with an overnight bag. Derringer had no idea where she had gone. And she wouldn't answer her cell phone, although he had left several messages for her. He knew her parents were still in Tennessee and wouldn't be returning for another week or so. Thinking she'd possibly driven out to their place to stay for the night, he had gone there too, only to find the Conyers's homestead deserted.

It was after midnight when he returned to his place and rushed over to his phone when it began ringing the moment he opened the door. "Hello?"

"This is Chloe. I just got a call from Lucia. She's fine and asked that you not try seeing her or calling her. She needs time."

"No, she needs me just like I need her. She should have told me about Ashira's visit and I would have straightened things out then. I need to talk with her, Chloe. I can't stand to lose her."

"And why can't you stand to lose her, Derringer? What makes her so different from the others?"

He knew why Chloe was goading him. He was well aware what she was trying to get him to admit, not only to himself, but to her as well, just how he felt about Lucia. "I love her." He drew in a deep breath. "I love her so damn much."

"Then somehow you're going to have to convince her of that, not only in words, but with actions. Good night, Derringer."

Chloe then hung up the phone.

Chapter 12

Lucia sat behind her desk and stared at the beautiful arrangement of flowers that had arrived that morning. She then glanced around her office at the others that had arrived during the week. The cards all said the same thing: *You are the only woman I want.*

She drew in a deep breath wishing she could believe that, but for some reason she couldn't. Maybe it had to do with the haughty I-told-you-so look Ashira had had on her face when she had left that day with Derringer. The two of them had a history. The woman had been after Derringer for years and it seemed as if she had him. And according to Ashira, no matter who he messed around with, *she* would be the woman he married.

So, Lucia couldn't help asking herself, why was she wasting her time and her heart? The latter she knew there was no answer for. She would continue to love him, no matter what. Always had and always would. But she could do something about the former. To spend any more time with him was heartbreak just waiting to happen. Of course, he wouldn't see it that way. Men had a tendency to look at affairs differently. They didn't have a clue when it came to emotions.

At least he was respecting her wishes and hadn't tried

contacting her again. She figured he and Ashira were now a hot item, although Chloe insisted otherwise. Of course, she had come up with an excuse for the reason he'd left, which Lucia was certain was the one he'd told everyone. Little did he know that Ashira was spreading another story. She wanted to make sure word got back to Lucia through mutual acquaintances that she and Derringer had left the party to go to his place and have hot, blazing sex. It deeply pained Lucia that he could leave her bed that morning and hop into bed with another woman less than twelve hours later.

Lucia glanced up when she heard the knock at her office door. "Come in."

Chloe stuck her head in and smiled. "Word is around the office that you got more flowers."

She came in and closed the door behind her, admiring the arrangement sitting on Lucia's desk. "They are gorgeous, but then, all the bouquets Derringer has sent have been gorgeous. You have to admit that."

Lucia smiled slowly. "Yes, they've all been gorgeous, but they don't mean a thing."

Chloe took the chair across from her desk. "Because of what Tanya McCoy called and told you yesterday? That she'd heard Ashira and Derringer left my place and had hot, rousing sex over at Derringer's Dungeon? I don't believe that and neither should you. Ashira is just trying to save face. I was there when Derringer returned in Pete's patrol car. Don't let Ashira continue to mess with your mind like that. You need to take Derringer's message on those cards you've been getting with the flowers to heart."

Lucia fought back tears. "I wish I could, but I can't. All these years I've loved him and was fine with loving him from a distance. But then I had to go ruin everything by admitting I loved him and letting him into my space. From now on it's going back to status quo."

"Does that mean you won't ever visit your goddaughter at my place, for fear of running into Derringer?"

"No, but I'm trying to get beyond that."

"Then I think this coming Saturday is the perfect way to start. I suggest you change your mind about coming to the Westmoreland Charity Ball. If you see Derringer, no big deal. Now is your time to show him once and for all that you've gotten over him and you're moving on and won't be hiding out to avoid him."

Lucia nervously nibbled on her bottom lip. "And what if he's there with Ashira?"

"And what if he is? It's his loss. And if he wants her instead of you then more power to him. But if I were you, I would definitely let him see what he gave up. Um, I think you and I should go shopping."

Lucia wasn't convinced making an appearance at the charity ball this weekend would be the right thing to do.

"Just because you think one Westmoreland acted like an ass is no reason to ostracize yourself from the rest of us," Chloe added.

Lucia knew what Chloe just said was true. Gemma had called her this morning and she had yet to call her back. So had Megan and Bailey earlier in the week. They had been friends long before she'd met Derringer. It wasn't their fault that she had fallen head over heels in love with their brother, a man who would never settle down, fall in love and marry any woman. Except maybe Ashira one day when he got tired of playing the field.

She tossed her pen on the desk and met Chloe's gaze. "Maybe you're right. I can't avoid the other Westmorelands just because my affair with Derringer went sour."

A smile touched Chloe's lips. "No, you can't. So are we going shopping this weekend?"

Lucia chuckled. "Yes, and I know this is more about you

than me, Chloe Burton Westmoreland. You'll do anything, come up with any excuse, to shop."

Chloe stood, smiling. "Hey, what can I say? A woman has to do what a woman has to do."

Derringer glanced around. He was surrounded by Westmorelands and he couldn't help but smile. Once a year all the Westmorelands—from the south and west—got together for a family reunion rotating between Atlanta, rural Montana and Denver. At other times they got together to support each other for various events. Earlier this year they had traveled to Austin to be with their cousins: Cole, Clint and Casey Westmoreland had honored their deceased uncle during the Sid Roberts Foundation annual charity ball. And usually every year there seemed to be a Westmoreland wedding. The last one had been Gemma's a few months back.

And now all the Atlanta and Montana Westmorelands were gathered here in Denver with their wives for the Westmoreland Charity Ball. They had begun arriving a few days ago and were all accounted for as of noon today when Thorn and Tara had arrived. Thorn had come straight from Bikers' Week in Myrtle Beach, South Carolina.

"Thanks for putting us up for the next couple of days, Derringer."

He glanced around and smiled at his cousins, the twins—Storm and Chase. But then there were several sets of twins in the Atlanta Westmorelands' group. Storm and Chase's father had been a twin, and his cousins, Ian and Quade, were twins as well.

"Hey, no problem. If there's anything you need, just let me know." At that moment his cell phone went off and when he saw it was Chloe he smiled. "Excuse me while I take this."

He went outside to sit on the porch. "Yes, Chloe?"

"You owe me big-time, Derringer, and I swear, if you screw up, I'm coming after you myself."

He believed her. "Trust me, I've got everything planned. I'm just grateful you got Lucia to agree to come to the charity ball."

"It wasn't easy. Ashira and her girls are out spreading lies, claiming that when you left the cookout, you took her to Derringer's Dungeon and got busy."

Derringer's mouth dropped. They hadn't gone near his home. "That's a lie."

"I know, but she's intent on spreading that rumor. I don't know what you have planned for the ball, but it better be good, and hopefully it will put a stop to Ashira once and for all."

Derringer nodded. "Trust me. It will."

"You sure you're all right, sweetheart?"

Lucia glanced over at her parents, namely, her dad, who had a concerned look on his face. "Yes, Dad, I'm fine."

He smiled. "Well, you look simply beautiful."

And considering everything, she felt beautiful. Chloe had nearly worn her out last weekend. They hadn't just shopped in Denver but had caught one of those commuter planes to Boulder to do some shopping there as well. In the end, she felt like Cinderella entering the ball. And just like good ole Cinderella she feared she would leave the ball without her man.

The moment she and her parents entered the huge ballroom she drew in a deep breath at the number of people in attendance. But then, she really wasn't surprised. The Westmoreland Foundation provided funds to a number of charities and for that very reason the people of Denver were always supportive.

It didn't take long to pick out all the Westmorelands, especially the males. Whether they were from the north, south, east or west, they had similar looks and builds. In their black tuxes, they were all tall, dashing and ultrahandsome and, not surprisingly, even with their wives on their arms most of the other women present had their eyes on them with wishful expressions on their faces.

She had met all of them at Chloe's wedding and again at Gemma's. They were a nice group of people and she thought Chloe was blessed to be a part of the Westmoreland clan.

It seemed Chloe spotted her the moment she arrived and eagerly pulled her from her parents' side, telling her over and over just how ravishing she looked. So did Bailey, Megan, Gemma and a number of the other Westmoreland women. All the men spoke to her and as usual Zane gave her a naughty wink, which made her chuckle.

She released a deep breath, glad no one was acting or behaving any differently toward her, although all that might change once Derringer arrived with Ashira on his arm. She was just speculating and couldn't help doing so when both he and Ashira didn't appear to be present. No sooner had that thought left her mind than she glanced up and Ashira walked in with a couple of her girlfriends. Lucia was surprised she wasn't with Derringer.

A short while later, Lucia was dancing with Jason when Derringer cut in. She glanced up and tried her best not to narrow her gaze at him. The last thing she wanted was to let him know just how badly he had hurt her, although she was sure he had a clue, which was the reason for the flowers. But if he thought he could woo her and sleep with Ashira at the same time then he had another thought coming.

"Lucia."

She wished he didn't say her name quite that way. With that same throatiness she remembered so well. "Derringer."

"You look beautiful."

"Thanks. You look handsome yourself." That was no

lie. For some reason, tonight he looked more handsome than ever.

"I'm glad you came."

"Are you?"

"Yes, and I hope you liked the flowers."

"I did, but they mean nothing as far as rekindling our relationship. It's over, Derringer."

He shook his head. "Things will never be over between us. If you read all those cards then you know you're the only woman I want."

She rolled her eyes. "Yeah, right, go tell that to someone else."

He smiled. "I don't have a problem telling anyone else. In fact, I think I will tell everyone."

He turned and gave the orchestra a cue to stop playing and everything got quiet. Also, as if on cue, someone handed him a microphone. "May I have everyone's attention, please?"

Aghast, she tried tugging her hand from his. "What do you think you're doing?" She wanted to run and hide when her words got captured on the mic for all to hear. She was certain before the night was over she would die of shame.

"I'm about to speak from my heart," he said, holding tight to her hand.

"When it comes to the ladies, I didn't know you had a heart, Derringer," Pete called out.

She tried not to glance around since she knew all eyes were on them. They were in the middle of the ballroom's dance floor, and everyone, curious as to what was going on, had moved closer to watch. The Westmorelands, she noted, were standing in a cluster behind Derringer as if to show a united front.

A smile touched Derringer's lips, but when he turned around and met her gaze, his expression got serious. Then he said in a loud and clear voice, "I didn't know I had a heart either until Lucia captured it." He paused and then added, "And that is something no other woman has been able to do."

She glanced away, refusing to believe what she thought she heard him saying. She didn't want to make a mistake about what he was saying. There was no way it could be true.

As if he'd read her thoughts, he tugged on her hand to make her look back at him. "It's true, Lucia. I am so hopelessly in love with you I can't think straight. You are so filled with goodness, warmth and love, I can't imagine not loving you. And it's not anything I discovered upon waking this morning. I knew that I loved you for a while, but didn't want to. I have this fear of loving someone and then losing that person. I think a number of us Denver Westmorelands can't help but feel that way due to the catastrophic losses we've endured in the past. It can do something to you. It can make you not want to take a chance and get attached to anyone.

"But I want to get attached to you. I have to get attached to you. You make me whole. Without you I am nothing."

Lucia couldn't stop the tears that began falling from her eyes. She couldn't believe what he was saying. Derringer was declaring his love and his need for her in front of everyone. His family. Her parents. Their neighbors and friends. Ashira. Ashira's girlfriends. Ashira's parents. Everyone who wanted to hear it.

Evidently, Ashira and her girlfriends didn't. Lucia watched them walk out. It didn't matter to her. The man she had loved for a lifetime was letting her know in front of everyone that he loved her back.

"And when a man has that much love for any woman," Derringer was saying, bringing her attention back to him, "he will choose that woman as his mate for life. The woman he wants for his wife."

She then watched in shock as he eased down on bended knee, gripped her hand tighter and then held her gaze. "Lucia, will you marry me? Will you take my name? Have my babies? And continue to make me happy? In turn, I will be the best husband to you. I will love you. Honor you and cherish you for as long as I live. Will you marry me?"

While she was still swooning from his public proposal, she felt a ring being slid onto her finger. She glanced down. The diamond sparkled so brightly it almost blinded her. She could only stare at it in amazement.

"You have a proposal on the table, Lucia. Please answer the man," someone called out from the crowd.

She couldn't help but smile as she swiped her tears. That had been her father's voice. She met Derringer's gaze. He was still on his knees waiting. "Oh, Derringer," she said through her tears. "Yes! Yes! I will marry you!"

Smiling, he got to his feet and pulled her into his arms in a deep, passionate kiss. She was not sure how long the kiss lasted. The only thing she did know was that the orchestra was playing music again and others were dancing all around them. They didn't care. Tonight was their night and they were going to take full advantage of it.

Hours later, Derringer and Lucia lay together naked in the bed where their adventure all began at Derringer's Dungeon. Upon hearing her wake up during the night, he was ready and leaned up on his elbow and looked down at her, his gaze hot as it roamed over every inch of her naked body.

He leaned down and kissed her and moaned deep in his throat when she returned the kiss with the same hunger he was giving her. Moments later when he pulled back he could only draw in a deep breath in total amazement. Would he always want her to this extreme? He smiled, knowing that yes, he would.

"I love you," he whispered softy. "I regret all the years I didn't make you my one and only girl."

Lucia smiled up at him. "You weren't ready for that type of serious move back then, and in a way I'm glad." She chuckled. "Besides, you needed to impress my dad."

"And you think I did?"

Her smile brightened. "Yes. Going to him and asking for his permission to marry me scored you a lot of brownie points for sure. You're going to be a son-in-law for life."

"Baby, I intend to be a husband for life as well. And you will be my wife for life."

He ran his fingers through her hair as he leaned down and captured her mouth with his. She was definitely a wife for a Westmoreland. She was his, and their love was just the beginning.

Epilogue

A month and a half later

"Okay, Derringer, you may kiss your bride."

A huge smile lit Derringer's features when he pulled Lucia into his arms. She was the woman he wanted, the wife he desired, and as he captured her mouth with his he knew they would share a long and wonderful life together.

He finally released her and turned to their guests as the minister presented them to everyone as Mr. and Mrs. Derringer Westmoreland. He loved the sound of that and wondered why he'd let his fear keep him away from the altar for so long. But as Lucia had said, he hadn't been ready until now.

A short while later, with his wife's hand tucked in his, they made their way around his property, which the women of the family had transformed from Derringer's Dungeon to Derringer and Lucia's Castle. Gemma had returned the week before the wedding and had worked alongside the wedding planner to give Lucia the wedding she deserved.

He glanced down at her and tightened her hand in his. "Happy?"

She smiled up at him. "Immensely so."

He thought she looked beautiful and doubted he would

ever forget how he felt the moment he saw her walking down the aisle to him on her father's arm. She was the most beautiful vision in white that he'd ever seen. They had decided to travel to Dubai for their honeymoon, and while they were across the waters they planned to visit Callum and Gemma in Australia before returning home.

"Time for you to throw your bouquet to the single ladies, Lucia," the wedding planner came up to say.

Lucia turned to Derringer and placed a kiss on his lips. "I'll be back in a moment," she whispered.

"And I'll be right here waiting," was his response. He watched her walk to an area where over thirty women—that included his sisters—stood waiting.

"I've never seen you so happy, Derringer," Jason said, smiling as he walked up. "Congratulations."

"Thanks, and I'm going to give you the same advice I gave Zane, Riley, Canyon and Stern this morning at breakfast, although I could tell they didn't want to hear it. Being single is nice, but being married is much sweeter. Trust me, two is better than one."

Derringer figured if he could get any of his single cousins to take his advice it would be Jason. He had been standing with Jason at the charity ball the moment old man Bostwick's granddaughter had made her entrance. It had been obvious that Jason had been spellbound, entranced by the woman's beauty.

He looked over at Jason. "So, have you officially met Bostwick's granddaughter yet?"

Jason smiled. "Yes, I introduced myself at the ball. Her name is Elizabeth but she prefers being called Bella."

Derringer nodded. "Did you let her know you were interested in her land and in Hercules?"

"Yes, we spoke briefly before Kenneth Bostwick interrupted us. I hear she's trying to make up her mind about what she wants to do. I don't think she's interested in hanging around these parts. This is no place for a Southern belle and besides, she knows nothing about ranching."

"But you do. You can always show her the ropes."

Jason looked shocked at the suggestion. "Why would I want to do something like that? She has two things I want—her land and that stallion. The sooner she decides to sell and return to Savannah, the sooner I can get both. I'd do just about anything to get the land and that horse."

Derringer glanced up at Jason and saw his cousin was serious. "Just remember what I said, Jason. Worldly possessions aren't everything. The love of a good woman is."

He then watched as Lucia began walking back over toward him. She was a good woman. She was his life and now she was his wife.

* * * * *